NOBLE SEED

Noble Seed is the compulsive sequel to *Noble Beginnings* and *Noble Deeds*, and the concluding novel in the gripping story of the community in a small Argyllshire powermill town. Anna McIntyre, now eighteen, has enjoyed her time of respite while her brutal father Roderick has been sent away to work by Sir Malaroy of Noble House. With her kind employer, Lady Pandora, and her friend Beth Jordan, only the depraved behaviour of her brother, Adam, her secret devotion to her half-brother, Magnus, and the return of Roderick can cast shadows of anxiety over her happiness. But little does Anna know that her life is about to be changed radically—all because of the chance discovery of the Luckenbooth locket given to her years ago by her estranged mother. As events of the past—acts of murder, abuse and outrage—are avenged and the truth is finally revealed, there is no telling whether the McIntyre and Noble families will be liberated at last, or whether the price of justice will be too high for them all.

NOBLE SEED

Christine Marion Fraser

CHIVERS PRESS
BATH

First published 1997
by
HarperCollins Publishers
This Large Print edition published by
Chivers Press
by arrangement with
HarperCollins Publishers Ltd
1998

ISBN 0 7540 1064 3

British Library Cataloguing in Publication Data available

Photoset, printed and bound in Great Britain by
REDWOOD BOOKS, Trowbridge, Wiltshire

CHAPTER ONE

THE LUCKENBOOTH

The Seaside Resort of Dunmor, Argyll, 1895

It was dim and rather mysterious in the jeweller's shop. So thought Anna as she stood at the counter waiting for Duncan Lauder, the proprietor, to emerge from the bead-curtained doorway at the back of the shop. He had disappeared into this domain fully ten minutes ago and a total silence had descended over the premises.

It was a bit like an Aladdin's cave, Anna decided, as her eyes roved round the glass cases where precious gems winked in the half-light and the walls dripped gold in the shape of rings, necklaces and earrings, all enclosed in leaded glass cabinets, which were, in themselves, objects of rare and unusual interest.

Anna was entranced by all the beautiful things that surrounded her and became so absorbed in looking at them she barely heard the rattling of the bead curtains and jumped with surprise when Duncan Lauder suddenly loomed up in front of her.

'Sorry I startled you, Miss McIntyre.' The jeweller gazed at her apologetically through his thick spectacles. 'And forgive me for taking so long to serve you, but I wanted to make sure everything was alright with your necklace before I showed it to you.'

Anna wasn't convinced by his excuses. She could smell the whisky on his breath. It was a well-known fact that Duncan Lauder could take a 'good bucket' and was 'always nipping off for a nip', according to Tell Tale Todd who thought he knew everything about everybody. But despite his drinking, Duncan Lauder was adept at repairing and making adjustments to all sorts of jewellery and it was with a flourish that he removed a shiny object from its wrappings and set it down carefully on the counter.

'There you are, Miss McIntyre,' he said in a breathy, reverent voice. 'I hope you'll see I haven't been wasting my time. I gave it a bit o' a clean to bring up the sparkle and I've put the inscription that you wanted on the back.'

Anna's hands trembled as she picked up the exquisite ornament; it was fashioned into a pair of entwined silver hearts surmounted by a gem-encrusted crown. For years it had lain unused in her small leather writing case, and only recently had she come upon it while searching for something else.

She had been seized by guilt at the sight of it, and wondered how she could have neglected the gift her mother had given to her all those years ago. Six! She had been six years old when

Lillian McIntyre had presented her with the necklace, telling her it would protect her from evil.

On seeing it again in the writing case, Anna had fingered the broken chain, remembering how it had snapped when her father, in a fit of unbridled rage, had almost beaten the life out of her with his shaving strop. That had been two years ago, when she was sixteen. The marks were still on her body, marks that would never completely fade, as long as she lived. After the beating she had lost faith in the charm and put it away, feeling that it hadn't done a very good job of protecting her from her father's tyranny. It was better for it to be locked away where he couldn't find it and sell it, as he had done with most of the other little bits and pieces that her mother had left behind when she had been taken away to the asylum in Kilkenzie.

Some of the trinkets had found their way into the possession of Roderick's one-time fancy woman, Nellie Jean, but he knew a good thing when he saw it, and that was why Anna had never let him see her necklace.

Now it read, *To Anna from Mother, 1883,* and as she traced the words with a gentle finger she whispered, 'You've made a fine job, Mr Lauder. I've been saving up to have it done and I'll pay you now.'

'No, no, lass,' he objected. 'It isn't properly finished yet. I've still to clean it up and put on

3

the catch for the chain. It's such a heavy thing it will need to be done properly. As a matter o' fact, I'm a bit uneasy about it hanging on the end o' a chain. I don't want you losing it so don't go rushing me. I've always taken pride in my work and I'm not going to change for anybody.'

Anna looked disappointed, being of the opinion that he'd had more than enough time to fix her necklace.

'Ach, I'm sorry, lass,' he said, seeing her face. 'I've no' been feeling so well lately and it's taking me longer these days to get through my work.' Peering at her over his spectacles he went on, 'I don't know if you realise it, but you have a unique piece of workmanship there, my lass. It's been around a bit from what I can make out and I just wondered if you knew what it was.'

Anna shook her head. 'It's always been special to me because it was a present from my mother, but I also have this feeling that there's more to it than I know.'

'You say you wore it as a necklace but it is in fact a Luckenbooth brooch, crafted in the days when sweethearts gave them to each other to seal their love. It was also believed they protected babies from evil spells cast by the witches of old.'

'That's what my mother told me.'

'Ay, and she was right enough there, for they were sometimes pinned to newborn babies to

4

keep them safe. But this is no ordinary Luckenbooth ...' Leaning over the counter he took the brooch from her to better demonstrate his meaning. 'See here, this silver backing has an unusual depth to it, it has been put on by someone at some time for some reason, but for the life of me I can't see why, though I've examined it back to front. In many ways it's been fashioned like a Mauchline box—they had tiny wee secret hinges on them that no-one could see, an art known only to a few craftsmen in and around Cumnock.'

'Does that mean you think the backing is hollow?' Anna asked excitedly.

'Och, no, lassie, I'm not saying that at all, but it could be—though it would take a more knowledgeable man than me to find out how it opens, if it opens at all.'

Her eyes were brilliant with curiosity, her skin was pink and glowing, and the jeweller wondered, as he had often wondered before, how a lovely young woman like Anna could have a brash and boorish father like Roderick McIntyre. They bore no physical resemblance to each other whatsoever, there was nothing in their make-up to suggest compatibility of any sort, and Duncan Lauder shook his head sadly at the strange quirks and ironies that nature so often produced.

'Are you alright, Mr Lauder?' Anna asked.

He put his hand over hers and sighed, as he was wont to do frequently. 'Just thinking my thoughts, lass, just thinking my thoughts.'

Then he smiled, a smile of warmth that lit his rather tired face. 'You take care now, lass, and don't worry about your Luckenbooth. I'll put a safety clasp on it so it should be alright.'

Anna thanked him. The bell above the door tinkled to admit another customer who politely stepped aside to let her pass. But before going into the street she paused for a moment to put up her sun parasol, a recent gift from Lady Pandora and one that was still such a novelty to Anna she seized any opportunity to make use of it. Satisfied that she was ready to face the world she lifted up an inch of her skirt and made her exit from Duncan Lauder's.

CHAPTER TWO

A CHANCE ENCOUNTER

As she stepped out of Duncan Lauder's doorway, Anna ran full tilt into Sir Malaroy as he was walking briskly past. As quick as a flash he put out his arms to save her from falling and when they had both recovered from their fright he tipped his hat to her and smiled somewhat wryly.

'Anna McIntyre! It would seem I am destined to bump into you in unusual circumstances. I haven't forgotten our meeting

6

in a ditch a couple of years ago. I seem to remember also that you expressed your feelings in such a forthright manner I still smile to this day when I think about it.'

Anna reddened. She straightened her hat and glanced away from the laughing expression in his eyes, though her own were twinkling when she said, 'Sir Malaroy, I hope that isn't all you remember about that day. I can recall a very refined gentleman falling from his horse, and yelling his head off with temper because he felt he had made a fool of himself in front of a lady.'

He smiled sourly. 'I stand corrected. I still owe you an apology for that little incident and take this opportunity to say I'm sorry.'

'And I'm indebted to you for saving my dignity just now and can only say thank you. You're a perfect gentleman and a very understanding one.'

Tilting her head to one side she smiled at him and thought how aristocratic and handsome he looked in his immaculate, three-piece, grey linen suit with a dark red silk tie at his neck. His keen eyes were very blue in the flushed fair skin of his face and, with his neat Van Dyke beard, she couldn't help thinking he looked young and fresh and not at all like a man in his late forties.

'Anna.' He said her name as though he just felt like saying it. She looked so attractive in her summer finery, with the sunbeams dancing

7

in the white-gold of her hair, and dimples of mischief showing at the corners of her wide, sweet mouth.

Seeing the admiration in his glance she caught her breath and moved away from him slightly, her deep purple-grey eyes showing the sudden confusion of her feelings. This was her first meeting with him since that day, two years ago, when she had fallen off her horse into a ditch and he had come upon her struggling to get up.

'Come on, I'll show you how not to fall off your horse,' he had teased, and had ridden away to the stables to tumble promptly from his own horse when his foot had caught in the stirrup.

Since that day she had only caught glimpses of him in and around the House of Noble policies and she was still of the opinion that he tended to avoid her if he could. But he had always been a quiet, reserved man, and there was no reason at all why he should seek her out. She had been brought into his home at the insistence of his wife, who had wanted a companion and had chosen Anna McIntyre of The Gatehouse to fill the role.

Anna was aware that Lady Pandora looked upon her as the daughter she had never had. That didn't mean, however, that Sir Malaroy saw her in quite the same light and Anna often got the feeling that he didn't entirely approve of the place she held in his wife's affections. He no doubt saw her as just another employee, but that didn't stop Anna wishing that he would occasionally stop and speak to her as he had done on that warm spring day of yore.

'Anna,' he said again, his cultured, resonant voice very pleasing to her ears. 'You were in a hurry just now. Were you perhaps fleeing from the temptations of spending too much money in Duncan Lauder's shop?'

'Och no, Sir Malaroy, I don't have that kind of money to spend. I was just in seeing Mr Lauder about a necklace that got broken a long time ago. He was fixing it but it isn't ready yet, so I'll have to come back some other day.'

'You need no ornaments about your pretty throat to make people notice you, Anna,' he said softly.

'Oh, sir, I must hurry.' Blushing, she turned away from him. 'I have some things to collect for Lady Pandora.'

'So, you're running errands for my wife?'

'Yes, she was supposed to come with me but at the last moment didn't feel well. I thought she would have told you that.'

'I left the house before my wife came down to breakfast.' He spoke rather abruptly. 'I had business matters to attend.' He spread his long fingers expressively. 'My wife is like a butterfly, flitting from one bright flower to the next. Very often I don't know where she'll be at any given time.'

There was an indefinable message in his

9

words; also there was about him a strange aura of sadness, the pain of which seemed to reach out and touch Anna like a physical thing.

But before she could speak he brisked himself up and said lightly, 'If I had known you were coming into Dunmor we could have accompanied one another. As it was I had a pleasant but solitary journey in my gig. How, pray, did you get here, child?'

She smiled. 'By my wits! Ben McLeod took me as far as Munkirk in his cart and then I had a ride in a rumble. I didn't want to impose myself on Neil Black who was busy this morning. Anyway, I enjoyed the freedom. With Father away at Canon Point I can suit myself for a while.'

Sir Malaroy merely grunted and frowned. It was he himself who had negotiated Roderick's temporary transfer to Canon Point in order to assist the new manager there. At least, that's what he had told Roderick. All he had really wanted was to get rid of him for a while. The sight of the man made him sick and nothing would have pleased Sir Malaroy more than to make Roderick's removal from the Glen Tarsa gunpowder factory a permanent arrangement.

For too long now he had been a very painful thorn in Sir Malaroy's side and the day was coming when something drastic would have to be done about him. But he was a cunning bastard, and always seemed to be one step ahead of everybody else. No-one seemed able

10

to get the better of him, not even those who had tried their best to wreak their revenge on him.

There was only one consolation: no-one who lived as recklessly as Roderick did could get away with it indefinitely, not even someone as swaggering and indestructible as he seemed to be.

Initially Roderick had been none too pleased at Sir Malaroy's proposals to send him away and he hadn't been slow to say so.

'You're going, McIntyre, and that's final,' Sir Malaroy had told him. 'I would have thought you would be glad to get away from Glen Tarsa for a while. Nothing's been the same here since young Ralph ran away and never came back. Her ladyship was very upset over that incident. As well as all that, there's still the question of what happened to Andrew Mallard and Peter. The belief in these parts is that someone murdered them and we've yet to find out who that someone is.'

Peter and Lucas Noble, Robert and Ralph, had all lived together at Noble House, and all four boys had been tutored by Andrew Mallard. Lucas had been quickly sent to an English school after the death of his brother, but Ralph and Robert had remained at the big house to continue their education under the rule of that prissy pants, Michael Dick. The boys must have discussed the deaths of Mallard and Peter with one another, so if Ralph knew so much it followed that Robert

11

would possibly know it as well.

Roderick had never felt easy in his mind since the death of young Peter Noble, Lady Pandora's nephew. That swine Mallard had deserved all he got, but Peter had just been an innocent bystander who had somehow got in the way ... As for Master Ralph, Lady Pandora's protegé, it had been rumoured that he knew who had killed Andrew Mallard, had actually witnessed the murder taking place.

With all this to consider Roderick had been in a very uneasy frame of mind for quite some time now, and the more he thought about a break away from Glen Tarsa the more he began to warm to the idea. He couldn't however let Sir Malaroy see this. The old sod had to be kept on his toes all the time. It would never do to slacken vigilance on him. He had to pay for what he had done all those years ago—he had to pay for Anna—and he had conveyed all of this to Sir Malaroy. Right up to the day of his departure to Canon Point he had made life very unpleasant indeed for his lordship and swore he'd be back to collect his dues before too many weeks had passed.

Anna's words had brought it all flooding back to Sir Malaroy and his thoughts were bleak at this juncture. He could only take so much! There had to be a breaking point. Roderick had pushed him almost to the brink, Roderick and Pandora between them. Rumours were spreading about them; it was said that they had been seen together in compromising circumstances: rumours, whispers, gossip. How could Pandora even begin to contemplate any sort of liaison with the man she had sworn she hated?

It all boiled down to one thing: Roderick had to go, but how? How?

'Sir Malaroy, are you alright?' Anna's voice seemed to come from a very long distance.

He pulled himself together and looked at her rather dazedly. 'My dear child, of course I am, but how are you to struggle home with all these packages?'

'If I'm at the coachbuilders before noon Mr Walters said he would give me a ride back in his cart.'

'What have you still to do?'

Anna consulted a list she withdrew from her pocket. 'Collect Lady Pandora's new shoes from the cobblers. Real calf leather they are and all of eleven shillings and sixpence.' Anna sucked in her breath at the very idea of such an exorbitant price for shoes. 'Then I've to call in at Larchwood to see if Miss Fiddly Fingers has finished a dress and after that I've to get some Pears soap from the pharmacy.'

Sir Malaroy's eyes sparkled. 'Miss who-did-you-say?'

'Sorry, I meant Miss Fletcher ...' Anna put her hand to her mouth and giggled. 'She *is* all fingers and thumbs and I wonder sometimes how she ever manages to sew anything

13

straight.'

'Oh, Anna.' Sir Malaroy shook his head. 'You're such a tonic to me on the few occasions that we meet ...' He gazed thoughtfully towards the pierhead where a number of brightly painted coaches were waiting for the holiday makers to arrive on the next steamer.

It was a calm, sunny morning in mid-June. After an indifferent start, the summer days were now golden and warm. The stretches of shore that skirted the town were busy with people pottering about or just relaxing. Children in sailor suits were making sandcastles; others in less formal attire were having a wonderful time frolicking in bare feet and eating ice-cream; young ladies promenaded with their parasols; young men in shirt-sleeves, waistcoats, and bowler hats, splashed about in rowing boats and generally showed off to the young ladies; fat women lay on the beaches like miniature mountains; husbands tied hankies on their bald heads and pretended to sleep whilst keeping one eye fixed firmly on the bathing belles dipping tentative toes in the water.

Sir Malaroy experienced a rising of the sap. This was life as he seldom knew it and suddenly and impulsively he wanted to be part of the whole, happy, summer scene.

'Anna,' he began briskly, 'my business here is finished and I have some time on my hands. How would you like to come with me on the

14

Loch Gorm coach tour?'

'Me?' She stared. 'Oh, but I can't. There is so much yet for me to do.'

'Anna, you know that isn't true. Your father is away, Magnus left early this morning to bring some beasts over from Bute. I passed him on the Drove road in the company of some other lads and he won't be back much before nightfall.'

'I said I would go home to see to things—Adam...'

'Adam is a big lad now and well able to look after himself. Come now, my dear Anna, you have no excuses left. The day is perfect, the time is right. My horse will keep at Jock's Stables—and don't worry your pretty little head about my wife, I will take her things back to her and you can see her again this evening, or surely tomorrow will do.'

Anna felt herself weakening. 'I—I suppose so...'

'Well then.' He crooked his arm in a dashing manner. 'Step out with me, little maiden. I'll collect her ladyship's shoes while you run along to the pharmacy. Give me your parcels, I'll leave them with the cobbler for collection later.' He grinned. 'That takes care of everything except the soap but I think we can just about manage to carry that between us. Come along now, we mustn't dally or all the best seats on the coach will be taken.'

His enthusiasm was infectious. Bright-eyed

15

with excitement she took his arm and they walked along the street together before parting at the corner to go on their separate errands.

* * *

'Hurry up, Anna,' was his impatient greeting some ten minutes later and she was surprised because he was normally so restrained about everything. 'I see the steamer coming and we must dash if we want to get good seats on the coach.'

So saying he grabbed her hand and they went running towards the pier, tall distinguished Sir Malaroy of the House of Noble, fair little Anna McIntyre of The Gatehouse, she holding on to her hat as she struggled to keep up with his long stride, he laughingly urging her along, ignoring the turned heads, the curious faces that watched and whispered and wondered.

CHAPTER THREE

A DAY WITH SIR MALAROY

The Lady of Bute was sailing into the pier, packed from bow to stern with day-trippers who were abuzz with anticipation, all trying to talk at once over the frantic threshing of the ship's reversed paddles.

'Run, Anna!' yelled Sir Malaroy. 'They're lowering the gangplank.'

'I can't go any faster!' Anna panted breathlessly, one eye on the colourful crocodile of people swarming out of *The Lady of Bute.* 'Your legs are longer than mine!'

The coaches were filling rapidly, the horses jibbing and frisking and pawing the ground as they sensed that soon they would be off.

'Sir Malaroy.' The leading coachman, James McMorran, a dashing figure in his red-coated livery and tile hat, recognised the lord of Glen Tarsa at once and touched his hat respectfully.

'Climb aboard, Sir ...' Raising his voice he cried authoritatively, 'Make way for his lordship, two seats at the front! Sit you down, Sir—and you too, Miss McIntyre. Her ladyship not with you today, Sir?' he added in a polite, almost disinterested tone.

Sir Malaroy knew better. 'No, McMorran, she had to opt out due to unforeseen circumstances. She did, however, give Miss McIntyre and myself her blessing and told us to enjoy our trip.'

'Ay, Sir, just as you say, you couldn't have picked a finer day for it. All aboard now, everybody. Hold on to your hats, ladies!'

Thus Anna found herself seated in an open coach next to Sir Malaroy, squeezed up against him to be more precise since the seat they occupied was hardly generous in its proportions. Her emotions span in circles. She didn't know if it was either right or proper to be here on this touring coach with Lady Pandora's husband, but that didn't stop her feeling elated, excited, and joyous all at the one time.

It was as if tiny bubbles were bursting inside of herself, a bit like the fizz in the champagne she had sampled at the Christmas Ball held at The House of Noble last year for all the servants and estate workers. Her spirit was flying higher with each turn of the coach wheels and the doom-ridden sampler above her bed in The Gatehouse, was wrong. She *hadn't* missed the way to heaven through being too exuberant and carefree, because heaven was here, on earth, on a mid-summer's day in 1895, and she was flying on wings of perfect joy that took her higher and higher to the very summits of the hills.

The yachts on the Firth of Clyde were like butterflies in flight, their white sails filling with the breezes that flurried the greeny-blue water; the clip-clop of the horses' hooves had a rhythm all of their own; the scent of new-cut grass came wafting in the wind, mingling with salt and seaweed and all the other smells associated with the seaside. And all around, about and above, was the eternal dome of the azure sky, glimpsed through banners of foliage that hung over the road and brushed the coach as it passed by.

Anna took a deep, shuddering breath and tried to still her fast-beating heart. But how could she? On a day like this, in a place like this? With Sir Malaroy so near, overwhelming her with the knowledge of how things had changed so much for her over the years. No more was she a tiny wee creature who had feared the night and the daytime hours alike, for neither darkness nor daylight had lessened the strength of her father's wrath in those not-so-long distant childhood days.

Now she was eighteen and no longer dependent on him to feed and clothe her. She had spread her wings beyond the four walls of The Gatehouse, and a lot of the ugliness had been erased from her life; she now knew the joy of lovely things and wonderful people and the delights of travelling to new places in comfort and style. She knew however that she could never completely break free from the ties that bound her to home and family. Not as long as her mother lived and breathed and might possibly be set free herself some day from the fetters of her hurt and fragile mind.

Then there was Magnus, the elder brother that she adored; as long as he needed her she could never leave him, nor Adam, her younger brother, so pitifully insecure and unhappy and not strong enough to break away from the domineering hold that his father had over his life.

But today she didn't want to think of all that,

not with the warmth of Sir Malaroy's body shafting through hers, making her so aware of everything that was bright and beautiful in the sunny world around her.

As if reading her thoughts he turned his head to look at her and the smile that he gave her was lazy and warm and intimate in the way it included only her in its light. 'Happy, Anna?' he asked gently.

'I don't know, there's so much happening to me I find it difficult to tell.'

'Anna.' His thumb touched her shoulder. 'Today is our day. After this, everything will go back to the way it's always been between us. You'll never know how much I've wanted to enjoy your company, but many things have prevented that. Some day you'll have to know what they are—and you will hate me.'

'Oh, no, Sir Malaroy, I could never do that—never.'

'Dear little Anna, don't look so tragic, just appreciate this special day that's been given to us.'

Minutes later they were laughing together, everyone was in a holiday mood, someone began to sing, then another and another, and in a moment of abandon Sir Malaroy pulled off his jacket and threw it carelessly over the seat in front. He looked cool in his fine cotton shirt but when he settled himself back, the heat of him burned against Anna fiercer than before.

'Won't Lady Pandora worry if you aren't

home by lunch-time?' Anna asked quietly, bewildered suddenly by everything that had happened to her since morning.

'I often dine out when I'm in Dunmor for the day. Stop worrying, child, my wife has plenty to occupy her, she won't miss me for a few hours.'

Anna sensed a sudden bridge between them and she fell silent. Deep in her heart she knew that relations weren't as they had once been between Sir Malaroy and his wife. In some strange way Anna knew that it was all somehow connected with her, a small web of intrigue that had sprung up from nowhere yet was growing stronger as the days went by. Anna had tried to turn her mind away from it, she didn't want to know too much of it because always she was afraid that the threads of love and loyalty that bound her to The House of Noble would be broken for all time.

The coach went spanking along the leafy lanes and was soon passing through the sleepy little village of Munkirk on the shores of Loch Longart. Here the green hills were reflected in the still water, small boats puttered in and out of the jetties, white yachts sailed serenely along. Nothing hurried, or worried, or moved, unless it had to.

The open country beyond the loch was a patchwork of green and golden fields dotted with sheep and cows, the purple hills of Glen Tarsa looked distant and mysterious, and

Anna thought of her life there and how peculiar it felt to be passing it by on the way to other places, and no-one knowing that she was doing so with Sir Malaroy at her side.

By the time the coach reached the jetty at Loch Gorm, the lord of Glen Tarsa was himself once more, charming, gallant, delighted to be alive that enchanted sunlit day when so much that was good belonged to anybody who could appreciate it.

He held on to Anna's arm as they stepped aboard the *S.S. Kelpie* and climbed to the upper deck to watch the ship gliding away from the jetty and out into the deep dark depths of Loch Gorm. Together they stood at the rails and gazed towards the towering heights of the surrounding hills where the sun slanted into rugged corries and glinted on burns tumbling over the stones.

'I love this loch,' Anna said quietly. 'I and my brothers passed this way two years ago when Mr Simpson was taking us to see our mother in Kilkenzie. *The Kelpie* was sailing on the loch that day and I remember wishing I could have a sail in her—and today you have made my wish come true.'

The smile he gave her was oddly tender. 'Your wishes should always come true, Anna, always...'

He gave himself a little shake and went on briskly, 'Did you know that *The Kelpie* is a Royal Mail carrier with a postbox on board?

22

Why don't you buy a postcard and send it to your mother?'

'Oh, could I? But—I'm not sure if she would understand it. She—well—I don't know if she reads anything anymore.'

'She may like to look at the pictures—and a nurse will read it to her.'

'Yes, oh, yes!' Anna's eyes were shining. 'I'll send her one right away. Come with me, Sir Malaroy, you can show me where to go and what to do.' A short while later she popped the card she had written into the postbox and then she went to join Sir Malaroy at the rails.

'Thank you for suggesting that,' she said softly. 'Since my visit to my mother I've tried not to think about her too much. Oh, it's shameful, I know, but it hurts to remember how she used to be and how she is now. I'll never forget that day at Kilkenzie. The journey there was wonderful, with the minister telling us everything he knew about the places we passed. But the nearer we got to Kilkenzie the more jittery we all became. Adam was the worst, though when we started off, he seemed to be the calmest. When we got to the hospital it was only Magnus and me alone with Mother and we both felt that she knew who we were. She was so gentle, like a little girl, and then Adam came in and she just—went wild, shouting, screaming, saying that she didn't want him near her. He was terribly upset and frightened—we all were.'

Sir Malaroy gripped Anna's arm tightly and when he spoke it was with an intensity that surprised her. 'I'm so sorry! Oh, my dear little Anna! You don't know how sorry I am. She shouldn't be in there—she ...' Abruptly he halted and turned away. Anna stared at him, and without knowing why she began to speak in a strange, faraway voice that didn't seem to belong to her.

'Father told Magnus and me that we will gradually go mad like *her*, like our mother. He asked us never to let Adam know because he feels he isn't strong enough to take it.'

Sir Malaroy said nothing. The knuckles of his hands had gone white on the rails, his face had grown sad and somehow old in the last few moments.

Anna drew in her breath. 'What is it, Sir Malaroy?' she asked fearfully. 'You sound as if—as if you know my mother as well, or better, than I do myself. Why are you saying these things about her? What makes you say she shouldn't be in the asylum?'

Slowly he turned his head to look at her and in his piercing blue eyes she saw pain, stark, dark, and terrible, clawing its way up out of the depths of his soul till it became like a tangible creature that reared up its ugly head and reached out to enfold her in its clutches.

'Anna,' Sir Malaroy spoke huskily, 'believe me, please believe me when I tell you this; your father has no right to say these things to you,

24

they have no foundation in truth whatsoever. You are a sane, beautiful young woman, Magnus is a healthy, normal young man, and may God in the heavens above grant that it will always remain so.' Putting his hand on her arm he stared deep into her eyes. 'Anna, trust me and listen to what I tell you. I *know* what I'm talking about, but I have to beg you not to ask any more questions. The day will come when you will know everything but not now, Anna, certainly not now on this day of nature's bountiful blessings.'

Anna shivered. 'Mystery surrounds me and my family, doesn't it, Sir Malaroy? I think I've always known that, ever since I was a little girl watching my mother walking away from me to an unknown place, leaving me and my brothers to fend for ourselves. Yet she loved us, and she wouldn't have gone away if she hadn't been driven to it by my father.

'From the beginning he said strange things, hinted that he'd never had a hand in my being. He's always predicted doom and gloom for my future and I have this terrible feeling that one day, the people I love most will be terribly hurt by the things he has kept hidden all these years.'

She gazed unseeingly over the dark water. 'You're a good man, Sir Malaroy, and I take comfort from the things you said to try and ease my mind. But I have to face the reality of my mother's mental condition and prepare myself for what lies ahead of me and my family.'

'No, Anna, no!' The protest was torn from Sir Malaroy. 'You mustn't think like that! It isn't true and it grieves my heart to know that you won't listen to me.'

'Oh, Sir Malaroy, not only are you a good man, you're a compassionate one also.' Her voice was hushed as she spoke, and it seemed to her, on that sun-dappled day of many mixed emotions, that she and her tall distinguished companion were the only two people in the whole of the summer world.

'I—I feel a great affection and admiration for you,' she went on shakily. 'More so now than at any other period in my life. But you mustn't feel that you have to be sad for me. I live only for the present. Every day that I awake is a new start for me and I'm so aware of God's beautiful earth I sometimes feel I can reach out and hold it in my arms.' Her hand tightened on his. 'When I'm alone and afraid I think of Lady Pandora and you, and I remember Peter, and how wonderful it was to have loved him, even for so short a time.'

She paused for a moment, remembering Peter, Lady Pandora's nephew; together they had known a magical snow-filled winter and they had played like starry-eyed children in wonderland. Then had come spring, filled with light and laughter, the days merging into perfect summer through which they had

26

wandered hand in hand, picking wildflowers, talking, laughing, loving. Wild and free. He had said that, his tanned skin glowing, his blue eyes shining as they gazed upon her face, filled with the wonder of the love he and she shared...

Neither of them could have dreamed that he would never see the glories of that autumn, because by then he was dead, killed in a fruitless attempt to save the life of his tutor, Andrew Mallard, whom he had found hanging from a tree near the Rumbling Brig in Glen Tarsa.

That had been almost three years ago now, and still no-one knew what had really happened to cause the tragic loss of two young lives. Anna was convinced that her father held the key to the mystery. He had said some pretty strange things after the bodies had been discovered, implying his hatred of Andrew Mallard and his sorrow that Peter had also died. 'Too bad about Peter, it wasn't meant for him, I know how much he meant to you ...' These were words that Anna would never forget for the rest of her life. She had become more and more convinced that her father was a murderer and would somehow have to be brought to justice.

Other people were convinced of it too, and young Ralph van Hueson, a distant cousin of Lady Pandora's, had, after months of tortured nightmares, admitted that he had been at the

Rumbling Brig at the time of Mallard's death and had actually witnessed Roderick knocking the tutor senseless and tying the fatal noose round his neck. Ralph had promised to tell the police everything he'd seen, but at the last minute he'd taken fright and had run away, and no-one had set eyes on him since.

Anna brought her thoughts back to the present with an effort. Sir Malaroy was watching her anxiously and she laughed and said simply, 'I told you before, don't worry about me, I've got many things to be thankful for and of course, there's Magnus, he means so much to me. We talk all the time, we comfort one another, and long ago we decided it's only today that matters, yesterday is gone, tomorrow must bring what it will.'

'Oh dear God!' Sir Malaroy's hand went to his eyes. 'It's all so wrong! I can't allow this suffering to go on, and yet if I speak it will hurt so many people ... my wife ...'

Anna could see that he was in torment. It was difficult to know what he was trying to say, he looked dazed, bewildered, afraid.

'Please,' she said urgently, 'I know how unhappy you are and I also know it's got something to do with my father. He seems to be at the root of everything that causes unpleasantness. He's a materialistic man and I know that, through me, he benefits from Lady Pandora's generosity. I used to be of small worth in his eyes but I have been the means of

28

opening new doors for him and he is making full use of all the opportunities. Perhaps—it might be better for everyone if I didn't come back to Noble House. In that way my father would have no reason to go there either since all he's interested in is the money he gets from my employment.'

'Dear child,' Sir Malaroy said huskily, 'it is not entirely a question of money—if only it were. You have made many people happy, and of course you will not stop your visits to my house. I insist on that, and after today, not just for Pandora's sake but for my own as well. Come now, let's stop being morose and enjoy the rest of this lovely morning.'

After that, neither of them mentioned Roderick's name again. *The Kelpie* continued its enchanting tour of the loch and Sir Malaroy indicated various things of interest to Anna.

'That's the hill where a Danish prince was said to have been slain in the days of King Haakon back in the thirteenth century. And over there,' Sir Malaroy pointed, 'do you see that deep, dark, hole in the mountainside? Legend has it that the witches of the loch lived there. On stormy nights, when the wind shrieks over the water, it is really the wrathful breath of the old she-devils venting their temper on some giant or other who rolled a huge stone over one of their smelly old caves. This caused a bit of a furore among the witching population because after that they were a wee bit short of living accommodation and were apt to fight among themselves as to which witch cave belonged to which witch family.'

Anna burst out laughing. He was a lively, entertaining companion, showing a frivolous side to his nature that she had never seen before. She was sorry when the sail on *The Kelpie* came to an end and the passengers had to disembark at the little jetty at the top of Loch Gorm.

But the tour wasn't over yet. Fresh coaches were waiting to whisk everyone to a tiny inn halfway along the lochside where tea, sandwiches, and cream cakes, disappeared in no time.

Anna and Sir Malaroy ate as hungrily as anyone and afterwards they wandered down to a sheltered bay hidden from the road by slender birch trees. Silently they stood at the water's edge, letting the peace of the golden day wash over them. The hills rose up in front of them, majestic and dour; blue wood smoke, from a hidden chimney on the opposite shore, spiralled lazily into the surrounding trees.

Anna picked up a stone and dropped it into the water. 'Plop,' she said, and smiled.

Solemnly he followed her example. Glistening rings of bright water spread out in ever-widening circles.

'Our cares have gone to the bottom of the loch, Anna,' he said lightly and taking her hand he helped her back up the slope to the waiting coach.

CHAPTER FOUR

A DINNER INVITATION

Glen Tarsa, Argyll, 1895

The trip to Loch Gorm was over, and very soon Anna found herself sitting beside Sir Malaroy in his pony trap, heading away from Dunmor, taking the high hill road into Munkirk and from there to Glen Tarsa. Both he and she were very quiet, and when he slowed the pony to a gentle trot she knew he shared her reluctance for the day to end.

'Anna,' he said at last, his voice low, 'I don't want to let go of this wonderful day. It has meant a great deal to me. This morning I was a middle-aged man going about my business, hardly aware that the sun was shining and the birds were singing. When I met you I not only knew the sun was there, I felt the heat of it, I smelled the perfume of the flowers, and heard the singing of the birds. And all because you allowed me to share in your life, even if ever so briefly, and while I was about it I borrowed some of your youth and knew what it was like to feel young again.'

Anna's face went hot. 'You are a very poetic

man, Sir Malaroy—no-one has ever spoken to me in quite that way before.'

'I'd have thought that a girl like you would have had dozens of young poets queuing up at her door, all of them eager to impress with their mastery of the romantic word.'

She smiled appreciatively at this. 'No, not dozens, maybe just the odd stray one now and then.'

He sighed, 'Ah, well, that is their loss, is it not, and leaves me free to ask you not to go home just yet but to do Lady Pandora and myself the honour of dining with us tonight.'

It was her turn to sigh. 'That sounds wonderful, and I would love to accept, but I promised old Grace I would go along to Moss Cottage to help her make rhubarb jam. Also, there's Adam, I ought to get a meal together for him.'

'But I thought Nora McCrae looked after such matters now.'

'Only for part of the day. She's a good soul, though, and often leaves something prepared, ready for me to heat up at teatime.'

They were nearing the gunpowder factory now, a solidly built construction situated amidst the grandeur of Highland glens and bens. It gave employment to many people in and around Glen Tarsa and was also the means of providing housing accommodation for workers and their families. The busy clatter of the working day now over, several mill workers were wending their way homewards, and to add to the familiarity of the scene, the well-kent voice of Donal McDonald was ringing through the glen, proclaiming to all and sundry that the hour had come for everyone to lay down their tools and go home.

Donal was one of a family of three mentally handicapped children whose parents had died many years ago, leaving the trio to fend for themselves. Although twenty-six, Donal had the capabilities of a six-year-old, but was possessed of such a sunny disposition that everyone genuinely liked him and tried their best to make life easier for him by supplying him with food and clothing whenever they could.

His forward-leaning gait carried him swiftly along and as he neared the trap carrying Anna and Sir Malaroy he waved both hands at them and cried exuberantly, 'Time to stop! Shut up shop! Time to stop!'

So busy was he, trying to impress the laird of the glen with his little ditty, he failed to look where he was going and ran full tilt into a crowd of youths coming out of the mill gate.

'Hallo, daftie!' one or two of the men cried in delight. 'Got any more old watches to show us and we'll show you where to put them!'

Recognising her brother, Adam, among the group, Anna requested Sir Malaroy to stop the trap.

'Anna!' Adam had spotted his sister. He

swaggered over to her, a crudely handsome seventeen-year-old, with snapping dark eyes and a head of tightly curled hair that was the colour of autumn leaves. He wore his cap jauntily, his thumbs were hooked into his braces, his deep barrel of a chest strained against his shirt; everything about him suggested supreme confidence, but Anna knew differently.

Roderick was a wrathful and dominant figure in all of their lives but Adam was the only one who had never been able to stand up to him. Ever since he was a young boy he had feared and hated the bully who was his father and would do almost anything to see him brought to his knees. Despite his resolution to bring Roderick to justice after he had found the incriminating pipe hidden near the murder scene, he was too afraid to do or say anything that might bring about such an event, and so he said nothing, just simmered away quietly and took his feelings out on those weaker than himself, harassing people such as Donal and Donal's sister Sally, both of whom had been on the receiving end of Adam's vengeful fury before.

Outside the four walls of The Gatehouse it was a different matter altogether. Adam came into his own then. He was the leader of his own particular gang of cronies, with whom he boasted and strutted and held sway with stories of startling sexual adventures and feats of superior strength. The older he had grown, the more vulgar and unruly his behaviour had become, trends that were exacerbated by wild drinking bouts that brought out the undesirable elements in his strange, contradictory nature.

At times he seemed to lose control of himself altogether and Anna was afraid that one day he would do something so catastrophic it would have far-reaching effects on all whose lives it touched.

But he could be entirely charming and good mannered if the mood took him and at the sight of Sir Malaroy he touched his cap and grinned disarmingly.

'Just the young man I want to see,' Sir Malaroy addressed Adam in kindly tones. 'I have this minute issued an invitation to your sister, requesting that she have dinner at my house tonight, but she has refused on the grounds that she has to look after you. What do you say to that, Adam?'

Adam regarded Sir Malaroy with respect and affection. The lord of Noble House had always been courteous and friendly towards him, despite the fact that there had been a point when Adam had displayed hostility towards anyone of note from the big house, imagining them all to be haughty and patronising. His attitude had softened with time however, Sir Malaroy in particular earning a special place in the boy's rebellious heart.

'Don't you listen to her, Sir,' he advised with a great show of generous spirit. 'I'll get myself a meal in no time at all. I will not have a sister o' mine sacrificing herself for me.'

His tone was a mite too plausible, his attitude too humble to be true. Anna's suspicions were immediately aroused. She knew her brother only too well and feeling that he was up to some mischief or other she looked at him quickly and attempted to catch his eye. He avoided her gaze and muttering something unintelligible he dug his hands into his pockets and went on his way, followed reluctantly by his cronies who had been eyeing Anna appreciatively and nudging one another to see who would be first to gain her attention.

'You have got quite a following there, Anna,' Sir Malaroy commented dryly. 'Perhaps it might be too tedious for you to have dinner with an ancient creature like myself?'

Anna giggled. 'You are neither ancient nor tedious and I never said I would have dinner with you. By hook or by crook I am going this evening to make jam with old Grace—even though she herself can be ancient and tedious and occasionally downright impossible. She's always been good to me, however, and I just can't break my word to her.'

He threw back his head and laughed. 'You are enchantingly loyal, Anna, and I wouldn't dream of letting you break your promise to dear old Grace. She is as much a mother to me as she is to you and she too shall come to dinner. She can bring her jars and her rhubarb and we will all make jam together after we have eaten. The last time I made merry with the jam pan was when I was a lad of twelve. Our old cook, Bella, let me help her make it, but when she caught me scooping it out of the pan with my fingers she chased me away from her kitchen with a broom and I was never allowed to make anything with her again.'

His mood of elation rubbed off on Anna and she allowed him to drive her along the road to Moss Cottage, where he helped her step down from the trap and escorted her to the door of the neat little dwelling.

Grace was greatly put about when she saw her tall distinguished visitor standing on her doorstep. Without ado he put his dinner proposal to her, then stood listening politely to a long list of reasons why she couldn't possibly accept, the main one being that she wasn't dressed properly for such an occasion and had no intention of even trying to 'doll herself up' at such short notice.

'My dear Grace,' Sir Malaroy said with an engaging show of humility, 'if that is all that is bothering you then you needn't fear, I'll be glad of an excuse not to dicky myself up either, and I'm sure my wife will feel exactly the same as I do. One gets tired of all the formalities and it will be grand to be oneself for a change. Please, dear lady, don't deny me this treat. I'm looking forward to making jam in my own kitchens and to have you smacking me on the fingers if I dare to dip them in the jam pan.'

'It doesny seem right, a fine gentleman like yourself wanting to do domestic things like that.'

Grace shook her white head and looked reproachfully at Anna standing in the doorway, her face alight with mischief. 'I don't know what's gotten into you, Anna Ban,' the old lady scolded, 'you should never have brought his lordship here to my house. It isn't right, it isn't decent, and you should know better than to put me about like this!'

'Grace,' Sir Malaroy gazed at her pleadingly, 'I am not a god, I am a human being, and when I was a lad you used to take me into your cottage and ply me with girdle scones piled high with jam and fresh cream, which you made from the milk of that bonny little goat you had. Chin-wag, that was her name, don't you remember her, Grace?'

'Ay, I remember,' the old lady's bright blue eyes grew dreamy. 'It's so near sometimes it's as if it all happened yesterday. My Jim would scold me for spoiling you but he never meant a word for he spoiled you too, just as if you were his own laddie.'

'Yes, Grace,' Sir Malaroy said softly. 'It was all a long time ago but I'm the richer for those days. I spent a good portion of my boyhood hours in the homes of the people of this glen

38

and I've never forgotten any of them. I stand now in your cottage, as I did long ago, with Jim in his rocking chair and Chin-wag browsing at the door, and I can see it all as plainly as I did then. I haven't changed all that much, Grace, inside of myself I'm still the laddie who ate your scones and drank milk from a pitcher, only these days I have to try and be a dignified gentleman, even when I least feel like it.'

Grace's hanky was out, she was dabbing at her eyes.

'Bigger homes don't necessarily have finer bricks, Grace,' he went on gently. 'You do see what I'm trying to say, don't you?'

'Ay, laddie, I think I do,' she agreed huskily, and Anna held her breath because the moments between the two were laden with emotion.

'Right, that's settled then.' Sir Malaroy laughed as he helped Grace out of her apron and into her coat. When that was done they all went into the tiny scullery to seek out jam jars and bundles of rhubarb and soon all three were clanking merrily down the path to the trap and the pony waiting patiently in his shafts.

'Oh, my cat!' At the last minute Grace remembered she hadn't fed the feline in question and both Anna and the 'dignified gentleman' had to wait till Grace was satisfied that her adored Woody was not only fed and watered, but that he had been made as comfortable as any cat in the land could ever hope to be on top of a nice plump cushion in front of a carefully guarded fire. The window was opened a peep in case he got the wanderlust, and a saucer of milk was placed at his nose, 'for fear he should get thirsty and nobody there to see to all his little needs'.

Only then was Grace satisfied that she could leave her home with an easy mind. After one final check to ascertain that all was well she shut her door behind her and went to join Anna and Sir Malaroy at the gate.

CHAPTER FIVE

MID-SUMMER MADNESS

Since early childhood, Lady Pandora had been taught to deal with all sorts of unusual situations that might arise in her life. She was therefore able to hide her surprise very well indeed when her husband appeared before her with Anna and Grace in tow, all three of them burdened down with bundles of rhubarb and carrying between them an assortment of jam jars.

In no time at all the maid was instructed to inform Molly the Cook that two extra dinner guests were to be catered for, and it was as well that that lady's reaction was not repeated upstairs since Molly was not fond of sudden changes in her daily routine.

Lady Pandora on the other hand was always a willing hostess. She was delighted to receive her visitors and directed Mary, the maid, to bring this, that and the other till that young lady thought herself to be very put upon and began puffing and panting in an effort to convey her feelings to those around her.

Mary was not familiar with the etiquette that went on in the upper realms of The House of Noble, her place was normally below stairs in the kitchens, but Betty, the parlourmaid, was ill in bed with the cold and Mary had been dispatched upstairs to help out. Lady Pandora did not like Mary. She was shifty-eyed, foxy-faced, and lacking in refinement, she had very little in the way of good manners and had been seen once or twice snooping about in parts of the house she had no business to be in.

Lady Pandora had recently been on the point of dismissing her but then she remembered the girl's background, an all too familiar tale of poverty and deprivation in which Mary and her six younger brothers and sisters struggled to survive. So Pandora shut her mind to Mary's faults and allowed her to stay on in her employ. She had never expected to see her upstairs however and now here she was, huffing and puffing like a pregnant sow and looking as if she would like to put a dagger through the hearts of both Anna and Grace for causing her all this bother.

Mary had a soft spot for Adam McIntyre which did not extend to his sister, Anna. Who did she think she was to merit such attentions anyway? No better than herself and maybe a mite worse than some. She and the old woman were only people from the village after all. Anna was just an employee of Noble House, and old Grace had no place here at all, except to boast about how his lordship used to visit her when he was young—as if that should gain her any privileges. All this gave Mary a great sense of resentment. She glowered meaningfully at Anna, and looked down her nose at Grace; her nostrils flared and she gave an extra loud snort.

'Mary,' Pandora's voice was cold, 'would I be correct in thinking that you are about to have some sort of seizure?'

Mary was caught off guard. She wasn't too sure what having a seizure meant, and she stared at her ladyship and stuttered, 'Begging your pardon, ma'am, no, ma'am, at least I don't think so, ma'am.'

'Good, Mary, I'm very pleased to hear that, it will therefore not hurt you to go and fetch the port and sherry this minute—and silently, Mary, as if you had little wings on your feet carrying you effortlessly along.'

Mary looked startled, she glided away as softly as her clumsy feet would allow, and old Grace, ensconced comfortably on the couch beside Anna, nodded her white head approvingly at her hostess and told her she was 'just the boy for the likes o' Mary McIntosh, a ferret if ever there was one.'

After that, the little drinks trolley arrived in double-quick time, and Lady Pandora settled herself back in a claret-velvet occasional chair to sip her port wine while Anna and Sir Malaroy between them regaled her with enthusiastic accounts of their day's adventures.

'I feel I've missed out on something rather special,' Lady Pandora said with a sigh. 'Loch Gorm is one of my favourite places. The water is always so green and filled with reflections.'

'Oh, I wish you had been with us, my lady!' Anna was flooded with remorse, and a strange feeling of guilt, as if she had done something she shouldn't have, having allowed herself to be whisked off for the day by another woman's husband.

Mary was watching her with narrowed eyes, old Grace was listening with her head tilted to one side, every so often shaking it as if she too was surprised by the revelations she was hearing.

Lady Pandora didn't immediately answer Anna, instead she turned to Mary and very coolly dismissed her. Only when the door had clicked shut behind the girl did she speak. 'I had no idea she was still there, I'm afraid she gives me the shivers. Now, what were you saying, Anna?'

43

'The trip on the loch, you would have enjoyed it.'

'Oh, it sounds wonderful, but I have had a very busy day making preparations for next week's Mid-summer Ball, I'm so looking forward to it.'

'I got all the things you asked me to get in Dunmor,' Anna said quickly, still feeling that she had somehow to make up for her day's lapse from routine affairs. 'And if Sir Malaroy is late then you must blame me because it was I who bumped into him this morning and . . .'

'Anna, Anna!' chided her ladyship with a light laugh. 'Pray control yourself, child, my husband is a grown man and doesn't have to answer to me for every move he makes. I am not his keeper.'

'We are home now, anyway,' Sir Malaroy said quietly. 'And I for one feel like a breath of fresh air before dinner. It's a perfect evening out there.' He inclined his head towards the window. 'Just right for a game of croquet on the lawn.'

'The midges will be out,' protested Grace. 'And I'm too old for these fancy games you gentry folk play. Leave me here, I'm enjoying my sherry and might have forty winks before my dinner.'

But Sir Malaroy would have none of that. Gently but firmly he led Grace outside and was soon showing her how to hold her mallet properly. Before long she was bossing him

44

about, laughing with him, telling him what to do as if he was an overgrown schoolboy.

Anna and Lady Pandora were sitting together on a rug spread out on the upper lawn. It was a perfect summer evening and the grass was freshly cut, its scent mingling with the perfumes from a riot of blooms in the borders.

'Look at him.' Lady Pandora was watching her husband with a strange light in her eye. 'He so loves the long summer days and it's a long time since I've seen him as happy as he is now. You have enchanted him today, Anna.'

Anna looked startled. 'Enchanted him? Och, my lady, you are even more fanciful than I am. I only went out on the loch with him. We kept each other company—we talked—that was all.'

'It's enough, I have seldom seen him so carefree, even with me he is very often reserved and quiet. I can't seem to touch him sometimes and I have known him more than half my life.'

'My lady, it isn't me,' Anna's dimples showed, 'it's mid-summer madness. It makes me want to do something really outrageous, like take off my stays and throw them away! It's so hot, and they're so tight, I feel like tossing them away forever, maybe into the River Cree where they will float out to sea and never be heard of again!'

A chuckle of delight escaped her ladyship's lips. 'Let's do it! You're right, it is mid-summer, there's magic in the air. Grace has

45

said she hates dressing up for dinner and I agree with her. I'm tired of being stiff and starchy and doing what is expected of me. The river runs past the east wing, we'll go there and toss our cares out of a window.'

'But,' Anna glanced down at the smooth swell of her bosom rising above her muslin dress, 'won't everything fall down?'

Lady Pandora emitted a very unladylike snort of mirth. 'Nothing of yours certainly, your body is young and firm, and nature has been kind to me, gravity has not yet had its way with me.'

They looked at one another, they stood up, they took each other's hand and fled towards the house, their peals of laughter ringing in the scented air.

Old Grace watched them go and she smiled. 'Her ladyship is like a girl when our Anna is in her company.'

Sir Malaroy nodded in agreement, his keen blue eyes filling with tenderness when he said, 'Anna is a child of light and she spreads it to all who are lucky enough to meet with her.'

'Ay, indeed she is, but there was a time when her wee world was a cheerless dark place. The House o' Noble has brought brightness to her day. It's as if she was meant to be here wi' you and her ladyship. I aye knew there was something different about Anna, she and that fine laddie, Magnus, have got breeding in them. It's a different story with that rascal

46

Adam. He's his father's son alright, but the others ...' She shook her snowy head. 'They must have taken their goodness from their mother. I never kent her well, she was only in the glen a short while before she was taken away to the asylum, but I mind she was a kindly soul wi' a look o' gentleness in her. Roderick McIntyre put her where she is, drove her to it wi' his badness and madness. From the look o' him this whilie back I'd say he's heading for just such a place himself. Justice will be done, ay, and the Lord Himself has his own way o' doing it, just you wait and see if I'm right.'

Sir Malaroy had gone very quiet while the old lady was speaking. Now he gazed at her and said almost to himself, 'Justice *will* be done, my dear old friend. Every passing day brings the judgement hour closer. In my bones I feel it creeping nearer and nearer, like a grey ghost who will only be laid to rest when the truth is revealed.'

'Laddie?' Old Grace was staring at him in questioning wonder. The sound of her voice seemed to startle him out of himself. With an effort he laughed and tried his best to be as jovial as he had been minutes before.

'Come on,' laying his hand on her shoulder he gently steered her towards the house, 'we've had enough croquet for one night. I don't want you becoming addicted to it. Sweet old ladies do the oddest things. I knew one in London, butter wouldn't have melted in her mouth, yet I observed her drinking gin like water and pushing snuff up her nose with great expertise. You aren't a secret snuff sniffer by any chance, are you, Grace?'

'*Sir Malaroy!*' she exploded indignantly, and they carried on up to the house in the best of spirits, though Grace couldn't quite forget the look in Sir Malaroy's face when he had been talking about ghosts, and truth, and justice being done. He was a man with a troubled heart, the old lady decided, and she felt sad because she had always respected and loved the lord of Noble House and she didn't like to think of him being troubled and unhappy.

*   *   *

Up in a room in the east wing, Anna and Lady Pandora stood at a window, hugging one another with glee as they watched the white specks that were their corsets gliding merrily along the River Cree's fast-flowing current. In and out of eddies and swirls the corsets went, till they reached calmer water. For a few minutes they bobbed tranquilly and then they were off again, keeping pace with one another for quite some distance before one set of laces got caught on a stone. The girl and the woman watched ecstatically, their hands at their mouths, hardly daring to breathe as they waited for the next step of the little drama to unfold.

'Oh, look!' Lady Pandora pointed. 'I don't think that one can hold on for much longer.'

The corset was free suddenly and went sailing swiftly along to re-join the other and a few moments later both garments disappeared over the edge of a little waterfall with a final flourish of laces and suspenders.

There was an enthusiastic burst of applause from the window. 'I feel marvellous, Anna!' Lady Pandora cried. 'And I'm going to eat what I want without feeling I'm going to burst out of my stays halfway through the meal. Oh, it's so good to have you here, my child,' she went on with sparkling eyes, 'I never seem to enjoy myself as much with anyone else. I can be just me when I'm with you and I look back sometimes and wonder what I ever did without you in my life.'

Anna drew in her breath. 'So you aren't angry at me anymore for going off with Sir Malaroy today?'

'Angry? My dear girl, why should I be angry? A trifle envious perhaps, because the pair of you enjoyed yourselves so much without me, but in a way I'm glad that I wasn't there. You and he have never really talked or gotten to know one another properly, so it was high time you did.'

'He's great company,' Anna said slowly. 'We did talk a lot and I lost some of my shyness with him. He seemed to know quite a lot about my mother and spoke as if he knew her in some way. I don't see how he could though, do you? She wasn't here in Glen Tarsa all that long before she had to go away and I was wondering—has he ever said anything about her to you?'

A frown marred the older woman's brow. 'Not that I can recall. I'm sure he would have mentioned it to me if he had known her at all well. Although I told you he has always been a quiet man that doesn't mean to say that we didn't talk to one another as husband and wife and as friends. He always listened to what I had to say and he would confide in me too—except ...' She hesitated, then went on rather sadly, 'In the past year or so I feel that we have drifted apart. I love him very much and it has never been my intention to hurt him, but we all have our little secrets, things that are private to us as individual human beings...'

She grew rather red at this point and Anna looked at her curiously as she went on, 'Oh, it is nothing, Anna, don't look at me like that. We all do things that we regret, but sometimes it is so difficult to know which way to turn...'

She spread her long fingers and was quiet for a moment, then she shrugged. 'Oh, why am I being so silly? My husband is a busy man and I'm just being selfish wanting all his attention. Come on, we must make ourselves presentable before we go downstairs. I would hate to fall apart at the seams in front of old Grace. She's the soul of discretion, I know, but even she has her limits and she might be rather shocked if something moved that shouldn't. So we must button each other up as best we can and hope we remain in one piece for the rest of the evening.'

*   *   *

Everybody enjoyed themselves that evening. Dinner was a carefree affair and no-one paid too much attention to etiquette. There was a good deal of banter and fun between Sir Malaroy and old Grace which did not end at the dinner table.

Sir Malaroy had ordered that extra rhubarb be picked from the kitchen gardens. The servants did as they were bid in a rather bemused fashion and looked at one another askance when the dinner party descended below stairs armed with their bundles of rhubarb and their jam jars.

Molly the Cook was utterly taken aback at this intrusion into what she considered to be her inviolable domain. 'Make jam?' she repeated when Sir Malaroy explained what he was about. 'In my kitchens? At this time o' night! Och, no, sir, it will have to wait till I'm ready to see to it. Mary can do it if she has any spare time in the morning.'

'Out, Molly.' Gently but firmly the gentleman of the house propelled the protesting cook away from the table to which she had anchored herself with two tightly clenched fists. 'Don't worry about a thing, dear lady,' he told her soothingly, 'we'll attend to the washing-up and make sure we leave everything spick and span.'

Thus it was that a red-faced, mortified Molly, gave up her below-stairs premises to the master and mistress of the house, forever more to recount the tale to anyone who would care to listen to it.

As soon as the kitchen was empty the invasive party got to work, merrily hacking up sticks of rhubarb on the scrubbed white wooden table and throwing the resulting pieces into the big jelly pans that Sir Malaroy had manhandled down from their hooks in the white-painted utensils closet. In the course of the evening the jam jars ran short, resulting in a hilarious search of the cupboards when everybody got in everybody's way and no-one seemed in the least concerned about anything.

Lady Pandora's hair parted company with its restraining pins and went tumbling about her shoulders in attractive disarray; Anna lost a button from her cuff; Sir Malaroy's beard became sticky from licking the hot jam off the back of a big wooden spoon; old Grace pottered in a long white apron and thoroughly enjoyed herself, bossing everybody about.

Halfway through the evening Molly looked in to see if she could help and was promptly chased away by a few choice words from Sir Malaroy as he tested the jam for the umpteenth time.

Molly snorted, glancing meaningfully at the sinkful of dirty utensils, and then she flounced away with her nose in the air.

'She'll never forgive us,' laughed her ladyship. 'But it's been such fun I don't care what Molly or anyone else thinks. We'll probably never do anything like this again and will look back on this night with affection and gratitude.'

'Ay, and never let it be said that we left an untidy kitchen,' nodded Grace. 'We'll clean everything up and put it back the way we found it; that way no-one will have cause to speak about us behind our backs.'

By ten-thirty the pots and pans had been washed and returned to their rightful places, along with everything else that had been commandeered for use in the jam-making session.

Sir Malaroy hadn't helped with the dishes; he was quite content sticking labels on the jam pots and arranging them into neat rows, as if he was loath to leave the results of his labours behind.

'No-one will steal it, darling,' his wife laughed. 'It will still be there in the morning and I'm perfectly sure we'll get our share of the spoils. And just think, next time you bite into a pancake spread with jam you'll know it was made by your very own fair hands and will enjoy it all the more for that.'

Grace, who was a creature of habit, announced her intention of wanting to go home to see to her cat before bedtime. Since she rose at six each morning her request was not an unreasonable one and Sir Malaroy said he would take her down in the pony trap.

'Havers!' she objected without enthusiasm, as she was tired and a jaunt home in the trap was tempting. 'Anna will take my arm and we'll be down that road in no time.'

'I insist, I'm in need of some fresh air after slaving over a hot stove all night. Will you come too, Pandora?'

'No, I think I'll have a bath, I haven't been so sticky since I stole a jar of honey when I was five years old and ate it with my fingers in a cupboard under the stairs.'

'You did that?' An oddly tender smile touched his lips. 'My perfect little Pandy actually dipped her dainty fingers in the honey pot—a stolen one to boot?'

She smiled back at him. 'Your not-so-perfect Pandy committed many such misdemeanours but didn't think they were all that terrible at the time.'

'Ah, innocent childhood,' he sighed sadly. 'Would that we could have remained as untarnished as we were then. But time changes everything and everybody and there is no turning back—for anyone.'

He went off to arrange for the trap to be brought to the door and she stood looking after him for several long moments, a sad, strange expression in the depths of her wondrous violet eyes.

So much that was frank and forthright remained unsaid between herself and her husband these days. More and more he was showing indications of the unrest that was in him and she knew that the time was coming when they would have to be honest with one another—before it was too late for them both.

CHAPTER SIX

WILD OATS

It was lovely riding along the glen road. The air was refreshingly cool, the sky filled with honey-rose light on that long day in mid-summer. Grace was soon delivered to her door, to be met by her adored cat mewing a rather reproachful welcome.

'We'll send you down your jam,' Sir Malaroy called as he took up the reins once more. The old lady nodded and stood at her gate, waving till the clip-clop of the pony's hooves could be heard no more.

'You don't want to go home just yet, do you, Anna?' Sir Malaroy asked, guiding the pony off the road and into a little hidden glade at the edge of the woods.

Anna thought how quiet it was without the rumble of wheels under her, but soon other sounds became apparent, the blackbirds still singing from lofty perches in the woods; a fox barking from far in the glen; the trees rustling in the breezes blowing down from the hills.

'A perfect midsummer's eve,' said Sir Malaroy, breathing in the soft air appreciatively. 'Will you get up at dawn, Anna, to wash your face in dew and wish that soon you will meet the young man of your dreams?'

She made a wry little face. 'It sounds wonderful but I don't think it's likely. I'll get up at dawn certainly, but only to milk Clover and to prepare breakfast, and my face will be washed as usual in cold water from the pitcher on my dresser.'

'Are you telling me that you don't have a young man? A girl who is as pretty as you are?'

'I've never met anyone I liked well enough.'

His hand curled over hers and she felt breathless and strange and somehow unreal as he said, 'I want to thank you for crossing my path this morning. It's been a rare and wonderful day, one that I shall never forget for as long as I live. You gave me something that I haven't had in a long time, true joy, the bright, pure joy that one gets blind to as the years pass. When I was a boy I used to feel as if a lamp was burning inside of me. As I grew older it became

56

dimmer. Today you polished up my lamp for me, my dear little Anna Ban, I could see and feel and hope for the first time in years.'

He pulled her close to him, then his lips touched her cheek with a kiss that was warm, sweet, fleeting, yet somehow everlasting.

'Anna,' he murmured softly, 'I've wanted to do that all day. I just couldn't help it...'

She stilled his lips with her fingers, trying to savour the moment. She knew that nothing like this would ever happen to her again. It was mid-summer, there was enchantment in the air, for that night only she and the lord of Noble House were locked into a magical sphere that belonged to them and them alone.

She bit her lip. 'I really must go home now, Magnus might be back from Bute and I want to be there to get his supper for him. He'll be tired after such a long day.'

'You're very fond of your older brother, Anna.'

'I love him,' she answered simply.

Sir Malaroy said nothing more as he guided the pony out of the clearing and on up the road to The Gatehouse. With his hand under her elbow he helped her alight from the trap; their eyes met and held for a brief moment, then she turned and walked the short distance to her door, knowing that he stood where he was without moving, watching her go.

*   *   *

57

The kitchen was stifling after the heat of the day. Magnus hadn't yet returned from his day's droving and all was quiet and still with an air of peace about it that was lacking when Roderick was at home. Without his surly, unpredictable presence, the house seemed to have shrugged off a shroud of gloom; the atmosphere was sleepy and warm and friendly.

Despite Roderick, Anna had always loved The Gatehouse with its nooks and crannies and its windows looking out to the hills and the green fields stretching down to the river.

Everything was relaxed tonight and Anna allowed herself to relax with it as she stood meditatively by the door, her eyes dreamy and faraway as she allowed her thoughts to wander. Her emotions were running high. She had hoped that Magnus would be here when she came in as she hadn't wanted to be alone so soon.

All at once the house seemed to be too quiet, and she suddenly remembered how her cat, Tibby, used to hurry to meet her, its tail high in the air, its welcoming meows and purrs filling her ears as she lifted it into her arms to cuddle it and kiss its dainty pink nose. Anger shafted through her, anger at her father for taking the life of a small creature that had been so generous with its affections, so sparing with its demands. It was Adam who had found the cat, in the ashpit where Roderick had thrown it after choking it to death.

Anna remembered the hopeless rage in Adam's eyes when he said, '*He* killed her, didn't he, Anna? Just throttled the life out o' her with those bloody big meat cleavers of his. I was never a great lover o' cats but I liked Tibby, she was always pleased to see me when nobody else was.'

Roderick had affected great surprise at the discovery of Tibby's body in the ashpit and had quickly blamed it on one of the mill workers.

'Who came into our garden and killed our cat, then buried her in a fit of remorse for what he had done,' Adam had said sarcastically, earning a clip on the ear for daring to speak his mind.

Anna could recall that scene quite clearly and she would never forget the look in Adam's eyes; it had burned with such hatred she shuddered every time she thought about it.

Softly she closed the kitchen door, unwilling to disturb the tranquility of the house. Her mind was filling again, this time with sweeter memories; the trip on *The Kelpie* with Sir Malaroy; the interlude with old Grace in Moss Cottage; dinner at Noble House...

A picture came unbidden to her mind, that of two pairs of corsets merrily swimming along in the river, diving and dipping and finally disappearing over the rocks in a cascade of foaming water.

She put her hand to her mouth and chuckled as happiness overwhelmed her again. It had been such a good day, filled with laughter and unexpected happenings, and she hugged the secrets of it to her heart. She felt exhilarated at the thought of her newfound closeness with Sir Malaroy. He had awakened in her a great depth of emotion, although she couldn't explain the reason why.

She moved about restlessly. Oh, if only Magnus were home, she needed him here beside her, she hated it when he wasn't in, nothing was the same without him, nothing. He might be her brother, but she had always loved him in a way that no sister ever should. It was an impossible, unnatural, forbidden love, and she was afraid even to think about it ...

Thinking that he might have come in earlier and gone straight to bed, she pulled off her hat and went to the boys' bedroom to throw open the door.

A jumble of impressions hit her: Adam, and Beth Jordan, cavorting naked in the double iron bedstead in the corner, oblivious to all but their lusty explorations of one another's bodies; Beth's long legs curling around Adam's muscular buttocks, a dew of sweat gleaming on her brow, her pale blue eyes dazed and unfocused; she looked sleepy and contented, the way a cat looks after feasting on cream.

For a few moments Beth appeared to be unaware that the door of the room had opened, then slowly she turned her head to gaze at Anna standing there. Seconds passed, each one seeming longer than the other, then her eyes grew round and became filled with annoyance rather than surprise.

'Get off, Adam!' she hissed into his ear. 'Your sister has just come in. Get *off* me, do you hear!'

For Adam, the intrusion was an untimely one. Beth's hungry demands on his body had whipped his blood to fire and he was in a frenzy of excitement. For more than a year now they had been making love wherever and whenever they could, usually in places sadly lacking in home comforts but well hidden from prying eyes. Tonight was their first time in a bed; tonight it wasn't his father in the next room with Nellie Jean, now it was his turn, and Beth had driven him crazy because she knew how to make him wait for his release, had forced him time and again to hold back till her own demanding needs were met.

And now, here was Anna, at the crucial moment—and he couldn't hold back, he couldn't. There, right in front of her, he gasped, moaned, and cried out in an agonising blend of pleasure, humiliation, and sorrow that the sister he loved so dearly should see him like this, with Beth Jordan, her best friend since childhood.

'*Anna!*' His heart was thudding, his lungs bursting, as he called out her name, his body doubled over as he fought to regain breath. 'Anna,' he repeated, his voice growing soft with shame, 'I didn't expect you back so early.'

'So I see.' Anna forced herself to speak steadily though her face was burning. No wonder he had been so anxious to have her out of the way when he had spoken to Sir Malaroy earlier in the evening. Just like Adam not to miss out on any opportunity that chanced his way and he would do anything if it meant having Beth to himself for a while. Anna had known of course that the two of them had been seeing one another for some time.

Beth had laughed about it and had tried to pass it over as a casual friendship. She certainly didn't want her parents to find out about it. Her designs on Adam were purely physical.

Now, she was more annoyed than ashamed that Anna had caught her 'with her bloomers down' so to speak, but she trusted the girl who had been her most enduring friend since their schooldays, spent under the reign of Miss Priscilla McLeod in the tiny village school. She began wriggling into her clothes and Anna looked at her, surprised to see that the girl she had always thought so beautiful wasn't so at all without her layers of finery. She was certainly tall, with good long legs, but her body was unattractively gaunt, her waist was surprisingly thick, her shoulders square and unfeminine, her swinging breasts too large and too pendulous for a girl of seventeen.

'Well! Are you seeing enough!' Beth was glaring at Anna, her voice high with rage. 'You always did gawp, Anna!' She tugged viciously at the laces of her corsets. 'Oh, damn these things! They get tighter every day. C'mon, Adam, do me up, you were quick enough to get them off. I'll *have* to get dressed properly. I daren't risk Mother seeing anything amiss, she's got eyes like a hawk.'

But Adam was hurrying into his own clothes, anxious to get both himself and the big double bed back in order before Magnus arrived home. Once upon a time the two brothers had shared this bed but Adam now had one of his own, a single bed at which Beth had turned up her nose, saying the other was far more suitable for what they'd had in mind when they came sneaking into The Gatehouse earlier on.

'I'll put on clean bedcovers,' Anna said woodenly, the idea of Magnus lying on soiled bedlinen making her shudder. Going over to the furiously struggling Beth she swallowed down her feelings of annoyance at her friend and offered to do her up.

The sweaty odour of Beth's body cloyed into her nostrils. It had never occurred to her that this girl, with all her airs and graces and snobbery, could smell anything else but nice. In the space of just a few minutes Anna had lost some of her illusions about Beth Jordan of Corran House, who had always at least given the appearance of being a young lady of refinement.

But Magnus had always known differently. As a boy he had told Anna, 'Beth might look like a little lady but inside she's common and vulgar and one day you'll see the truth for yourself.'

Anna had shut her mind to things like that and had told herself that everyone had their faults. All through the years of her growing up she had tried hard to think the best of Beth, though there had been times when she gladly could have wrung that young lady's long, white, swan-like neck.

One by one, Magnus's predictions were coming to pass, tonight's little episode having put the cap on everything. Even so, Anna knew she would never easily abandon Beth, and she was even able to smile a little when Beth swung round to say eagerly, 'Oh, *would* you, Anna? Thanks ever so. I wish we didn't have to wear these horrid stays, I can hardly breathe when I've got them on. Don't do them up too tightly.'

A few minutes later she looked like the Beth that Anna had always known, demure, well-dressed, elegant—but slightly on the dishevelled side for all that, and definitely not as sweet-smelling as usual.

'Walk with me to the door, Anna, there's a dear,' she requested, and Anna followed her friend, wishing with all her heart that none of this had happened. It wasn't exactly a perfect end to a perfect day and she felt uneasy as she wondered what would come of it all.

If Beth could have chosen to have had any sort of meaningful relationship with a McIntyre lad it would most certainly have been with Magnus, whom she had always loved and admired. Magnus however didn't want Beth, and made that fact quite plain while remaining friendly and pleasant towards her. If Mrs Victoria Jordan, Beth's mother, could have had her way, her daughter would be engaged to a 'proper young man' by now and mixing with the right kind of people while she was about it. As it was, Beth had stormed her tempestuous way out of two boarding schools and had lasted only weeks at the English finishing school for young ladies she had been sent to two years ago.

'I am fed up trying to be a proper young lady,' she had told her mother when she had been dismissed with a letter that proclaimed her to be a disruptive and unfavourable influence on the rest of the girls.

She keeps trying to escape, the headmistress had written. *Twice, at an unseemly hour of night, she has been caught, making her way into town to sample 'other forms of life', as she puts it. She's unhealthily fond of the company of undesirable young men and with all this taken into account I see no other option but to dismiss her.*

Mrs Jordan had been shocked and horrified by all this. She was unable to understand a daughter who turned her back on life's niceties in favour of the crude and common elements of society. Mr William Jordan, with his wider understanding of the world, recognised his daughter's rebellious need to escape the rules set down by her mother. He knew that his wife was a woman playing out her own high-flying social ambitions through her daughter. In the process she had closed her mind to the dangers of trying to manipulate someone else's life and so she blundered on, never succeeding in anything she tried to arrange for Beth, blaming her for everything that went wrong.

It was a form of retaliation that made Beth go her own sweet way. At the moment she was marking time, recklessly sewing her wild oats with Adam while waiting for bigger fish to turn up. She had her eye on one or two possibilities but the favourite was Lady Pandora's nephew, Lucas Noble of Noble House who had, on quite a few occasions, risen to the lure of Beth's willing charms. She had never quite succeeded in fully baiting him however. He was away at school in England for a greater part of the year and Beth was always afraid that he would meet and fall in love with someone of his own social standing. He had finished, or so he said, with that snobby little Miss Chastity Belt as Beth had called her, even though she was really Lady Something or Other and as pretty as a picture to boot. But she was empty-headed and priggish, and Lucas himself had told Beth that he had never met anyone as exciting as she was.

'We'll enjoy ourselves next time I'm home, Bethy,' he had said, his dark eyes flashing in his handsome, sanguine face. That had been at Easter, and Beth was in a ferment of impatience waiting for that 'next time'. She was hoping desperately that he would be present at the Mid-summer Ball which was being held at Noble House next week. She and her parents had been invited, the result of which had meant another shopping spree for her mother and a headache for William Jordan, whose financial budget was already under a terrible strain.

Beth herself, her wardrobe already bursting at the seams, felt she had enough new clothes to last her a lifetime, but she knew her mother and went along willingly enough with her plans. It was mid-summer after all, and she did want to look her best for Lucas.

So all in all, she was in a fever of anticipation waiting for Lucas but for now she amused herself with Adam, who satisfied her physical appetites admirably well but knew better than to push himself into any other aspect of her life.

CHAPTER SEVEN

ADAM'S UNDOING

Once in the tiny lobby, Beth grabbed Anna's hand and said urgently, 'You do know, don't you, that Adam is most awfully persistent and just won't leave me alone? I like him too, of course, and with your old Iron Rod away and my parents out for the evening—well—it seemed too good a chance to miss. Anyway,' she tossed her head, 'we haven't done anybody any harm, have we, Anna?' Without waiting for an answer she rushed on, 'It won't happen again, I can promise you. Lucas will be home soon and he must never find out. My parents mustn't hear of it either, especially Mother, she would die if this came to her ears and I would never hear the end of it.'

'You should know me better than that, Beth.'

'I know, best friends and everything.' Beth's pale blue eyes were slightly mocking as she spoke. 'But do we *really* know one another? Now that we're all grown up? What, for instance, do you get up to in your spare time?' Leaning forward she whispered, 'Sir Malaroy is an exciting man, isn't he? Mother's old gasbag of a friend, Fanny McWhirter, said she saw you both strolling arm in arm through

68

town this morning. Never fear though, I won't say a word to anyone else.'

'Oh, but there's nothing to say!'

'Och, wheesht, Anna,' Beth smiled wickedly. 'You *are* human like the rest of us, and what Lady Pandora doesn't know won't hurt her. Oh, I am well aware that everyone thinks you're a little angel, especially her ladyship, but you and I know better—don't we, Anna Ban?'

Closing one eye she gave her friend a slow, deliberate, conspiratorial wink. She looked so funny Anna might have laughed if she hadn't felt so annoyed. As it was she countered Beth's remark by saying, 'Aren't you ever worried that you might get pregnant, Beth?'

'Don't be silly,' Beth answered with an incredulous laugh. 'I always bathe afterwards. Besides, I've never been regular with my monthlies. I missed a whole twelve weeks once and it's been off and on ever since. People don't have babies when they're that irregular. If they did, I would have bagged Lucas long ago!'

Anna was stunned into silence as it dawned on her just how little Beth must know about the facts of life. Anna herself had gleaned much of her own knowledge from the animals of the surrounding countryside as she grew up. She had witnessed matings and birthings many times; to her it was all just a part of nature's pattern. She was aware that Mrs Victoria Jordan had always shielded her daughter from the 'cruder aspects of life' but, until now, Anna hadn't realised how limited Beth's knowledge of her own womanly functions must be.

'You can still have babies, Beth,' she hazarded carefully. 'Why don't you ask your mother to take you to the doctor for an examination?'

Beth examined her nails restlessly. 'I've often thought about it, but you know what Mother's like. She would fuss, fuss, fuss, and probably die of shame into the bargain. She's never spoken to me about things like that and has a bad enough job trying to understand her own body without having to deal with mine as well.

'I truly cannot imagine how she came to have me. Poor Father. It can't have been a picnic for him. I'm sure he must have fumbled about a lot in the dark while she shut her eyes and prayed to God for forgiveness. As to my actual birth, did she think I was going to pop out of a cabbage in the garden, I wonder? Or perhaps materialise out of the sky in the beak of a stork? All neatly wrapped up in a pretty little bundle? It must have come as a great shock to her when I started coming out of her body. She probably thought she was falling apart at the seams or that she had been taking too much syrup-of-figs.'

Anna felt a great rush of affection and sympathy for Beth. She seemed to have everything yet she had none of the things that really mattered. As a result she was always dissatisfied with her lot, always searching for something and never quite finding what it was she was looking for. 'Take care, Beth,' Anna whispered, putting her arms round her friend and hugging her tightly. 'If you ever need me for anything I'll always be here.'

'As a matter of fact I do need you, Anna,' Beth said promptly. 'Could you possibly spare a half-hour tomorrow evening to come over and tell me what you think of my new frock? I'm not quite sure I really like it and when I look through my wardrobe I can't see the wood for the trees. I know you have next to nothing yourself, but you've always had a good eye for style, so what do you say? Around eightish? A good chin-wag and a fashion show, followed by tea and some of Fat Jane's delicious hot crumpets spread with cream and jam?'

Anna burst out laughing and nodded, and the pair of them parted on the best of terms, their differences forgotten for the moment.

*   *   *

When Anna returned to the kitchen it was to find Adam seated by the smouldering wood fire, his chin in his hand as he stared moodily up the chimney.

'I'm sorry, Anna,' he mumbled without looking at her. 'I never meant for that to happen. Beth can be a real bitch sometimes and told me she wouldn't see me again unless I

71

provided her wi' some home comforts. Say you'll forgive me, Anna, say it.'

'I'm not your keeper, Adam,' she told him softly.

'I wish you were! I wish somebody was!' he said savagely, and getting up he blundered past her out of the house, banging the door behind him, and she knew she wouldn't see him again that night.

More and more of late he had taken to nocturnal habits, drinking, staying out late, often not coming home at all, laying down his head where he could, sleeping rough when the drink took the feet from under him and he couldn't stagger another yard. If something happened to really upset him his behaviour became even worse and once or twice he had been admonished by the local policeman for unruly conduct in the inns and taverns he frequented.

Anna stood alone in the kitchen, her mind on this younger brother of hers. She had never been able to understand him, often she had hated him for all the cruel things he had said and done to her over the years. But there was something terribly pathetic and lost about him that tugged at her heartstrings and made her want to help him all she could. With Adam that was never easy, he despised what he called 'softness', and had a habit of mistaking kindness for pity. With a sigh she went to put on the kettle for her bedtime cocoa, hoping that Magnus would come in soon and share it with her.

Eleven o'clock came and went and still he hadn't appeared; he was later than usual. Tired out after her busy day she made her way to her tiny cubby-hole of a bedroom. Until fairly recently it had been no more than a large walk-in cupboard containing all sorts of discarded household junk, Roderick being of the opinion that nothing should ever be thrown out as there was no telling when it would be needed again. But Magnus had told his sister it was high time she had her own room, and in defiance of his father he had cleared everything out of the small enclosure and in it he had installed Anna's bed and a few other necessities.

'It isn't much, but at least you can have a bit o' privacy now,' Magnus had told her. 'It's even got a little window so you'll be able to see out and get fresh air when you want it.'

Anna loved the tiny room, and she loved Magnus for his thoughtfulness, blessing him as she undressed and got into bed. It was his habit to come in and say goodnight to her, but she was asleep by the time he got home and she didn't hear him when he stole softly into her room to kiss her lightly on the cheek and stroke the flaxen hair away from her face. He sat there at the edge of her bed for a long time, his hazel eyes tender as he gazed at her lying in her repose. She was very beautiful and childlike in

73

her white gown, with her hair tumbling over the pillows, and he was glad that she was asleep so that he could just sit there and look at her for as long as he wanted. But he was exhausted himself after his travels of the day and his eyelids were growing heavy. 'Goodnight, sweet Anna,' he whispered, and went through to his own room to tumble into bed, thinking that he would fall asleep instantly. Instead he tossed and turned restlessly, thinking of Anna in her little room, as alone as he was, the house all quiet and still around them, with never a groan or a grunt or a curse to disturb the peace.

It was heaven with Roderick away, but how much more heavenly it would have been, Magnus thought, if he could have shared the love and the wonder of it with Anna, lying here beside him, her arms around him, loving him in a way a sister would never love a brother.

*   *   *

It was the next day and Adam was in a foul mood. He had just asked Beth if he could see her later but she had rejected him, telling him she was seeing his sister that evening and anyway, she had decided it would be better if they didn't meet again as it was 'all getting too risky for words'.

All that day Adam fretted and fumed, and by late afternoon he had worked himself into a state of outrage and was ready to vent his anger on anyone or anything who dared to cross him. As soon as it was time to stop work in the mill he and a gang of his mates made their way to The Coach House Inn, there to feast on pies and beans for their tea, while they boasted to one another about women and laughed uproariously at dirty jokes, the coarser the better.

As the evening wore on they competed with each other to see who could drink the most beer in the least possible time and by nine o'clock they were decanted from the establishment by John Grier, the proprietor, for upsetting everyone with their swearing and rowdiness.

'Swine!' Adam swore, wiping his mouth with the back of his hand and making to go after the innkeeper.

But Danny Black grabbed him and pulled him away and the gang went on up the road, swaggering and laughing.

When Angus Johnson, son of Jimmy, head gamekeeper for the Leanachorran Estates, announced that he had a bottle of whisky hidden in the woods they all went to dig it up and sat giggling round the bole of 'the whisky tree', taking turns to swig from the bottle, growing more intoxicated with every mouthful.

It was quiet in the woods, with only an occasional whinney from the nearby stables to break the silence. Dusk was merging into darkness when Charlie Kennedy spotted Sally McDonald wandering along the lane from the direction of the village. She was in one of her relatively calm moods and was singing to herself, a surprisingly sweet little melody that came out in short snatches, in between puffs of her clay pipe and bites of a jammy scone that had been given to her by Kate McLeod on her way past Knock Farm. She was as happy and as contented as she could possibly be and was so engrossed with her simple pleasures she wasn't aware of anything that was going on outside her own small world.

'Let's get a hold of the silly old bitch,' Adam suggested with a snigger. 'We could get her into the hayshed and take her knickers off. I've always wanted to pay that family back for what Davie did to me—nearly beating me to death.'

The others took up the idea eagerly and didn't waste time about it. Creeping through the trees they pounced on Sally, threw her to the ground and roughly muffled her cries with a grimy rag. They then proceeded to half-carry, half-drag her, into the hayshed, then threw her on to a bundle of bedding straw in a corner. She was kicking and struggling furiously, her bare legs flaying the air, violently tossing her head from side to side.

Freeing herself for an instant she bit as hard as she could into the nearest hand and Danny Black jumped back, cursing as he stared in disbelief at his torn flesh.

'Bitch!' he spat malevolently, and tore off his neckerchief to stuff it into her mouth, so viciously that he drew blood.

The others had a hold of her limbs and were struggling to pin them down. Soon she was lying spreadeagled on the straw but she was like a wildcat in her panic and managed to free one hand to gouge a furrow of bloody streaks along the length of Charlie Kennedy's arm with her long dirty fingernails. With an oath he let go of her and she fought tooth and claw to escape the rest of her captors, all the forces of her untamed spirit unleashing themselves in the arching and writhing of her agile body. 'Hold on to her!' ordered Adam. 'I don't want the bitch kicking me!'

'Hurry up, then,' panted Danny. 'Christ! She's like a crazed animal. She ought to be kept in a cage in the woods out o' harm's way.'

Adam lurched forward, throwing back Sally's ragged dress. 'Her arse is bare!' he laughed. 'I never thought o' that! Silly Sally doesn't wear knickers.'

'We canny let it go at that,' Charlie spoke in disappointed tones. 'I was hoping for a bit o' fun wi' her myself.' His eyes gleamed. 'I know, I dare you to have a poke at her, Adam.'

Adam screwed up his face in disgust. 'Poke that! No bloody fear. What d'you take me for?'

'What's the matter?' Danny asked sarcastically. 'Aren't you up to it? Maybe all that boasting you do about women is just a lot o' hot air.'

'That's right!' The others took up the cry, their faces flushed with drink. 'How do we know it isn't just a pack o' lies?'

'It's likely just words,' taunted Angus. 'Could be he's hung no bigger than a rabbit.'

Adam's eyes blazed. 'Want me to damned well show you?'

'Ay, go on, show us what you're made of!'

Slowly and deliberately Adam pulled his braces down over his shoulders. His trousers fell to his feet and he kicked them away.

'Go on, Adam,' urged Angus.

Sally was fighting harder than ever, her legs still flaying the straw. Adam glanced at her not-unshapely limbs and felt a surge of excitement. The whisky was glowing in his belly, dulling his sensibilities, making him feel big and fearless. Weaving his way over to the pile of straw he stood towering over her. Her eyes went black with dread. She knew this particular McIntyre alright, had suffered badly at his hands when he had half-killed her in a fit of pique and rage some years ago. Her brother Davie had soon sorted him out for what he had done, but Davie wasn't here now and Sally felt stark terror rising in her gorge.

Adam laughed. She whimpered but the pathetic little sound raised no sympathy; instead it only added to the feeling of power that was mounting within him.

'Hold her, lads,' he ordered, and began to torment her, pulling faces at her, calling her names, the guffaws from his mates goading him on, and all the while Sally moved her matted, dark head from side to side in a frenzy of fear and tried to free herself from the bruising hands that held her.

'God, she smells!' Adam screwed up his face. 'Get that bucket o' water and throw it over her. I'm no' going near her till she's cleaned up a bit.'

Charlie scurried for the bucket and slopped some of the cold water over Sally, who drew her legs up with shock.

'Obliging, isn't she?' sniggered Adam, his coarse yet handsome face alight with devilment. 'See that bit o' rope over there, get it and tie her arms to these posts.'

'That's going a bit far,' objected Danny.

'Look, you lot wanted this. It's got to be done properly or not at all. Do as I say and tie her arms.'

Danny and Charlie looked at one another apprehensively. Somewhat soberly they fetched the pieces of rope and carried out Adam's orders.

Adam, really carried away by now, was wasting no more time and threw himself down on top of Sally. In spite of his words of bravado to his mates he really didn't want to hurt her, just frighten her a bit, but he couldn't very well back out now, not with Danny and Angus chanting out words of encouragement to him and Charlie telling him to hurry up because he was feeling sick.

Adam took a deep breath; shutting his eyes he thought of Beth and he began to move, slowly at first, then more urgently as memories of his times with Beth filled his veins with fire. Sally gave a muffled scream of pain as brutally he entered her. Blindly he pushed and sought, sweat breaking on his brow as the first pleasurable sensations made him forget all else.

Sally had stopped struggling. Above the choking gag that covered her mouth her black eyes were glazed with terror and pain.

The others were gaping in awe at the sight.

'Go easy, man,' breathed Danny uneasily.

But Adam was beyond hearing. His eyes were staring, fixed on the wall in front of him, but he wasn't seeing it; his whole being was concentrated on the fire that burned within him and his need to release himself from its pitiless ecstasy.

'He's gone mad!' cried Danny. 'I'm getting out of it!'

'Me too,' said Charlie.

There was a scramble to the door, a creak as it opened and shut, leaving Adam alone with Sally. The crude sounds of his enjoyment were growing in volume, filling the hayshed for several long moments before he fell back, panting with his efforts, unaware that he was alone till he opened his eyes and looked around.

'Cowardly sods!' he cursed. The whisky bottle was lying in the hay where it had been dropped. It was still a quarter-full and raising it to his mouth he drank deeply. Coughing and spluttering he drew a hand over his mouth and lay back to look at Sally, who was lying quite still, gazing blankly up at the rafters.

'D'you know what I think?' he began chattily. 'I think you enjoyed that, silly old Sally.'

He gazed thoughtfully into her fear-filled eyes and throwing back his head he let out a shout of laughter. When he had regained his breath he got up and stood over her, his voice filling with menace when he said, 'Say a word o' this to anyone and I'll kill you. Do you hear?'

There was no response. Bending down he grabbed her by the throat to pull her head up till her eyes were level with his. 'Do you hear me, Sally? Don't try to defy me if you know what's good for you. Say a word to Davie about this and I'll break the two o' you in half. Answer me, you stupid bitch.'

Wordlessly she nodded and roughly he pushed her away from him and straightened up. She was beginning to tremble with a mixture of cold and shock.

Feeling uneasy, Adam struggled into his trousers before untying her wrists and removing the gag from her mouth. 'Here.'

Taking pity on her he tossed the whisky bottle at her. 'Revive yourself wi' that. I know how much you like booze, you old soak, so thank your lucky stars you met me tonight and got everything you ever wanted out o' life.'

He gave an insane giggle, burped, took a last, long look at her and was about to stumble away when a wave of utter exhaustion washed over him. Staggering back to where Sally lay, he dropped down beside her and fell instantly into a comatose sleep.

Beside him Sally drank her whisky and cried. A few minutes later she began to sing softly and forgot to cry. She depleted the whisky bottle and hiccuped. Getting up she hoisted her dress around her thighs. Straddling the prone figure on the floor she urinated all over him, making sure she soaked as much of him as she could.

Then she smiled, a slow, soft, secretive smile, and staggered away out of the shed to splash water over herself from a nearby burn. It was a warm night, and Sally was used to having the sky as a roof over her head; sometimes it was safer than being at home with her brother Davie when he was in one of his tempers.

CHAPTER EIGHT

INTERLUDE

Anna and Beth were having a lovely evening in Beth's own little sitting room, which was situated just off her bedroom. Because the evening air was cool, Beth had requested that a fire be lit and the atmosphere was altogether warm, friendly, and inviting.

The decor of the room was individual to say the least, stamped as it was with Beth's own distinctive style. She had chosen the drapes and furnishings herself and while her mother was throwing up her hands in horror at such 'Bohemian tastes', her daughter had calmly gone on to pick out the carpet of her choice— one, of course, of which her mother entirely disapproved.

'Really, Beth,' she had scolded. 'I have no idea where, or from whom, you get your ideas. The whole exercise is a waste of good money as far as I am concerned and it's as well that it is only yourself and your friends who will get the doubtful benefit of sampling such peculiar surroundings.'

Anna thought nothing of the kind. To her the room was cosy and comfortable yet utterly fashionable, and she was delighted to settle herself in one of the pink-and-green chairs and relax a little after her labours of the afternoon.

For the last two years she had been painting a portrait of Lady Pandora. It had been a long process. Lady Pandora wasn't a particularly restful sitter. In fact she was a fidget if ever there was one and would make any excuse not to pose.

'I'm always too busy doing something else,' she would tell Anna, and for nearly a year the project had been suspended, 'till further notice'. Now the painting had once more been resurrected, with a shame-faced Pandora apologising to Anna and promising to be 'a model of patience from now on'. But she was too much of a butterfly to really keep her word and Anna's good nature was stretched to the limit as she strove to capture all she could in the scant time allotted to her.

'One day it will be finished, Anna,' Lady Pandora laughed. 'Then the world will see what a great artist you are.'

To which Anna nodded and sighed and said, 'Yes, m'lady, and by that time I might be dead and buried and forgotten by all who knew me, and they might be dead and buried too, and there would be nobody to remember who or what we all looked like when we were alive.'

'Dear child!' Her ladyship had pealed with delighted mirth at this. 'You are such a funny wee thing when you talk like that ...' At this point her eyes had grown misty and faraway and she had gone on to say dreamily, 'There was only one other person in my life who used to say such things—a man with smiling Irish eyes and a nature so beguiling...'

She had stopped her reminiscences there, but Anna had never forgotten the look of love in her eyes as she was speaking nor the pink sweet flush that had diffused her face, making her look like a sparkly-eyed young girl whose thoughts had carried her away on wings of rapture.

These were the sort of confidences that the lady of the house was wont to share with Anna, who felt honoured to be trusted in this way. Sometimes, however, it all proved to be rather exhausting, especially when portrait sitting was on the agenda, and Anna was very glad to relax in the quietly luxurious surroundings of Beth's room and let her do all the talking, something that Beth had been good at for as far back as Anna could remember.

Beth was in one of her more humorous moods that evening and set out to amuse her visitor with a one-model fashion show. Rapidly she changed from one outfit to another, mincing round the room and giving hilarious running commentaries on the merits of each garment.

'This wonderful ensemble with the wicked bits of moth-eaten lace has been loaned to us tonight by Madam Droopy Drawers of Brothel À La Paris; this next creation of threadbare threads and see-through spider's webs is straight from the rag cupboard of Larchwood just down the road, and this masterpiece of wobbly seams has been personally hand-crafted and ruined by old Grace of Moss Cottage just up the road.'

Beth was at her best. She posed, pouted and paraded, and when she grew tired of that she impersonated people like Fat Jane the Cook, and Fanny McWhirter, her mother's friend, till Anna was rolling about in her seat with merriment.

'Oh, Beth,' she said at last, wiping her eyes, 'you were always so good at making me laugh. I wish we could be together more often but everything's changed so much since our schooldays.'

'I know.' Beth looked quite sad for a moment. 'They were the best days ever. I've never been as happy as I was then. Still,' her eyes gleamed, 'some things change for the better. I've just heard Lucas is coming home for the Ball next week and I just can't wait for him to see me in my new dress.'

She jumped up. 'I've been saving it to the last, Anna. Close your eyes and don't look till I tell you.'

When Anna was finally permitted to open her eyes she saw in front of her a vision of lilac satin and cream lace, close fitting, low cut, utterly feminine and breathtakingly eyecatching.

'It's a bit tight.' Viciously Beth tugged the

straining material at her waist. 'Mother will have to see about getting it altered.'

'Oh, but it's beautiful, Beth.' Anna ran her hands over the luscious cloth. 'Lucas won't be able to take his eyes off you.'

'And you, Anna? What will you be wearing?'

'I don't know yet.'

'You don't know! For the Ball of the summer! You are going, aren't you? Everybody will be there.'

'Och, of course I'm going. Magnus said he would take me, even though he's never been keen on large social functions. If he really wanted not to go, I wouldn't either.'

Beth stared. 'You'd do anything for Magnus, wouldn't you, Anna?'

'Just about.'

Beth's pale blue eyes narrowed. 'You know, I've always found it strange, the way you and Magnus behave towards one another, more like sweethearts than brother and sister. But you'll have to let go of him sometime, Anna, your lives are very restricted as things stand and Magnus is a virile young man. Soon he'll want more out of life than just a sisterly hug and a kiss.' She looked at Anna askance. 'I've always fancied him for myself. Too bad he's only a farmer, otherwise he *would* be mine by now. As a matter of fact ...' She made a show of studying her nails, a habit of hers when she was getting ready to make one of her profound statements, 'If things don't turn out the way I want for Lucas and me, I fully intend asking Magnus to pledge himself to me. I could do a lot worse, and once he's mine I would soon push him on a bit. He doesn't have to remain a farmer all his life. Yuffie Smythe of Deerfield would help me there, I'm sure. If she thought I really wanted it, she would soon create a post for Magnus.

'And that need only be the beginning. Who knows where it could lead? I would simply die altogether if I had to betroth myself to one of those dreadful pimply boys that Mother's got lined up for me, like James Heatherington. It's bad enough having him escort me to the Ball, I would rather have let Adam do it, just to spite Mother, but for some reason he's taking the Noble House kitchenmaid. Her name's Mary and she's a dreadful little sneak, but she's besotted by him and he didn't want to let her down. She is, of course, more on his level, so I didn't press the point—and anyway, Lucas mustn't find out about him, I can't have someone like Adam McIntyre ruining things for me.'

Anna felt her temper bubbling up and it was all she could do not to slap Beth's infuriatingly smug face. Despite her sense of humour, she was an egotist as well as a snob and thought she could do anything, say anything, get anything—just by snapping a finger and asking for it. Going to the window, Anna threw up the sash and took a deep breath of fresh air. It was a mild, calm night, and the sounds of the countryside were borne to her on the sweet-smelling air.

It wasn't quite dark yet, the hills were outlined against a clear, honey-gold sky. She gazed at the powdermill on the opposite side of the road. It was dark in there, a shadowy dark that made everyday objects look sinister and unfriendly. Some of the buildings looked like grey old men crouching among the trees and Anna shuddered as suddenly she thought of Roderick.

He had been away at Canon Point for several weeks now and she hoped he would remain there for a long while yet. Life was so good without him ... except for Adam. More and more these days he seemed to be angry about something. At the moment it was Beth; she had the ability to send him crazy one way or another, and Anna sighed as she wondered where their affair would lead them in the end.

Her train of thought was interrupted by strange sounds coming from Stable Lane. Leaning further out of the window she listened harder. Was that someone crying out for help? A faint, sad, human voice begging to be heard? Anna shuddered. It was eerie out there in the gunpowder factory at this hour of dusky day. Mist lurked in the hollows, ghostly sighs drifted, despairing echoes of human voices seemed trapped in the secret places among the stones.

A muffled shout of laughter came to her, followed by another. It was only people enjoying themselves, nothing to worry about. She started to breathe again...

'Anna!' Beth's voice came peevishly. 'Do shut that window. It's causing a draught. Supper's here and I don't want it getting cold.'

Mrs Higgins, otherwise known as Fat Jane, the excellent Corran House cook, had brought the supper tray herself. It was brimming over with plates of hot crumpets, pots of jam, butter, and cream, dishes filled with tiny pink and white meringues, pastry horns stuffed with cream, dainty sandwiches containing all sorts of fillings, and a large pot of tea covered over with a cheerful sunflower-yellow tea cosy made by the cook par excellence herself.

'There you are, m'dears.' Fat Jane set the tray down on a little occasional table and stood back, beaming from ear to ear, hands folded over her ample stomach as she nodded and said, 'A feast fit for royalty, even though I do say so meself.' Looking at Anna, her smile deepened. 'Anything for you, my little lovely. When I heard that Miss Beth was 'aving you over I just set to and gave it the works.'

'It looks wonderful, Mrs Higgins,' Anna cried in ecstasy.

'Too wonderful,' said Beth, ruefully indicating her waistline.

'Ah well, you're only young once.' Fat Jane moved to the door. 'Enjoy yourself while you

90

can. Me and Maggie May gave up on our waistlines long ago but at our age it doesn't matter and we're 'appy being fat.'

The door closed, Beth gazed at the goodies on the table and helped herself to a pink meringue. 'I really will have to stop eating Fat Jane's cakes,' she declared with a sigh. 'Trouble is, they're so awfully good I can't seem to help myself and I'm putting on so much weight I feel as if I'm going to burst out of my stays at any moment.'

So saying she popped another creamy morsel into her mouth and both girls collapsed in a heap laughing.

*   *   *

It was late when Anna took her leave of Beth to make her way home to The Gatehouse, which was situated just across the road from Corran House. William Jordan courteously offered to accompany her but she declined, saying it was such a short distance she would be there in two shakes of a lamb's tail.

The glen was very quiet and peaceful at this hour of the evening. The bleating of the sheep floated down from the hill slopes; a fox barked from some hidden corrie; the cows in the fields were lowing softly as they prepared to bed themselves down for the night.

The mill itself was still and silent; hardly a leaf rustled, and only the barest breath of a breeze swayed the tall ripening summer grasses. It seemed a serene and safe place to be but as she had grown older, Anna had begun to feel uneasy about the mill at night. It always seemed darker than anywhere else, a thick black darkness that skulked among the trees and shuffled and crept through the buildings like a living thing. Things had happened here in recent years, dark and dreadful deeds, ungodly acts of physical abuse that had violated all the laws of common decency. Her very own father had been beaten and left for dead down there among the stones; members of the McDonald family had met with violence here, and there were other unholy incidents, some of which were talked about in whispers, others which would never be fully known.

Now, as Anna passed the gates leading into Stable Lane, she shuddered and pulled her shawl closer around her shoulders. In the daytime the lane was an enchanting place, with sunlight dappling the earth and birdsong filling every tree, but when night descended it became eerie and seemed to lead into a tunnel of black nothingness where muffled footsteps stealthily moved and nameless shadows stalked the night...

Anna paused, every nerve tingling, every fibre alert. She strained her eyes into the blackness; something, someone, was coming out of that nothing-land to get her...

'Anna!'

A figure appeared on the other side of the gates and Anna gave a little scream.

'Sorry if I frightened you, Anna.'

The voice had a name now and Anna called out shakily, 'Danny! Danny Black! What on earth are you doing creeping about in there?'

Danny scrambled over the high gate with ease. He had sobered up considerably since leaving Adam in the hayshed and had gone home to try to settle himself for a while. But the memory of Adam raping Sally had been too much for his peace of mind and after a while he had gone back to the shed to see if he could talk some sense into Adam's head.

He had found Adam fast asleep, harmless and innocent-looking in his repose, the empty whisky bottle lying in the straw beside him. Of Sally there had been no sign, which meant that Adam had at least had the decency to untie her and let her go. Danny had quietly left the scene, feeling relieved that everything had turned out better than he could have hoped. He had seen Adam in action before, but never so reckless, never so mindless, as he had been that night with Sally...

And now here was Anna, Adam's sister, staring at him as if he was a ghost, her eyes dark with suspicion, a dozen questions trembling on her lips. Danny had always liked and admired Anna; he didn't want her thinking unsavoury things about him.

If any of the night's adventures ever came

out he wasn't going to take the blame for Adam's wrongdoings and at Anna's words he said quickly, 'It's alright, Anna, I just came through the mill for a shortcut. Me and the lads were having a quiet game o' cards at The Coach House Inn and now I'm on my way home to my bed.'

'Have you seen Adam?' Anna's question came out sharper than she had intended and she added in softer tones, 'He wasn't in a very good mood when he left home earlier and I just wondered if he was alright. I worry sometimes that he'll get into trouble when he's in one o' his tempers.'

The vision of Adam raping Sally floated into Danny's mind and a terrible sense of guilt seized him. He should have tried to stop it happening, none of them should have drunk so much, Adam was unstable enough at the best of times ... even worse, they had all encouraged him...

On the other hand she hadn't really been hurt, only a bit frightened, and *she* couldn't be all that innocent, God knows what went on in her own house with those two mad brothers of hers. Davie thought nothing of lifting his hand to her, so she knew what violence was all about.

Danny strove to convince himself that Sally was alright, that nothing could come of the bit of fun they'd had with her. She might look slightly battered and bruised after all that struggling, but she was a wild old bitch and could have hurt herself anywhere. She was tough, she would get over it. In fact, maybe she had enjoyed the whole episode so much she would come back for more. She might be soft in the head but everything else was intact, as they had proved when they had lifted up her dress...

Danny's eyes gleamed, and a chuckle escaped him. Anna was watching him, waiting for his answer. He took a deep breath and said glibly, 'Och, come on now, Anna, there's no need to worry your bonny wee head about Adam. You know what he's like when he gets going? He might no' be home tonight but there's no call to worry about that. It won't be the first time he's stayed out all night and it won't be the last. He might even turn up at my house, if so I'll make sure he behaves himself and I'll send him home in the morning.'

Danny wasn't giving anything away, although it was obvious he knew more. Anna looked at him for a long moment, then she bade him goodnight and let herself into the house.

Magnus was still up. Anna settled herself beside him and told him about her evening with Beth at Corran House.

'She can be so funny,' Anna enthused. 'She can also be very calculating and devious.' She went on to tell him about Beth's plans to marry him, depending on how forthcoming or

95

otherwise Lucas turned out to be.

'I thought you ought to know just what she's got lined up for you,' Anna told her brother, her eyes sparkling with amusement. 'Forewarned is forearmed, so they say.'

Magnus's reaction to all this was to throw back his head and roar with laughter. 'Beth's the last person I would ever want to marry,' he said at last. 'In fact, I can't see her ever settling down with anyone. She'd soon tire of them and cast them off like an old dress, even someone like Lucas Noble. Mind you, I can't see her having much success there. Lucas is just having his fling with her while he can. He'll marry into money and position. When all's said and done, Beth has none o' these things and can't afford to be fussy. Her mother's manipulated her all her life. Now she's so confused she can hardly tell what's what anymore. She doesn't even know which social scale she's supposed to be on.'

'Oh, poor Beth,' Anna sighed. 'She just seems to go around in circles and doesn't really know what she wants. I hope one day she finds what she's looking for.'

Magnus took her hand. 'Come on, don't get morbid. Beth's had your company all evening, now it's my turn and I don't want to waste it talking about her.'

After that they sat close together and for as long as possible in the ingle, each of them loath to go their separate ways to their sad and lonely beds. So far apart, so near, so pining to fulfil a love that could never be theirs yet which was steadily growing and stretching towards its ultimate destiny.

CHAPTER NINE

THE BALL OF THE SUMMER

The Balls at Noble House were an important part of the community and Lady Pandora's hospitality was legendary among the locals, who never missed an opportunity for some dancing, drinking and revelry with their fellow workers, neighbours and acquaintances. The 'Ball of the summer', as Beth liked to call it, proved to be a huge success for everyone who attended it—with the exception of Beth herself. Yet the days leading up to it had flashed by in a whirl of preparation. Clothes, hair, make-up, all had to be carefully considered, discussed, rehearsed.

Mrs Jordan was in her element. She liked nothing better than to be organising people and events. Little tea parties were arranged, ostensibly to discuss fashion, in reality just another excuse to exchange gossip in convivial surroundings with the added attraction of Fat Jane's baking thrown in for good measure.

The Saturday Ladies and the Sunday

Ladies, as Beth had titled the two factions, were pleased to accept the invitations. They could size up one another at their leisure and try to work out for themselves the individual merits that made Victoria Jordan single them out as first and second bests. So they gobbled cream cakes as fast as they talked, they drank sherry and sipped tea, and at the close of each little gathering the only conclusions that any of them reached were trivial and hardly worth bothering about. All they were really concerned with anyway was how they could make use of one another in the most profitable way possible. And so they name-dropped and spoke knowledgeably about people of note and made suitable noises of approval about each other's so-called good 'connections'.

In the process of all this sorting and sifting they were able to find out who was worth cultivating and who had to be dumped. If, at the end of the day, an invitation to wine and dine in a gentry home had been procured, then all the effort was considered to have been worthwhile and the victors went home happy.

As for Beth, she had taken so much time and care with her appearance that William Jordan had been moved to complain about the number of hours she spent in the bathroom, allowing him so few chances for his own personal needs he had to eventually resort to rudeness in order to make himself heard.

'I've got constipation, Victoria,' he loudly

told his wife, not caring who heard him. 'Beth is never out of the bathroom, neither are you for that matter, the result being that I am denied the opportunity to perform certain necessary bodily functions as and when the need arises. This is having a detrimental effect on my health and I wish you, Victoria, to do something about it.'

'Really, William, I've always said we needed another bathroom,' had been Mrs Jordan's answer. 'Elizabeth is a young lady now, in case you haven't noticed, and must have access to that small *room* whenever she wants it. Besides all that, she never listens to anything I have to say to her. Tell her about your problems yourself. Over the years you and she seem to have developed a rapport with one another that has never extended itself to me. Assert yourself with her, dear, she'll respect you for it in the long run.'

William Jordan had taken his wife's advice, and in the days leading up to the 'Ball of the summer' he had cajoled, berated, even threatened his daughter with mild violence, but all to no avail. Beth was too preoccupied with herself to listen to anything her father might have to say and that gentleman began taking himself off to The Coach House Inn of an evening, asking himself as he sat there amidst misunderstood husbands like himself why he hadn't done this sort of thing before, and from now on he damned well would and to hell with what Victoria thought!

Victoria not only thought plenty, she said plenty, ranting on so much about what she called 'common pleasure-seeking' that her husband began going to the inn on an even more regular basis and to hell with both Victoria *and* Beth!

Fortunately for all, this state of affairs only lasted till the evening of the long-awaited day itself. By then, not only was the Jordan household in a stew, so was every other household in the Leanachorran Estates, as well as its surrounding policies.

Everybody who 'worked to the big house' or who had ever done so, donned their glad rags and went to the Ball, accompanied by key members of their families, such as wives, husbands or sweethearts. It was a gala occasion, the doors of The House of Noble were thrown wide; streamers and baubles hung from the chandeliers; the sound of chinking crystal was much in evidence; buffet tables groaned under the weight of roasts and hams and suckling pigs; two refreshment tents had been erected on the lawns; people strolled about, partaking of food and drink as the mood took them; some played croquet, others played with each other, discreetly of course, down by the tree-fringed river where nobody could see them indulging in their flirtatious games.

* * *

Anna and Magnus had arrived with Beth and her partner, James Heatherington, a perfectly presentable and reasonably good-looking young man of twenty, sporting only two spots on his chin and a collar free of dandruff. James had always stuck faithfully by Beth, escorting her to various functions if she graciously condescended to let him take her. He knew he was just a standby for her, that if there was no-one else available she turned to him, and he had always felt honoured by these attentions, even if they were second-hand. Spots and dandruff in young men were medical conditions which did not meet with Beth's critical approval. In fact she positively bristled with indignance if any member of the opposite sex should dare to approach her unless they were pristine, clean and free of any physical defects, minor or otherwise.

That James should have not one but two pimples on his face was, to Beth, an indication that he either didn't wash as often as he should or that he was not as healthy as he ought to have been for a person of his age. She was therefore not at all keen to take his arm when he offered it to her as they wandered about in the warm summer sunshine. 'What's wrong, Beth?' he asked in his cultured, quiet voice. 'You're behaving as if I've got a disease or something.'

101

Beth gazed pointedly at his spots. 'Well, as a matter of fact ...' she began laconically, when she received a poke in the ribs from Anna who was near enough to have heard all that had passed between Beth and her partner. 'What is it?' Beth inquired sulkily of her friend, knowing full well why Anna had acted as she did.

'Och, Beth, you surely don't have to ask,' Anna hissed angrily. 'You're too hard on James, you should try being nice to him for a change or you might lose him altogether. You've chased all the others away and if you're not careful there won't be anyone left to take you anywhere.'

Beth gasped and glowered at her friend and immediately thought of a hundred things to say in retaliation. But it wasn't in her interest to create a bad impression at that moment, there were too many people about, and choking down her ire she put her arm through that of James and yanked him away before he knew what was happening.

Magnus grinned at the expression of surprise on James's face and looked in appreciation at Anna. She was wearing a gown of blue satin, and her white-gold hair was tied up with a ribbon the same colour and material as her dress; she had wanted to wear her precious Luckenbooth necklace, but it still wasn't ready due to Duncan being taken ill. But her purple-grey eyes, with their thick fringe of dark lashes, were huge and sparkling in the pale beauty of her face. There was nothing fussy or over elaborate about her appearance, yet she looked stunning and was the focus for many admiring glances, particularly from the menfolk.

'Good for you, little princess,' Magnus said quietly. 'You've got spirit as well as looks. Don't think I haven't noticed how the menfolk ogle you, you could get anybody you wanted yet you never seem to bother. Why is that? It's almost three years since Peter died, you have to start living again, Anna.'

Anna's eyes were very tender as she looked at this adored brother of hers, so handsome in his dark suit with the auburn lights glinting in his hair, his tanned golden skin smooth and glowing, his hazel eyes watching her intently as he awaited her answer. 'Because I have you,' she said softly. 'As long as you're here I'll never want anyone else—and you know you would hate it if I did.'

He didn't say anything but his hand curled into hers and they slipped away to walk along the cool riverbanks where the leaves in the trees whispered to them and the water slid smoothly and silently over the stones.

Beth was bossing James about something terrible and didn't notice that Anna and Magnus had wandered away down to the river. It wouldn't have mattered to her anyway, for the moment she didn't need them, she was too preoccupied with herself and her own affairs to care very much about those concerning other people.

She knew she was looking her best that evening: her hair was done up in elaborate sweeping curls, and her pale, freckled bosom swelled provocatively above the cream lace of her dress. She looked cool and composed but her eyes were too restless, darting hither and thither in an endless search for the one person she wanted to see among the many who were there that night. It didn't matter about James. If Lucas were to appear before her right now she would just simply up and off with him and leave her escort to his own devices.

James, on the other hand, was very attracted to her. He was aware that she was selfish and mercenary, but she was also a very exciting girl to be near. He had always sensed the turbulent quality of her nature, and had glimpsed the hungry fires that burned within her when once he had witnessed her kissing Lucas Noble as if she was possessed of the devil. Neither Lucas nor Beth had seen him watching them, and he had been able to enjoy the sight of Beth's bare bouncing breasts hanging out of her frock, Lucas suckling them before leading her into the barn near the Noble House stables, making sure to shut and bolt the door after them.

After that, James had known that an intimate relationship with Beth would have been exhilarating to say the least, but his inherent good manners and impeccable upbringing had prevented him from trying to take too many liberties with her. As far as he was concerned it had to be the honourable thing or nothing, and for a long time he had harboured notions that she might marry him someday. But Beth was not of the same mind as himself, she had never shown any inclinations for a serious commitment to him, and he had accepted this without rancour.

Now, however, he was beginning to want more from her than just the few kisses she had ever allowed him, and on that evening, surrounded as he was with colour and mid-summer magic, he got quite carried away by it all and, gathering both her hands in his, he gazed into her eyes and made a proposal of marriage to her.

Beth looked at the spots on his chin; one was red and angry-looking, the other had a yellow dot in the middle. It looked as if it might erupt at any moment and, shuddering, she stared at his earnest, shining, rather egg-shaped face; she took in his dark, slicked-back hair—and what she saw there filled her with such repugnance she was suddenly overcome with nausea. He had dandruff at his roots! White thick specks of it! Lying along his shed-line! Filtering down through his hair like dusting powder! So plain to see in that oiled dark hair of his ... why hadn't she noticed it before? Perhaps it was a new ailment. Another indication of how unhealthy he must be...

And he had the cheek to ask her to marry him! The nerve to expect that one day she would lie beside him in the same bed, his head next to hers, the dandruff pouring out of it like snow, billowing over her, getting up her nose and into her eyes, even her mouth ... Her imagination ran away with her. She was shocked, horrified and disgusted that he should so casually ask for her hand in marriage, and she began to stamp one of her elegantly clad feet.

'*No! No! No!*' she cried so vehemently that several heads turned to look inquiringly in her, and James's, direction. 'I won't! I won't! I won't!'

*   *   *

'That madam, Beth Jordan, is at it again, throwing tantrums like a bairn,' observed Moira O'Brady, the postmistress, to some of the other villagers. 'She's a spoiled wee bitch and no mistake.'

'Ay,' agreed Janet McCrae. 'But it would be a different story if it was Lucas Noble she was with. She sticks to him like a bee to a honey pot.'

'She keeps that lad Heatherington tied to her like a puppy dog on a leash,' was Tell Tale Todd's opinion. 'It's a wonder to me he puts up wi' it the way he does.'

106

'She might be making it worth his while,' old Shoris Ferguson said knowingly. 'She's been spreading her favours around from all I hear and it wouldny surprise me in the least if she gets herself into real trouble one o' these days.'

'Ach well, that's her problem.' Todd had his eye on the refreshment tent. 'It's no more than I ever expected and that mother o' hers is as much to blame as anyone. Right now I'm thinkin' we'd best get over to that tent before all the drams disappear and that would never do on such a thirsty night as this.'

*   *   *

James, aware of all the curious glances cast in his direction, reddened like a beetroot at his companion's outburst. 'Please, Beth,' he muttered in a tightly controlled voice, 'don't do that, not here, not in front of everyone.'

Beth was furious to be spoken to in this way by a young man she had always considered to be of little importance to her except as a general dogsbody. Her mother thought differently, and had never been slow to say so. 'The Heatheringtons are a good class family, Elizabeth. You could do a lot worse than marry James. He's a very respectable young man and anyone can see that he's quite besotted by you.'

Beth had never given any of this a second thought. To her, James was excessively boring

107

and totally devoid of spirit, especially in comparison to Lucas Noble. Both James and his brother Hector, who had also held a torch for Beth but who was now safely married to 'a horsey type like himself', were from an undoubtedly well-heeled and well-respected family. Beth knew, however, that she would die of emotional suffocation if she were to marry into such a family, which was why her reaction to James's offer of marriage was so violent.

'Really, Elizabeth,' Mrs Victoria Jordan, resplendent in green silk, stopped on her way past to positively glare at her daughter. 'What on earth's got into you tonight? You seem to have no self-control whatsoever, these days.'

Beth's nostrils flared. She said acidly, 'It is none of your business, Mother. What James and I have to say to one another has got nothing to do with anyone else.'

Mrs Jordan gasped. 'How dare you speak like that to me, Elizabeth? I am your mother, don't forget, and you're making sure it *has* to do with everybody, the way you're shouting at poor James.'

'Oh, come on, Victoria.' William Jordan had had enough. 'Leave the young people to sort out their own affairs. Beth's right, it has got nothing to do with you. She's old enough now to make up her own mind about what she wants.'

His wife was flabbergasted. First her daughter, now her husband! Ganging up on her! Making a fool of her for all to see. Had everyone taken leave of their senses? Something to do with the time of year and the feeling of levity in the air? Well, she wasn't the sort of woman to just sit back and allow herself to be browbeaten, and she didn't mince words when she told both her husband and her daughter exactly what she thought of them.

* * *

James stood, hands folded behind his back, watching the Jordan jaws at work, particularly those of Beth and her mother. He broke out in a sweat. Perhaps he'd had a lucky escape after all. If Beth were to turn out like that big bossy mother of hers there would be no living with her when she got older.

He glanced at William Jordan, who was standing with his back to a tree, a look of patient resignation on his face as he listened to his womenfolk squabbling. But was he listening? His expression was faraway, as if he was thinking of other matters entirely. Perhaps, over the years, he had become adept at shutting off his mind to the domestic family scene, turning a deaf ear to things he had no desire to hear.

James blinked. Extending his hand to William Jordan he excused himself and turning on his heel he walked away, over the lawn and down the Noble House driveway, away from

Beth, feeling lucky to have escaped the same sort of fate as William Jordan. Poor chap—he looked a decent sort.

James took a deep, purifying breath of fresh air. He had brought Beth to Noble House in a jaunting cart but to hell with all that. She would get home alright, she had her parents to see to such matters. It was a beautiful night; right now he felt like walking and Beth wouldn't miss him, not after her rejection of him. She would be far too busy posing and parading and showing herself off to susceptible young men—like himself, just a short few minutes ago!

*   *   *

James was right, Beth didn't miss him! She was too preoccupied having a fiery verbal battle with her mother to miss anybody.

Anna and Magnus, returning from their walk, were in time to see a visibly shaken James walking away over the lawn, leaving the two Jordan women to fight things out between themselves.

'Just look at that,' Magnus said grimly. 'Beth has obviously sent the Heatherington lad packing and her mother's interfering as usual.'

'Oh, I wish Beth would learn to hold her tongue,' Anna sighed. 'Even Adam is mad with her these days.' She glanced over at her younger brother, who was with Mary the kitchen maid, the pair of them presenting an agreeable picture as they laughed and talked together under the spreading branches of a big oak tree.

Mrs Jordan had now finished with her daughter, and grabbing her husband's arm she hauled him away, leaving Beth standing on her own, chest heaving, cheeks crimson.

She wasn't to be left in peace for long, however. Adam, his hand tucked firmly under Mary's elbow, walked with her over to Beth to say, mockingly, 'You just can't keep them, can you, Beth? I've just seen poor old Jimmy Heatherington, practically running in his hurry to get away from you. What's the matter, Bethy, isn't he hot enough for you?'

Beth's eyes bulged; this was more than she could take. She glowered at Mary who was watching her, a triumphant expression in her close-set eyes. 'Well, you should know all about that, Adam McIntyre!' Beth blazed. 'Have you shown Mary how we did it in the woodshed? On top of the logs? Or in the barn on all fours on the bales? We were good at it, you and me, Adam. Too bad you're only Rod McIntyre's little sod of a son! You and your sneaky Minky Mary deserve one another, she's about all you're ever likely to get, so try not to fall out with her.'

Beth was pleased with her performance. She stalked away, nose high in the air, leaving Mary to stare dumbfounded at Adam before she found her tongue and lashed him with it mercilessly.

CHAPTER TEN

A BITTER PILL

Everyone had moved inside the house. The atmosphere was wonderfully festive and alive. Lady Pandora was at her radiant best, enchantingly beautiful in a dress of emerald velvet, her fair hair upswept and piled on top of her head, little ringlets of it falling enticingly about her bare shoulders. She was feeling happier these days and it showed in the sparkle of her eye and the smile that sprang readily to her lovely mouth.

The reason for her buoyancy was the absence of Roderick McIntyre from the community. He hadn't been back to Glen Tarsa for several weeks now and she prayed that such a state of affairs would last for a long time to come. Perhaps he had found another woman! A man as lusty as he was couldn't do without female companionship for long. Oh, if only it could be so! It might mean that he would leave her alone, stop pestering her—for *that*. He would always want money, greed ran in his veins. She didn't mind, just as long as he didn't make any more of his vile sexual demands on her. It was all for the sake of Anna, the sweet waif she had loved since first seeing her six years ago. She had wanted Anna in her life but the child's companionship had cost her dear. Roderick's demands had been heavy, both in physical and financial terms, since he was still demanding wages for letting Anna be with her, even though Anna was now eighteen and able to make her own choices.

But it wasn't that simple. Roderick had made that clear enough. 'I know you adore the lass and would do anything to keep her in your life,' he had told her ladyship without preamble. 'If you withhold anything from me, Pandora, and I mean anything, I'll take her away and you'll never see her again, and I'm a man who always keeps his word, as you very well know, my dear.'

This had affected Lady Pandora greatly. She had become lethargic and uncommunicative, even towards her own husband, who was becoming increasingly suspicious of what was going on between his wife and Roderick McIntyre, under-manager of the powdermill.

Sir Malaroy himself had suffered at the hands of Roderick, who had been black-mailing him for years over matters connected with his past. Sir Malaroy knew that the man also had some sort of hold over Lady Pandora; the gossips had been busy, there were whispers of a romantic liaison between the two.

Romance! With that oaf! No-one in their right minds could possibly believe that her ladyship was interested in Roderick in *that* way! Sir Malaroy had fretted and fumed, wondering what it was all about, too afraid to ask for fear it might bring too many matters to a head, things that were best kept hidden in case people would get hurt, himself included.

So Sir Malaroy said nothing but took each day as it came, hoping that relations would improve between himself and the woman he had always loved. They had not got better, rather they had grown worse; he and she were cool towards one another and tried to avoid any sort of situation where they might be thrown together too intimately. But because each of them had been brought up not to show their true feelings in public, they were somehow able to put on a show of affection for the benefit of others. Tonight, however, they didn't have to. They were thawing towards one another, there was no doubt about it. Sir Malaroy couldn't keep his eyes off his beautiful wife and she was likewise with him, turning to him frequently to consult him about this, and that, her eyes smiling up at him as they stood close together by the great marble fireplace in the hall.

They were both greatly absorbed in a discussion about Lucas Nobel, Lady Pandora's nephew, who had arrived home from England the previous evening in time for 'the Ball of the summer'.

There had been a lot for Lucas to talk about with his Aunt Dora and Uncle Malaroy, a great many enjoyable plans for them all to make for the days ahead. Lady Pandora had been swept along on a tide of enthusiasm, she had enjoyed it when her 'boys' as she called them, had all been at home, confiding in her, asking her advice on various aspects of their young lives.

She had been devastated when Peter, Lucas's twin brother, had died. Peter had been very special to her, she had missed him terribly, Nobel House had been a sad and silent place without him, and to help Lucas get over his brother's death she had sent him away to a military academy in England. That had left only Ralph and Robert, her distant cousins, both boys continuing their education under the auspices of their tutor, Michael Dick. All that had changed too when Ralph had run away from home. It was said that he had witnessed the actual killing of Andrew Mallard, the death of Peter. In fear of his own life he had fled the scene and to this day no-one had seen him, no-one knew where he was.

That left only Robert, Lady Pandora's darling rogue of an Irish lad. Everybody had loved Robert, a boy filled with the joy of life, brimming over with blarney and cheek and love for his fellow creatures. But he had been lonely without his companions and very reluctantly Lady Pandora had decided she would have to let him go to. She had found a home and a family for him in Ireland and he had settled down there, though he had sworn that one day he would come back to Glen Tarsa to be beside all the folk he had grown to know and love with all the passion of his big Celtic heart.

So all the boys were more or less gone now from the big house and if it hadn't been for Anna her ladyship wouldn't have settled till she had gathered more little orphans into the bosom of the family. She needed to have young people around her and that was why she was always delighted when any of her boys came home.

Lucas, in his turn, was always pleased to return to Noble House to see his beloved Aunt Dora. Of all the boys he had been the most independent, knowing what he wanted out of life, pursuing his pleasures and ambitions often with heedless disregard for anyone else's feelings. He was thoughtless, selfish and, on occasion downright arrogant and sadistic, but he could also be charming, witty and amusing, and her ladyship loved having him around her.

He knew just how to woo and flatter women, he knew what pleased them and what didn't, he excelled himself with his good manners to ladies young and old and with his ability to appear interested in everything they had to say. And though later he might ape their small

116

mannerisms, he could do it in such a humorous and hilarious way as to have his rapt audience rolling about in their seats with helpless laughter.

Lucas thrived on attention and limelight, he enjoyed occasions of a grand kind, and he had looked forward to 'the Ball of the summer' for a great many reasons, though not by one twitch of his haughtily handsome face did he show it. He made it his business to be cool about everything, even when his insides were seething.

When he saw Beth in the hall, looking ruffled but decidedly delectable in her dress of clinging lilac satin, his stomach flipped over and he made his way over to her, a smile lifting the corners of his wide, cruel, sensual mouth.

'Beth,' he greeted her, his dark eyes flicking appreciatively over her comely figure. 'It's good to see you again. I must say, you look marvellous—ready—if you know what I mean.'

Beth's heart was beating a rapid tattoo inside her breast. Somehow the incident with James, the row she'd had with her mother, all faded into insignificance now that Lucas was here.

'Ready?' she tried to sound bemused. 'Ready for what, Lucas?'

He grinned at her, their eyes meeting in complete understanding.

'I can't wait for you, Beth,' he stated bluntly.

117

'No girl ever excited me the way you do.'

His fingers curled into hers and he murmured, 'Come on, my room, no-one will miss us for half an hour. Just one more time, that's all I ask.'

She allowed him to lead her up the broad staircase to his room, which was situated at the end of the first floor corridor. There was nobody about, no-one to see them entering his room, closing the door softly behind them. He wasted no time. In seconds he had unbuttoned, unpinned, and undressed her. Her hair fell to her shoulders, her clothes fell to the floor. She arched her neck to his hungry mouth and met his ardour with hers.

Tearing off his own clothes he lifted her up and threw her on the bed where he played with her till she was sobbing with delight and begging for more.

'Lucas!' she gasped as she writhed to his touch. 'It's been so long, three months almost. I've been sick waiting for you, really, truly, physically sick. I love it when I'm with you, you're so—so uncouth.'

He was speaking her name over and over, lost in a world of throbbing pleasure. 'Beth, Beth, there will never be another like you. You've always driven me crazy, always. Say you'll let me do it to you whenever and wherever we get the chance. No matter what happens, I can't let go of you. You can be my mistress, I'll see you want for nothing.'

She laughed, thinking he was raving in the delirium of love-making. 'Yes, oh, yes, Lucas, I'll be here, I'll always be here for you,' she gasped, as he and she rode to the pinnacles together.

'Beth!' he released a great cry, hung suspended by his arms for a few moments, before collapsing on top of her to kiss her and murmur in her ear. 'You did mean what you said, didn't you, Beth? You'll always be my little whore, won't you?'

She smiled and kissed the top of his dark head, contentment washing over her like a soft, warm bath. 'Of course I will, my darling Lucas. You and I were made for each other. We enjoy the same things, we have no inhibitions. In the eyes of the world I'll be your sweet, adorable, obedient wife. In the bedroom I'll be whatever you want me to be.'

'My wife!' The words were torn from him. Bounding out of bed he began donning his clothes as fast as he could. 'Don't be silly, Beth, you're a very presentable young woman but you could never fill that role in my life. Whatever made you think you could?'

She sat up, clutching the sheets around her. '*You* made me think it, Lucas Noble—just now. I thought it was your strange way of proposing.'

He laughed, that cruel, mocking laugh she knew so well. 'Proposing? In a way I suppose I was. I meant it when I said I wanted you to be my mistress. I've never had it as good with anyone as I've had it with you. You could teach the alley tarts a thing or two about pleasing a man.

'You're right, we're two of a kind, you and me. We're both unashamedly hot and dirty-minded but I have to be careful, I have my position to think about...'

He sniggered. 'To coin a phrase, I have the good family name to uphold and I must be seen to be a young man of impeccable character and to have excellent tastes in all things, women included. I couldn't however be a goody goody all the time, it would stifle me, that's why I took to you, Beth. I'll never stop wanting you, don't ever worry yourself about that.' Throwing her clothes at her he went on. 'Come on, get dressed, my real bride-to-be will be arriving at any moment, the one you've always hated, Lady Yvonne Marchmont of Hampshire ...' He laughed again. 'Miss Chastity Belt to you. I've still to find out if that's true or not, because you were right about her, she is a real little lady, the sort who will always remain faithful to her husband, just as it should be. You and I have been around, we just can't help ourselves. Yvonne is one of life's true innocents, and thinks only good of everybody.'

Straightening up he examined himself critically in the mirror, combed his hair, gave his tie a corrective tweak and said, 'I must dash, Yvonne might already be here. Later on,

Aunt Dora is announcing the engagement so it should be quite an evening all in.'

With that he left the room, leaving Beth speechless. She was shocked to the core by the things Lucas had just said. Too shocked to be angry, or to throw a tantrum, or do any of the things that Beth usually did when things weren't going her way. Misery bubbled up in her breast. How could he? How could he make love to her as he had just done and then coolly turn round and tell her he was waiting for his future wife to arrive at Noble House?

Feeling numb with hurt, the tears pouring unchecked down her face, she struggled into her clothes, her fingers fumbling with buttons and other fiddly bits of her apparel . . . And her stays wouldn't fasten! No matter how hard she tried to pull them together she just couldn't get them to lace up properly, and with a tearful, 'Damn,' she eventually gave up trying. Rolling them up she stuffed them down the front of her bloomers. She didn't care how she looked. For her 'the Ball of the summer' was over, finished before it had even properly begun.

She hated Lucas Noble, oh God, why had he done this to her? Why? It was cruel. So cruel. She felt breathless suddenly. A wave of nausea swept over her. She knew she was going to be sick but where was the bathroom? Where? Just in time she saw the vanity basin and rushing over to it she retched into the bowl without producing anything worth mentioning. For what seemed ages, she hung over the bowl, sobbing, and crying, and trying to be sick. After a while she scooped water from the running tap and splashed it over her face. Straightening her stiff shoulders she saw a white, tear-stained reflection of herself in the mirror above the sink, the sight of which set her off again.

The door opened and a maid came in. 'Oh, beg pardon, ma'am,' she apologised politely. 'I just came in to turn down Master Lucas's bed.' She immediately spotted the crumpled sheets and shaking her head she said indulgently, 'Och, would you look at that now? I don't know what he does in that bed, I really don't.'

She glanced sideways at Beth. 'It's as well he's going to marry that nice lass, Lady Yvonne. She's a real little lady and will soon make him toe the line. An angel she might look but anybody wi' half an eye can tell different, eh, Miss Beth?'

Beth let out a muffled sob. Gathering up her skirts she left the room and sped down the stairs. Not looking at anyone, praying that no-one would try to stop her, she somehow reached the door without incident. Out of the house she flew, hardly seeing where she was going for tears.

It was then that she saw the coach, just arriving at the main entrance, Lady Yvonne Marchmont alighting from it, aided by the coachman, and Lucas going forward to take

122

his bride-to-be into his arms and kiss her lightly on her pink rosebud of a mouth. She was exquisite, like a china doll, all frills and furbelows, and tinkly little-girl laughter.

No-one saw Beth. She had shrunk into the shadows. Through a watery veil she watched it all unfolding before her, feeling like some furtive thief of the night, stealing something which didn't belong to her.

Everybody went inside, the coach rumbled away, and Beth crept out from her hiding place, shivering and shaking. Once more her feet took flight. She was halfway down the drive when a voice hailed her. 'Beth! Beth! Please wait! It's me, Anna! Let me talk to you.'

It was like a re-enactment of a long-ago night when a frightened little girl had fled from a Hallowe'en party at Noble House, the folds of her ghost sheet flapping round her legs, the tears tripping her as she ran. Only this time it wasn't Anna who was running away, it was Beth, pounding down the driveway, hardly seeing where she was going for tears.

Beth faltered in her flight, half-turning to see Anna, her best friend of yesteryear, a vision in her blue satin dress, her hair a halo of pale gold in the afterglow of evening. 'Anna!' Beth crumpled, she fell into Anna's arms and cried her heart out.

Anna's own heart twisted with compassion, despite Beth's earlier behaviour. Sitting her friend down on top of a drystone dyke she let her cry and cry and cry until she had no more tears left.

It was then that she poured her sorrowful tale into Anna's ears. Anna listened; she had always been a good listener where Beth was concerned. Beth had hardly finished speaking when Magnus arrived quietly on the scene. 'I saw Anna leaving,' he explained succinctly, 'so I came after her.'

No more was said, and between them, Anna and Magnus helped Beth home. Without protest she allowed Anna to undress her and tuck her into bed and ply her with hot cocoa and warm words of sympathy.

*   *   *

And that was where Beth's mother found her some time later, wakeful but dry-eyed, sitting up on a pile of pillows, staring into space, pale, strained, woebegone.

'What on earth happened to you tonight, Elizabeth?' Mrs Jordan asked fretfully. 'First James, then Lucas. I must say, I'm very disappointed in you, your behaviour with James was shocking, so ill-mannered and hurtful.'

'We all get hurt at some time in our lives, Mother,' Beth answered tightly.

'Indeed we do, Elizabeth, but you seem to set out to do it deliberately, no matter who it is. James didn't deserve to be on the receiving end of your temper. No wonder he walked away from you. It will be all over the neighbourhood before we know where we are. Your rudeness, your bad manners will be the talk of the place.'

Beth made no reply to this, but her fingers tightened on the coverlet as her mother went on, 'And what on earth happened between you and Lucas tonight? I understood you and he had some sort of arrangement about the future and the next thing we hear an announcement to the effect that he is engaged to some milk and water young lady from England.'

Beth gave a mirthless laugh. 'There never was any arrangement between Lucas and me. He's simply interested in somebody else now—and she isn't milk and water, she's little Miss Chastity Belt, and she's more cunning than I am, and someday I'm going to pull out every one of her silly golden hairs—one by one—slowly, by the roots, and I'm going to enjoy every minute of listening to her screaming and begging for mercy.'

'Elizabeth! Really! You're utterly barbaric in the way you speak at times! Miss Chastity Belt indeed! What way is that for a young lady to describe another young lady? I don't understand you, Elizabeth, I've never been able to understand you.'

A glimmer of a smile touched Beth's lips. 'Mother, you're just an old gasbag,' she said without rancour, and slithering down in the bed she shut her eyes and pretended to go to sleep while her mother stared down at her in total shock and could hardly say what she wanted to say for the indignance that was choking her.

*   *   *

'We really must do something about Elizabeth,' Victoria Jordan told her husband when they were getting ready for bed later that same evening. 'She says the most awful things about people and never seems to know what she wants from one moment to the next.'

William Jordan paused in the act of removing his cufflinks. 'Do something, about Beth? But it's all been done for her years ago, everything that's ever happened to her was a foregone conclusion. Her path through life was mapped out for her from the minute she opened her eyes and drew breath into her lungs. You didn't give birth to a baby, Victoria, you gave birth to a puppet and you've tried to manoeuvre it to suit yourself ever since.'

'William!' Mrs Jordan was utterly shocked. 'Whatever do you mean by that? I've always done my best for our daughter. I've given her everything she ever wanted. I've tried my very hardest with her but none of it has ever worked and now you turn round and say these dreadful things to me as if it was all my fault.'

Mr Jordan removed his shirt, shook it, and

arranged it carefully round the back of a chair. 'Victoria,' he said patiently. 'The only things that Beth ever wanted was your approval and your love, but as far as I can see you've given her neither. She really doesn't know how to cope with her life anymore or what to do for the best. She's a stubborn little madam at times, I will admit that, but all she really wants is affection and I'm afraid she's going about getting it in entirely the wrong way.'

Mrs Jordan paused in the act of winding her hair into a thick plait and stared at her husband. 'And I suppose you're going to blame me for that too? Elizabeth's conduct is appalling, she's throwing away all her chances of ever marrying a decent young man. I've tried, God knows I've tried, to guide her on the proper paths through life and you've got the nerve to stand there and call it manoeuvring! Well! I've had enough of this for one night! I'm going to my bed and I'll thank you, William, not to say another word to me unless it is something *good* for a change!'

Wearing her most martyred expression Victoria Jordan arose from her dressing table. Flouncing over to the enormous brass bed with its canopies of heavy drapes, she pulled back the sheets and launched herself in between them to lie in a bristling mound of huffy rage.

William Jordan sighed. Wriggling himself into his nightshirt he went over to the bed and very carefully inserted himself into the cold cramped space that had been afforded him. His wife gave a snort and huddled herself into a tighter mound, her starched cotton back reminding him of a white-painted wall surrounding an impenetrable secret garden.

William was used to this state of affairs. He had forgotten what it was like to hold his own wife in his arms. He had never seen her naked except once when she had been bathing and had forgotten to bolt the bathroom door. Nothing had ever been spontaneous where Victoria was concerned, especially when it was connected to the human body. Before marriage she had seemed a strong, amusing woman, whose eyes had promised many delights to come. But after the wedding vows she had only ever allowed her husband to touch her on sufferance and then it had to be with the lights off, her nightclothes on, and with the condition that he didn't dally too long in her intimate places.

William had learned to make his life bearable in other ways. He had always enjoyed female companionship and after years of subservience to a frigid wife he had eventually succumbed to his natural instincts. But he had been careful, he had sought his solace well away from the marriage bed, away from the prying eyes of the village gossips.

Those little business trips he had to make to the south in connection with the mill had been his saving grace. There were plenty of warm, wonderful women out there, and that night, lying beside the rigid, uncommunicative bundle that was his wife, he knew he would have to get away again soon in order to salve both his manhood and his state of mind.

CHAPTER ELEVEN

AN ULTIMATUM

Glen Tarsa, Argyll, Autumn 1895

Anna made her way home through the sun-laced glen, smiling with appreciation as her eyes roved over the hills where the rowans made red splashes and the heather was purple against the golden ochre of summer's faded grasses. She had been working on Lady Pandora's portrait and had managed to make quite good progress before her ladyship had grown bored and had chased Anna away, telling her to go outside and get some fresh air while the sun was still shining.

'Come back this evening, child,' Lady Pandora had said with a yawn. 'Bring Magnus with you, the two of you can stay for dinner and we'll all have a nice little chat afterwards.'

Lady Pandora had grown very fond of Magnus in the last few months. He had danced with her at the mid-summer ball and she had

129

been charmed by his frankness and the way he conducted himself in company. Never too forward, never too shy, just a nice even balance that had appealed to her ladyship and had made her understand Anna's devotion to him.

Anna was humming a little tune as she made her way indoors. She was delighted to find Magnus at home, busily making a midday meal for himself and Adam who would be in shortly.

'Here, let me do that.' Anna rushed over to take the forks from Magnus's hand and proceeded to lay them out on the table.

'You don't have to run round after me, Anna,' Magnus said softly. 'Your days of that are over now, I can take care o' myself.'

'Shush.' She put her hand over his, their eyes met, stillness seized them, awareness passed between them like tiny electric shocks; their hearts seemed to entwine together; each pulsebeat brought them ever closer; each breath was swifter than the one before...

There was a knock at the door, the letterbox rattled. Startled, they jumped apart.

'Anyone in? It's Sam here! Sam McGuire. Are you there, McIntyre? Are you home yet, you cowardly sod!'

Anna and Magnus looked at one another, the questions piling in on them. Was this the start of more trouble? Was it all going to begin again? The tension; the lack of peace; the terrible feeling that arguments could erupt at any given time, without warning, without knowing what any of it was about.

Boxer Sam, as he was affectionately known, had once worked at the powdermill but had been wrongfully dismissed by Roderick for something he hadn't done. The young McIntyres had always expected Boxer Sam to return to the glen some day. A man as determined as he was didn't forget a man like Roderick so easily. But too bad he had to come back now, when everything was so good and peaceful at home.

'I'm coming, Sam,' called Magnus, and he went to open the door, feeling as he did so that all the old wounds were about to be opened, all the old hurts and humiliations brought back to the surface.

Boxer Sam strutted in, his dark, heavy-jowled face lighting into a warm smile at sight of Anna and Magnus. Nellie Jean was hanging on to Sam's arm, all voluptuous curves and wiggles, a new radiance flashing out of eyes that were filled with love whenever they came to rest on Sam's face.

He held out his hand and Magnus gripped it. 'Good to see you, lad,' he nodded, 'and you, Anna, not such a wee lassie anymore, three years has made a difference, you're a young lady now, a bonny one at that if you don't mind me saying so.'

He rubbed his hands together briskly, his muscles rippling under his jacket. 'I've come to see your father. A settlement, you might call it.' He grinned. 'I've got friends at Canon Point, and one of them has been keeping me informed about old Roddy's activities. He isn't happy biding where he is, I believe he's on his way home—I thought he would be here by now, but it looks as if he's going to be a wee bit late.'

'Oh, no,' Magnus groaned, while Anna held her breath. It was true, it was starting, her father was coming back, the lovely interlude of peace was over with, and Boxer Sam was the cataclysm that would set it all in motion. Adam came bounding in at that moment, his rough, handsome face lighting up at the sight of Boxer Sam, whom he had always admired. 'Sam! Great to see you!' He put up his fists, both men fooled about for a few moments, then Sam ruffled the boy's curly head affectionately.

'I heard you talking about my father,' Adam said eagerly. 'Are you going to get him, Sam, pay him back for getting you kicked out of the mill?'

'Wait and see, lad,' Boxer Sam said darkly. He crooked his arm to Nellie Jean and swept her majestically away. At the door he turned. 'I want a bit o' privacy when I come to see your old man. Arrange to be out, bairns, it's best for everyone, I warn you.'

*　　　*　　　*

Roderick let himself into The Gatehouse.

Dumping his bags in the lobby he stalked into the kitchen and stood for a while, resting one big meaty fist on the back of a chair as he surveyed the empty kitchen.

'Anyone home?' he roared, an unreasoning anger mounting in him when there was no reply. The silence of the house enshrouded him, emphasised by the ponderous ticking of the big heavy clock on the mantelpiece.

'Bugger Anna!' he cursed aloud. 'She should be here to see to me.'

He sank slowly into a chair. He was tired! God, he was buggering tired alright. And not a sod to welcome him home and give him his supper! He sat where he was for quite some time, sunk in lethargic gloom, his bitter thoughts twisting his thick lips. He'd make Sir Malaroy suffer for packing him off to Canon Point like a retarded child. He hadn't been needed at Canon Point. For almost six months he'd hung about like a spare post while the perfectly capable new manager had gone about his business and had treated him like something that had crawled out of the woodwork.

Sod! Roderick kicked the hearth fiercely, then went through to the larder where he sawed lumps from a leg of cured ham and slapped them between hunks of crusty bread. He was about to raise the thick doorstep of food to his lips when the door knocker banged imperatively.

Roderick jumped. His nerves weren't so good these days. 'Come in!' he roared. 'Whoever you are, come in, because I'm damned if I'm coming to open the door.'

There came the sound of the front door opening and closing, footsteps advancing up the lobby, stopping outside the larder. 'Evening, McIntyre.'

Roderick's heart began to pound. Slowly he turned to look into Boxer Sam's ruggedly handsome features. It was the first time that the two had come face to face since Sam's departure from the mill. Roderick had breathed easier once it was ascertained that the big burly Munkirk man had left Argyll to try to make good in England—now here he was, as large as life and twice as frightening, his lips twisted into a mocking smile, his looming frame filling the tiny lobby.

And behind him was the buxom figure of Nellie Jean, Roderick's one-time 'fancy woman', a smile on her rosy face that didn't quite reach her eyes which were cold and hard when they beheld the man she had once lain with before he had tossed her over for bigger game.

Nellie Jean hadn't been at all pleased when Boxer Sam had been sent packing from his job. She had always liked him and had never lost touch with him and now here she was, ready to do battle, judging by her determined expression.

Roderick felt the sweat popping out on his brow. His heartbeat swished in his ears, his knees were trembling, and his head seemed to be spinning away from him. Putting a hand on the doorknob to steady himself he managed to say gratingly, 'What the hell do you two want? I finished wi' you years ago, McGuire, and I'll thank you to take your carcase out o' my house.'

Sam's arm shot out to grab Roderick's collar. 'Ay, but I didn't finish wi' you, McIntyre. You surely didn't think I went away from here wi' my tail between my legs, feart to come back in case Big Bad Roddy might gobble me up! Oh no, I've been busy while I've been away, and I want you to hear about the nice cosy wee things I've been up to.'

His grip on the collar tightened. With a deft flick of his muscular wrists he spun Roderick around, screwed one hefty knee into the small of his back and bulldozed him into the kitchen to throw him into a chair and tower over him.

'Time to pay your dues, old man,' Sam snarled, 'to me and Nellie—and to Master Ralph. Ay, that's right, the lad who ran away from the big house because he saw things that terrified him, things concerning the deaths of Andrew Mallard and Peter Noble.'

Roderick made a strangulated sound and the other man laughed. 'Ay, you know what I'm talking about alright. Ralph's quite a lad for his age, he somehow found his way to

England and managed to find me as well. He was in pretty poor shape when he finally got to me but when he had recovered he certainly had a tale to tell, one that I can keep up my sleeve to use when the need arises.

'I'll let her ladyship know that the lad is safe, she'll be proud o' how well he coped on his own, he must have suffered quite a bit o' hardship, but all that's over for him now. I've found him a good place to stay, meanwhile I want you to realise just what a mean old bugger you've been to us all, Roddy. First you get rid o' me so that you can have Nell to yourself, then you all but throw her over when you sniffed something richer in the wind.'

Nellie Jean tossed her dark head, her eyes sparked fire. 'Ay, you used me alright, Roderick McIntyre, took your fill o' me then threw me off like an old blanket. Well, I've got news for you, you drunken old bugger! While you were having your use o' me I was making use o' you too! You thought I was too stupid to pay heed to your boozy ramblings but I was listening alright and listening a helluva sight harder after what you did to Sam. I hated you for that and we made a deal, Sam and me. Although I could hardly bear the feel o' your hairy paws on me I let you carry on wi' me and all the while you told me things, snippets about Lillian, your wife, your shady wee dealings wi' Sir Malaroy...'

Roderick had begun to breathe heavily, the

136

raucous sound of it filling the room. His ruddy, unshaven face had grown crimson, and his black eyes were bulging with chagrin. 'You slut!' he cried. 'You filthy slut!'

He made a lunge at Nellie but Boxer Sam's huge hands shot out to push him back into his chair.

'Now, now,' Sam's smile was cocksure, his tone deceptively silky, 'I'll thank you, McIntyre, not to speak to my wife in such a harsh manner.'

'Your—wife?'

'Ay, meet Mrs McGuire, we were married yesterday in Dunmor. I've been biding there for a few weeks—waiting for you to get back from Canon Point. To while away my time in your absence I had a word with William Jordan, the result being that I start back at the mill on Monday. He's a fair man is William Jordan, we had a long chat together, and he more or less implied that he felt I should never have been given the sack in the first place and said how nice it was to see me back in the glen.

'Och, ay, I think Nellie and me are going to be very happy here, our own little love nest just up the road, a good job to keep us in sillar. Oh, and before I forget, I found out that old Jock the foreman is retiring soon and Jordan is of the opinion that I might just fill the position very nicely. Nellie and I were wondering what your reaction would be to all this and it's quite interesting to see that we were both correct in our opinions.'

Roderick was inarticulate by this time. When he found his voice it sounded feeble and stilted as he stuttered, 'Over my dead body, McGuire, I'll see Jordan about this, I'll...'

Boxer Sam put his face close to Roderick's. 'Be careful, Roddy, you shouldn't make jokes about dying, you don't look too well, in fact I'd go as far as to say you're finished, you old windbag. Nellie tells me you've been going down the hill lately, not the same Iron Rod who used to strut about, drinking, womanising, beating children. If you were a nice man I'd feel sorry about your decline, but you aren't a very nice gentleman, are you? Even the animals can smell you a mile off. You stink, McIntyre, only this time you reek o' fear. Bullies like you can't last forever. And I'll tell you another thing...'

His tone became conversational. 'I don't mind being the foreman for a wee while, but my aim is to get further up the ladder. I have my eye on *your* job, Roddy.' Affably he patted Roderick's shaking hand. 'You're getting past it, anyone can see that, but I'm a fair man, I can wait, though from the look o' you I won't have to wait that long...'

Leaning forward confidentially he went on, 'I can see you're taking in all that I'm saying, old man, but I want you to listen even harder to the next part. Nellie and me, newly weds and all that, I want to give her the best money can

138

buy—*your* money, McIntyre. You aren't short o' a bob or two and won't miss a few pounds here and there if you get my meaning. Silence money, I believe it's called, the kind o' shady dealings that you yourself have been conducting for years now.'

Roderick fumbled in his pocket and withdrew his hanky to mop his perspiring face. He looked ready to burst and roared out furiously, 'For Christ's sake! Hit me! Beat me, McGuire! Get it over with, because you won't get a sou out o' me, even if you have to kill me!'

'Is that so?' Sam straightened so that his strong, bulky body loomed above Roderick. 'I'd like to kill you, McIntyre, nothing would give me greater pleasure, but I'm not going to harm a hair o' that bloody great bull head o' yours. Oh, no, I have other ideas, big ideas, I didn't wait three years to be done on a murder charge, you're the one who's got that coming if you don't shut up and listen to me.

'Nellie has told you she's been keeping a wee secret diary on you, so to speak. Well, she's been passing the snippets on to me. Your life is what you might call an open book to me, McIntyre, I know you drove your wife into the madhouse with your deceit and lies and I know about your cruel treatment of Anna over the years. There's also the question of your foul little game of blackmail with Sir Malaroy—her ladyship, too. I told you I was busy while I was in England. I got a job near where you used to live, I spoke to your old mates, I even paid a visit to your poor sister in the asylum.'

Roderick cowered down in his chair and put up his hands as if to ward off a blow. 'You're a buggering liar, McGuire,' he half-sobbed, 'my sister's dead, she's dead, I tell you!'

'Ay,' Sam's voice was soft. 'The poor old soul is dead now alright, she died a year ago and was buried in a pauper's grave. You buried her years ago though, when you shut her out o' your mind and would have nothing more to do with her. In a way I feel sorry for you, it's a hellish thing for anyone to bear, first your sister, then your wife, ending up in a madhouse, it's enough to drive anybody round the bend. If you had been a decent man I would take you in my arms this minute and give you a bit o' human comfort but you're a cold, wicked bastard and you deserve all that's coming to you.'

Boxer Sam stood back and put his arm around Nellie Jean's waist. 'I've said all I came to say, Roddy, now it's collection time. You know all about that, Mr Holy Wullie, bowing and scraping in kirk one minute, pinching the barmaids' arses the next, putting into the collection plate with one hand, taking it away with the other. Now it's my turn to play you at your own little game, a couple of hundred will do nicely, I'm not a greedy chap...'

'*You bastard!*' Roderick hauled himself out of his chair and lowering his head like an enraged bull he tried to use it to butt the other man in the belly. Sam's fist came out like lightning, landing his opponent such a crack on the jaw he staggered backwards across the room to bounce against the wall, an expression of pure amazement on his face as he slithered to the floor like a piece of jelly.

'Get the money, McIntyre,' Sam smiled pleasantly. 'Or I'll pulverise you—and don't tell me you haven't got any in the house, it's in a little black leather pouch in your bottom drawer in the bedroom, another wee secret that Nell just happened to discover.

'You like money, don't you, old man, you like the feel o' it, you enjoy counting it and gloating over it, well, I'll save you the bother of all that, let you save your energy for all those good works you profess to do. So, get up, go through to your room and bring me your money bag and we'll watch while you count out the sum of two hundred pounds. Then Nellie and me will go away like good little bairns and leave you in peace—for now.'

Roderick staggered away in the direction of his bedroom, leaving Nellie and Sam to look at one another in triumph. They had Roderick just where they wanted him, and it was a good feeling that, one that they would savour until the moment of his reckoning came.

But first he had to be punished. He had to squirm, and suffer, and worry, just as he had made others suffer all through the years of his tyrannical rule over his family and all the other victims of his cold and calculating manipulation.

CHAPTER TWELVE

PAYING THE PIPER

Beth stood at her window, watching Nellie Jean and Boxer Sam leaving The Gatehouse and flitting away up the road arm in arm. It was their second visit to the under-manager's house that day and Beth wondered what they wanted with old Iron Rod and him just newly back from Canon Point.

Then it dawned on her. Anna's father had been instrumental in Sam's untimely departure from the mill. Beth remembered the unpleasantness of the incident, how upset her father had been. He had always liked Sam McGuire and had been very loath to let him go.

Roderick had kept his head down for a bit after that. He had been uneasy about the role he had played in the affair and hadn't been happy till Sam had left the area. When that happened he had reverted back to his usual self, strutting around in his cocksure fashion, ordering everybody about. But he must have known that Sam would return to settle his old scores, that sooner or later the day of

142

reckoning would come...

That day had now arrived, and Sam had chosen a moment when he knew that Iron Rod's defences would be down, a moment when he would be tired and hungry after his journey and wanting nothing more than to put his feet up and relax. Beth had seen him letting himself into the house not more than an hour ago and she had thought at the time what an unpleasant surprise for Anna to come home to.

Well, it must be a surprise! Anna hadn't said anything about her father returning to Glen Tarsa. Beth's own father hadn't mentioned it either, which meant that Roderick had just upped and left the artillery unit at Canon Point probably because he'd had enough of it and had decided it was time for him to leave. Beth wasn't unduly amazed by this, it was just like Iron Rod to do such a thing. He had always done exactly what he pleased and in many ways Beth was surprised that he hadn't come back sooner, since it was a well-known fact that he didn't like Canon Point one little bit.

Not that Beth was overly concerned about Anna or her father at this particular period in her life. She was far too taken up with her own problems these days to bother very much about those concerning other people. With a sigh she left the window and ambled over to her dresser to stare at herself in the mirror. A pale, slightly haggard face stared back at her. She knew she was looking anything but her best just now and she was tired of her mother continually asking her if she was 'sickening for something'; maybe she was. She certainly didn't feel up to the mark. She was also getting stout! At first she had blamed this on Fat Jane's cakes, but as the days wore on, she had grown heavier and heavier, and had experienced more and more difficulty getting her clothes to fasten. She had become really concerned about this and had taken to wearing loose-fitting garments that helped in some measure to conceal the width of her waistline.

There was no fooling Victoria Jordan, however. 'Really, Elizabeth,' she had scolded. 'I can't think what's gotten into you lately. You mope about with no energy for anything. Your face is white and spotty, and you're putting on far too much weight for a girl of your age. Perhaps it's time I took you to see the doctor.'

But Beth hadn't wanted to see the doctor. There was nothing wrong with her, she told herself, but now, gazing at herself in the mirror, seeing the anxiety in her eyes, the pimples on her chin, she thought that she might, after all, have some sort of illness. She remembered how critical she had been of James Heatherington's blemishes, how hard she had been on him, and a feeling of regret welled up in her breast. She could have been more sympathetic towards him instead of treating him as if he had the plague. Now it was her turn! Poetic justice indeed!

And it wasn't only the blotches. Her nerves were also bad, she could feel them in her stomach at this very minute, twitching and jumping about, combining with the oddest sensation in her groin—as if somebody was kicking her, albeit gently. Fat Jane had often said that nerves did funny things to people.

On the other hand ... Beth's heart went cold in her breast. Perhaps it wasn't nerves, perhaps she was suffering from some really dreadful disease, one that manifested itself in plooks and boils and twitchy internal organs! With a sudden decisive movement she began peeling off her clothes. Wearing nothing but her birthday suit she went over to the full length mirror in her wardrobe and began to look at herself critically, turning herself this way and that, sideways, frontways, backways.

No matter which way she turned, the figure that looked back at her was decidedly misshapen. Her swelling breasts flopped on to a belly that was as round and as plump as one of Fat Jane's Christmas dumplings! The veins in her legs were enlarged, and there were funny white and purple marks under her belly-button. Breasts, buttocks, belly! They all reminded her of Ben McLeod's best breeding sow when it was in the advanced stages of pregnancy...

The truth hit Beth like a blow from a balled fist. She was pregnant! And judging from her girth she was too far gone to do very much about it, except have the baby. A rush of terror swept through Beth's veins, leaving her so weak she could feel her legs giving way beneath her. Hastily she sat down and closed her eyes. No no, no! she thought wildly, this can't be, it can't, it can't! But it very well could be, and she knew it as soon as she had recovered sufficiently to think rationally. She realised now that she was quite definitely pregnant. It had been staring her in the face for a long time but she'd been too ignorant of the facts to be able to see it. She remembered the nausea, the aching fullness in her breasts, the heaviness she'd felt on waking in the morning.

Her mind began to work frantically. She felt ill! She felt like dying! Her life was ruined—finished! This must be Adam McIntyre's child that she was carrying and she could never marry him, never! He was only a mill worker, a labourer, with no prospects for the future. It had only been a bit of fun with him, she hadn't expected this. She recalled how Anna had tried to warn her about being careful but she hadn't listened, she had fully believed that her womanly functions were too irregular for a thing such as this to happen. Adam's child, it was unthinkable! On the other hand—she brightened—Lucas Noble could just as easily be the father. She had allowed him to make love to her at every available opportunity. Whenever he had come home she and he had gone crazy together. Easter—yes, they had certainly done it then—as often as they could—it must have been round about then that she had conceived, she was at least six months 'gone' as Fat Jane would say. She stared in disbelief at her swollen stomach, and her face fell once more. If indeed it *was* Noble seed that she was carrying then it was too late for her to do anything that might have been to her advantage. Only last month, Lucas Noble had married his real little lady. The actual wedding had taken place in England but The House of Noble had been the venue for a huge celebration party beforehand, an event that had been well attended by everybody that mattered.

The social columns in the papers had been full of the Nobles and the Marchmonts, and Beth had hated both Lucas and Yvonne for daring to look so happy. Now she hated them even more. They were too wealthy for their own good. Mrs Goody Goody Yvonne was just an empty-headed socialite while he was nothing but a selfish philanderer. His silly little bride would soon regret marrying him—just see if she didn't!

Lucas! Adam! One married, the other mad! Oh, yes, she had always known there was a madness in Adam, but it had been exciting being with him and she hadn't cared. Now ... Putting her face in her hands Beth fell to a surfeit of weeping. How could she tell her mother about this? How could she tell her father? There was nobody who could help her now, no-one she could turn to, her life was over, over—unless...

She stopped weeping, she lifted up her head and gazed into space while her mind worked overtime. Yes, yes, that might just be the answer. Oh, please God, it would work! It *had* to work! She would see Anna tomorrow. After all, they had been best friends and best friends always helped one another out of difficulties, even if they were being asked to do something they desperately didn't want to do.

Beth arose from her chair and threw on her dressing gown. Going over to her dressing table she sat down and began to brush her hair slowly and methodically. One, two, three ... Each stroke of the brush seemed to soothe her fears about herself and her future. She didn't want to think too far ahead; her immediate prospects were what she had to concern herself with just now. Ten, eleven, twelve ... A quiver in her belly made her eyes pop. She sat up straight. It was real! It was alive! It was kicking! Oh, God! God! A baby! A horrible, smelly, real live baby! With eyes that cried and a mouth that bawled and a backside that emitted the most awful, foul unspeakable messes. She didn't like babies, she'd never liked them. Her experience of them was limited but those she had seen had looked like monkeys with sticky probing fingers and mouths that drooled continually.

Oh, if only she could have passed it off as Lucas's child. It might have been bearable then. He should never have married that sneaky, simpering, Miss Bossy Boots. If he hadn't he would be free right now to do as he liked, just as long as he'd done it with Miss Elizabeth Victoria Ellen Jordan!

Oh, what was the use of all this conjecture! It wasn't going to get her anywhere. Still, it was interesting to imagine what might have been—if only.

Beth shrugged and resumed brushing her hair: thirteen, fourteen, fifteen ... Of course, if it *was* Lucas Noble's baby it would be a gentry child, one with a worthy ancestral background and pots and pots of money in the family coffers, not that much could be gained by that now, it was too late, it was all too late ... Sixteen, seventeen, eighteen ... If it *was* a gentry child it still might be worth keeping—she could always try extracting money from Lucas for its upkeep, and perhaps a little bit extra for her own. After all, she would be the one with all the bother of giving birth to it, so she did deserve some compensation.

Yes ... Beth gazed thoughtfully into space. It could very well be worthwhile having Lucas Noble's child. On the other hand, it might be Adam's bastard that was growing inside of her, a poor, wee thing with no background worth mentioning and a streak of madness running through the maternal line. Lillian McIntyre, Adam's mother, was in an asylum. People didn't go to asylums unless they were mad...

Beth shivered. Life was indeed hard sometimes. It didn't really matter whose baby she was carrying, she might never know who had fathered it, unless it was the image of Lucas, or Adam—or both. Beth giggled, she felt better. It wouldn't do to allow her thoughts to wander too much at this stage. First things first, one stage at a time ... Nineteen, twenty, twenty-one...

Still brushing her hair Beth sauntered back over to the window in time to see Anna, Magnus and Adam arriving at The Gatehouse together. Beth sucked in her breath and tried to imagine what it must be like coming home to a bully like Roderick McIntyre. She shuddered. It would be horrendous. She could never have put up with it all these years as Anna had done. How could anyone tell a man like that anything? He would just shout and bawl, curse and swear, and never listen to anything you had to say.

Beth put her hand on her stomach and thought about her own long-suffering father. A sudden pang of remorse went through her at the realisation of what all this would mean to him. Up until that moment all her thoughts had been centred on herself; now they began to expand outwards to embrace all those who would be affected by the news she had to impart, and she wasn't looking forward to any of it one little bit.

*   *   *

The three young McIntyres entered the house in great trepidation, expecting that their father would be waiting to pounce on them with all his worries the minute they got inside. But the kitchen was quiet, no-one was about, the only evidence that Roderick had been there being the heavy smell of his pipe smoke lingering in the air.

'He's been here alright,' Magnus said grimly. 'You can tell the smell o' him anywhere.'

'Maybe he's gone back to Canon Point,' Adam said hopefully. 'Terrified in case Boxer Sam might get him and kill him.'

Anna said nothing. She was too sick at heart to make any comment about her father. Lady Pandora too had been oddly upset by the news of Roderick's return and Sir Malaroy had looked positively murderous at the idea of his under-manager just up and leaving Canon Point without so much as a by-your-leave from anyone.

'He simply can't bend the rules to suit himself!' Sir Malaroy had said angrily. 'And I'll tell him so as soon as I see him. I've had enough of Roderick McIntyre telling *me* what to do.'

Anna wished then that Sir Malaroy would reveal the secrets he had hinted at that day they had sailed together on the *S.S. Kelpie*. It was all to do with something that had happened in her past and she was growing impatient to find out the truth about herself.

'Be patient a little longer, Anna,' Sir Malaroy had said when they had a private moment together after dinner that evening. 'There are things you will have to know, but I have to pick my moment to tell you what they are. Everything will change after that, I may have to go away, it is all too hurtful to even think about just now, that is why I beg of you to go on as you are till I am ready to talk.

'You see, dear child, it isn't just your life that will change, it is mine, and Pandora's too, other lives will also be touched, some for the better, others for the worse. The issues are great and I just hope I'm strong enough to handle them when the time comes.'

Utterly mystified, Anna nevertheless agreed not to say anything more on the subject until he was ready to talk to her again, and she had walked home with Magnus, silent and pensive, hardly looking up when Adam had come bounding along the road to catch up with them, smelling of drink, brash, bold, doing his best to put a brave face on it even though he was more devastated than anybody by the return of his father.

Now all three stood in the kitchen, listening.

Nothing could be heard, except for the sound of the river rushing through the mill and the sigh of the wind in the trees outside the window.

Then it came, the sound of Roderick McIntyre coughing, filtering through from his bedroom, followed by a strange eerie monotony of a human voice, the words unintelligible, running together, like a malevolent presence that floated out to envelop every nook and cranny of the house. Anna, Magnus and Adam looked at one another in dismay.

'He's here and he's alive,' Adam said sarcastically. 'And he's talking to himself.'

Anna shook herself out of the state of lethargy that had gripped her for the last few minutes. 'I—I'd better go through and see if he wants anything.'

'No, I'll go.' Magnus pushed his sister gently aside and strode through the parlour to his father's room, with Anna and Adam at his heels. Throwing open the bedroom door they saw Roderick lying flat on his back on top of the bed, fully clothed, his hands folded over his chest, eyes staring up at the ceiling.

'Get me my supper,' he ordered without shifting his gaze. 'I'm tired out after my journey.'

'You'll get it when we have ours,' Magnus returned evenly. 'And in future, ask—don't order—we aren't your servants and the sooner you get that into your head the happier we'll all be.'

At this, Adam drew in his breath, while Anna's hand fluttered to her mouth. Roderick raised himself up on one elbow to glare at his eldest son. There was an electrifying silence in the room, Magnus's fists curled, as if he was getting ready for the onslaught that must surely follow his words.

But none came. With a grunt Roderick sank back on the pillows. 'Get out o' here and leave me in peace.' He spoke in a strange, flat voice. 'I had a buggering hard time o' it at Canon Point and I'm sore in need o' a rest. I'll be biding in my bed till I'm feeling better and all I ask is that you bring me food and drink at mealtimes and hot water for me to wash in each morning. Other than that I ask nothing of any of you, except that you just leave me alone. Don't let anyone into the house, no' even the minister. Tell Jordan I'll be back at work as soon as I'm able and no' before. All I want to do is lie here, read my bible and commune wi' my Maker. Right now I'm just having a think to myself so don't bang the door when you go out.'

He hadn't mentioned Boxer Sam or Nellie Jean. He hadn't mentioned Lady Pandora or Sir Malaroy or any of the people he was usually so keen to see when he had been away from Glen Tarsa for a while.

Roderick was afraid—and for the first time in his life he was showing it.

CHAPTER THIRTEEN

LAYING THE BLAME

Anna had been feeling terribly depressed by the return of her father into her life and when Beth issued her with an invitation to come over to Corran House for afternoon tea she was very glad to accept. Mr and Mrs Jordan were both out that day and their daughter had chosen to entertain her visitor in the little-used drawing room.

When Anna was shown in she found Beth sitting on an overstuffed sofa in a room that was packed with heavy furniture. Potted palms and aspidistras at the windows blotted out what little light filtered in through the thick drapes; fragile glass ornaments and vases sat on precarious-looking fretwork brackets; the walls were covered in photographs and pictures of all shapes and sizes. It was all too elaborate. Corran House was not a grand-sized dwelling but Mrs Jordan, who maintained that she was upper-middle class, had to have everything of the very best.

Anna hated the complexities of the class system. She didn't know which class she came into and cared less. Her status as an artist was

155

becoming more widespread in the area. Sir Hugh Cameron, a gentleman of note and an active member of the House of Lords, had been so charmed with her painting of his family he hadn't been slow in showing it off to his contemporaries who, amused at the idea of a virtually untrained, working-class girl having the temerity to call herself an artist, all wanted her to paint portraits and landscapes for them, if only out of curiosity.

The novelty of that had worn off now, the services of Anna McIntyre were eagerly sought, and Anna was glad that she had never worried about her position in the social scale. At the moment she considered herself to be living in the best of both worlds, always aware of how precarious life was and how easily the pendulum could swing either way.

Anna hadn't seen a lot of Beth recently and as she sat down beside her friend she couldn't help noticing how much she'd changed since their last meeting. Her face was all blotchy as if she'd been crying, and the voluminous frock she was wearing couldn't quite hide the fact that she had become really quite plump. A plump Beth was something that Anna had never visualised. She had always been slim, right from her schooldays, and though she had developed into a shapely young woman she had always managed to keep her slender appearance, in spite of being overly fond of Fat Jane's baking.

Anna was suddenly aware that this was going to be no ordinary visit. Beth was looking too serious for that. So far she'd had very little to say and Anna didn't say much either. She knew her friend's moods and how she would behave if she was spoken to before she was ready to enter into any sort of conversation. She would merely grunt, or grow annoyed at nothing, or she wouldn't say anything at all and perhaps get up and stomp about a bit until she decided it was time to talk.

'I'll ring for tea.' Beth raised a languid hand and pulled the servant's bell by the fireplace. A few minutes later a very thin, scared-looking little maid appeared with a laden tray which she nearly dropped as she was setting it down on the table.

'Be careful, Dot.' Beth frowned. 'You nearly tipped the teapot into my lap just now.'

Dot was a recent acquisition. Mrs Jordan had insisted to her husband that it was high time that people of their standing had a maid to see to them.

'We should have had one long ago, William,' Mrs Jordan had stipulated. 'Mrs Higgins can't always be expected to run about after us when she has got so much to do in the kitchens.'

'We can't afford a maid,' William Jordan had said, raising his eyes to the ceiling. 'It wouldn't hurt you to bring in the tea occasionally, Victoria ... and why do you always use the plural when you mention Mrs

Higgins's domain. We only have one kitchen, Victoria, this isn't the House of Noble, you know.'

'Me! Me!' Mrs Jordan almost had apoplexy. 'Kitchens! House of Noble! You speak in riddles, William. And you know full well that I'm far too busy for the mundane tasks you talk about. I'm surprised at you suggesting such a thing. I'll see Mrs Simpson on Sunday. She has trained numerous young girls in the course of her years at the manse and I'm sure she'll be able to suggest someone cheap but willing for us.'

So it was that sixteen-year-old Dorothy Ingles came to work at Corran House, fresh-faced, keen to learn, if slightly pert. Mrs Jordan and Beth between them had soon cut her down to size. On her first day she became just plain Dot, and on her second she was told to remove a pretty clasp from her hair and to stop goggling at Fat Jane every time she entered a room. When, on their allotted days, the Saturday and Sunday ladies were being entertained in the Corran House sitting room, she was ordered to move on tip-toe and not to dare try and address anyone unless she was spoken to first. All had gone reasonably well until Fanny McWhirter had accused her of denting a cream cake with her finger. When she had timidly denied this she had been severely rebuked by the lady of the house and had fled from the scene, red-faced and weeping.

Mrs Simpson, the minister's wife, feeling herself responsible for Dot since it was she who had recommended her to the Jordans, had stepped in at this juncture. Taking Mrs Jordan aside she had reminded her that the girl was just a young novice in a very exacting position and as such had to be handled with sympathy and understanding.

Victoria Jordan, had, of course, exploded at this, and had all but told Rachael Simpson to mind her own business.

'Dorothy *is* my business,' Mrs Simpson had returned firmly. 'And if I see that she isn't happy here I shall have to think about finding her another post. She's only a young girl and I got on very well with her while I had her at the manse.'

This had given Mrs Jordan food for thought. Becoming worried that she might lose the even-tempered Dot, she had withdrawn her horns a little and had tried not to be so peremptory. But by then it was too late. The girl was terrified of both Mrs Jordan and her daughter and was continually dropping things in her anxiety to please.

At Beth's sharp rebuke she just stood staring at the tea tray with big round eyes, then she rushed out of the room, banging the door quite loudly behind her.

'Really!' Beth's lips folded disapprovingly and it struck Anna how alike Mrs Jordan and her daughter could be on occasion. 'That girl

159

gets more hysterical with each passing day. I'm surprised at Mrs Simpson for expecting us to put up with it.'

Anna said nothing and Beth, acting the part of the polite hostess, poured tea and dispensed dainty sandwiches, before saying, 'I didn't ask you here just to drink tea, Anna, I want to talk to you quite seriously, and you needn't worry about us being disturbed. Mother and Father are both out and won't be back for an hour or two yet.'

She glanced at Anna under lowered sandy brows. 'I've always been able to talk to you, Anna, sometimes I think you're the only one who really understands me and that is why I'm turning to you now.'

She sounded very strange and Anna studied her assessingly, trying to fathom what all the mystery was about. Beth's eyes were veiled, she couldn't hold her friend's gaze, and dropping her head she played with her hair as she went on in a low voice, 'Anna, you aren't going to like what I have to tell you but if I don't tell someone I shall go quite mad. Oh God! Oh, dear God! It's so awful I really don't know where to begin.'

Her voice had changed, she sounded small and lost and afraid. A rush of sympathy swept through Anna and she got up to place a comforting arm round the other girl's shoulders.

'Wheesht now,' Anna said kindly. 'You

160

know you can trust me. We always used to confide in one another and nothing's changed all that much, we've just grown up, that's all.'

'I know, I know, you always listened to me, Anna, and tried to give me advice and I always loved you because you were the one person who cared enough to try and help me. I hated it when you had to leave school and it all changed. Nothing was the same after that—nothing!' Extracting her hanky from her sleeve she buried her face into the flimsy linen square and wept sorely, her shoulders shuddering with the turbulence of her grief.

Anna was overwhelmed with compassion. 'Tell me what ails you, Beth,' she said soothingly, 'I'll do anything I can to help.'

'Really?' Beth stopped weeping and lifted her head to gaze beseechingly at Anna through eyes that were pitifully swollen and red.

'You know I will.'

'Anything?'

'Ay, anything.'

'Oh, Anna, you can't imagine how relieved I am by your words. You see, I'm pregnant! And your brother, Magnus, is the father! I know he won't listen to me and that's why I'm telling you first, he'll heed what you say, Anna, and you'll both come to realise that the only decent thing he can do now is to marry me.'

Anna backed away, shaking her head, her eyes like coals in the sudden pallor of her face. 'No, Beth,' she whispered. 'I won't let you say

161

such things about Magnus. Don't forget, I saw you with Adam, if you're carrying a child it must be his.'

'Oh no, Anna,' Beth's voice was soft now, somehow threatening. 'What you saw meant nothing. Adam is just a silly boy, I've never cared for him the way I do Magnus. Can't you see my point of view in all this. I've suffered hell since I discovered my condition. I even thought of killing myself! Then there's the question of my parents, they'll die altogether when this comes out. At least if I'm married to Magnus things won't look so bad. He can't allow me to bear the shame of this alone, he will have to share the responsibility.'

'Why are you doing this, Beth Jordan?' Anna asked wildly. 'You had your chances with plenty o' young men, why pick on Magnus? You always wanted what you couldn't have! You covet things, you covet people. If Magnus married you it wouldn't last, you would grow tired of him. You said yourself, he's only a farm labourer, you would make his life a misery with ridicule, you would never be done pestering him with your wants and your wiles. I saw you with Adam, I know you and Lucas were more than just friends, you can't lay your predicament at Magnus's door, he doesn't have to marry you.'

Beth heaved herself up so that she was level with Anna's eyes. 'You know, you are right, Anna, Magnus is only a farm labourer, I could have done a whole lot better for myself but chance just passed me by. I might get tired of Magnus, but right now I want him and I mean to have him and he'll soon begin to realise how lucky he is to have me because, as I told you before, I could open new doors for him and give him a much better life than the one he has now.

'He'll try to deny he took advantage of me but who'll believe the word of a farm boy against that of a vulnerable young lady? If he doesn't do the decent thing by me, the McIntyres will never be able to hold up their heads again, so you go home and you tell Magnus he must marry me as quickly as he can.

'You can't hold on to him forever, Anna, you are only his sister after all, I can give him everything that he desires and the only thing I ask in return is that he gives our baby his name. One big happy family ...' Beth gave a slightly hysterical laugh. 'Fancy having Iron Rod for a father-in-law! Never in my wildest dreams could I ever have imagined such a fate. But never mind, we can all be mad together, you, me, Adam, Magnus—and, of course, the baby!'

CHAPTER FOURTEEN

MORE ENCOUNTERS

Todd Hunter was the last person Anna wanted to see after her talk with Beth. But there he was just the same, sauntering jauntily past the garden gate of Corran House as Anna was coming out of it, on his way to Janet McCrae's shop for his afternoon repast of tea and jammy doughnuts.

A few of the villagers maintained that Tell Tale Todd, as he was better known, spent far too much time in Janet's back shop, especially now that her husband, Keith, was so often confined to the house with arthritis. Janet, however, pooh-pooh'd these allegations, insisting that only fools could place anything more than simple friendship between herself and the Munkirk delivery man.

Todd himself was annoyed at this point of view of Janet's, not because of what she said, but because of how she said it, as if to suggest that he was a creature unworthy of any woman's attention, no matter how desperate for a man they might happen to be. So far, no member of the opposite sex had been desperate enough to try and proposition Todd; he remained unhooked, unfettered, and untrammelled, as he sometimes, rather wistfully, told his old cronie, Shoris Ferguson, who himself lived a solitary existence in his tiny cottage at the foot of Mill Brae.

Today, however, Todd was beyond caring about anybody's opinion of him. He had just consumed several drams in The Coach House Inn and was reeking of whisky when he paused to gaze at Anna with uninhibited curiosity.

'Anna,' he acknowledged with an inebriated hic, remembering to remove his cap from his head. 'It is yourself, lassie, a wee bittie upset lookin' and no wonder. I hear tell that your father is home from Canon Point and that he's taken to his bed wi' a nervous breakdown.'

Although Anna had lived most of her life in Glen Tarsa, it never ceased to amaze her how fast news travelled, and how exaggerated it was by the time it had gone the rounds. She wasn't in the mood for Todd at that precise moment in time. She wasn't in the mood for anybody, least of all the delivery man, with his broken, brown teeth grinning at her and his stubby fingers raking into the thinning sandy hair at his crown.

'You hear wrong, Todd Hunter,' Anna said with asperity. 'My father is *not* having a nervous breakdown. He was tired when he came home and is just resting in bed. No doubt he'll soon be out and about again—nothing ever kept Roderick McIntyre down for long,' she finished rather bleakly.

'Ay, ay, he's aye been that sort o' man,'

agreed Todd. 'But maybe this time he'll be glad to bide in his bed just for the sake o' keeping out o' trouble. I hear tell Boxer Sam went to visit him, along wi' Nellie Jean. They're sayin' she's Sam's wife now and I was just after thinkin' to myself how everything changes— seeing as how the widow woman was that thick wi' your father no' so long ago.' Slyly he glanced at Anna's red face. 'It just goes to show, tis never too late for a body to have a wee bit romance in their life. I have often wondered about it myself, even though it might be cheaper staying the way I am. Mind you, it can get real lonely in the long winter nights, a wee wife to cuddle up to would be just the job. She could mend my socks and make me nice meals and . . .'

'Anna.' A familiar voice broke into Todd's meanderings, and much to Anna's relief, Miss Priscilla McLeod, who had taught at the tiny village school since she was a young girl, hove into view.

Miss Priscilla, as she was known to most people, was matchstick thin in her long tweed skirt and jacket. Her steel green eyes seemed enormous behind her thick glasses; she had a peculiar habit of peering down her long thin nose as if she was viewing the world from a great height. In so doing she made children feel smaller than they were, which illusion ensured that she had no trouble at all in keeping the more unruly of her charges under control.

Some of them professed to dislike her and sniggered at her behind her back but despite everything they all respected her and admired the way she managed to extract the best out of everybody.

Over the years she had grown thinner and more boney, but there was no doubting her authority. She was *A Person Of Influence Even If She Was a Tartar*. This was how Todd always thought of her, in capital letters, bold, distinguished, and brave, and it was how he thought of her now as she walked up to stand in front of him, twitching her nostrils at him in a most disapproving manner.

'Todd Hunter, you have been drinking,' she stated sourly. 'In the middle of the day, too, and breathing the fumes all over Anna. You should be ashamed of yourself.'

Todd was, suddenly, very ashamed. The schoolteacher always had this effect on him, even though he was not normally intimidated by the female sex.

'Begging your pardon, Miss Priscilla,' he said humbly, twisting his cap around in his tobacco-stained fingers. 'Firth was thirsty coming up the brae and he just galloped me up that road to the inn before I could stop him.'

'But Firth is your horse, Todd Hunter,' Miss Priscilla said accusingly. 'Surely you cannot blame a dumb creature for your own deeds of mischief?'

'No, Miss Priscilla, I'll see it doesny happen

again.'

'I'm very pleased to hear that, Todd.' Miss Priscilla looked at Anna as she spoke and her eyelid came down in an almost imperceptible wink. 'But before you go I have something I wish to ask you. My sister, Kate, is a great knitter as you know. She wishes to personally deliver a baby's layette to young Mrs McNab of Corrie Farm. I know you sometimes pass that way and told Kate I would ask you to take her next time you are passing by.'

Todd blinked. 'Kate McLeod,' he muttered thoughtfully. Kate was the opposite of her schoolteacher sister, being plump, warm, womanly, and not at all fearsome. He had always had a soft spot for Kate and he acceded readily to Miss Priscilla's request before taking himself off up the road to his belated tea and doughnuts in Janet's back shop.

'That man.' Miss Priscilla turned to Anna. 'He would talk the hind legs off a donkey. I thought you needed rescuing and that is why I intervened. As a matter of fact, I wanted to see you myself, for several reasons, the first being to extend my sympathy to you and your family over the return of your father. I hope this doesn't mean a curtailment of your visits to Knock Farm.'

Anna had to smile. The teacher's polite condolences made it sound as if there had been a death in the family. 'It's alright, Miss Priscilla, nothing's changed in that way. I love

168

coming to the farm and it would take more than my father to stop me. As a matter of fact …' She hesitated before going on quickly, 'He's behaving rather strangely. As soon as he came home he went to his bed and says he wishes to stay there in order to rest himself and read his Bible. He doesn't want to see anybody and ordered us not to let anyone into the house—not even the minister.'

'Hmm.' Miss Priscilla lapsed into a muse. 'Is it true that Sam McGuire and Nellie Jean Anderson came to see him?' she asked at last.

'Ay, they did, but before they saw him they spoke to us. Sam was really keyed up, I think he had a few things to settle with my father.'

Miss Priscilla's eyes were very green behind her glasses. 'Of course, Sam was dismissed from the mill, wasn't he? By your father? Unfairly, everybody said. Mmm …' The teacher's eyes gleamed. 'No doubt the fur and feathers were flying when the two of them finally came face to face. Sam was once a boxer, I believe.'

Miss Priscilla positively glowed at the idea of Roderick getting 'his comeuppance'. She had never seen eye to eye with the under-manager of the gunpowder factory and felt that he thoroughly deserved any retaliation that was coming to him.

'Very good, very good,' she nodded, pulling back her shoulders and taking a long deep breath of the tangy autumn air. 'The chickens will come home to roost, Anna,' she said with satisfaction. 'Now,' she became brisker than ever. 'I know you must be busy and I won't keep you long. I just wanted to talk to you about Sally McDonald. She's been acting strange of late, even odder than usual. She's always been unpredictable, we all know that, but now the pattern of her behaviour has changed. She used to like to be on the top of the road, but now she hardly goes out at all and cowers in a corner if someone comes to the door. She doesn't seem to trust anybody anymore, even I have the most awful job keeping her calm when I visit the house. It all seems to stem from the summer. I was in visiting one warm day when she came home, after being out all night. She was in a dreadful state, filthy, demented-looking, bumps and bruises on her face, legs and arms. Davie tried to get her to tell him what had happened but she wouldn't talk. Ever since then she's been sick, ill, and terrified and I just wondered if you could throw any light on the matter. Strange things have been happening in this glen over the past few years, the mill in particular having been a venue for dark and gory deeds. It's a lot to ask, I know, but cast your mind back to the summer, Anna. Did you ever hear or see anything out of the ordinary? In the mill? Something that made you pause and wonder and think that all wasn't as it should have been.'

Anna frowned. She was finding it hard to concentrate on everything the teacher was saying. Her mind was on Beth, the things she had implied about Magnus, her ridiculous idea that he should marry her at once in order to give her child a name.

'I'm sorry, Miss Priscilla.' Anna forced her thoughts away from Beth Jordan. 'Now that you mention it, I went to visit Sally not so long ago and noticed that she was behaving oddly. It could be connected with some bad experience she's had but if so it could have happened anywhere, just let me think for a minute ...' There was silence for a few moments, then she said softly, 'There was one night. I was visiting Beth Jordan and I went to the window for a breath of fresh air. Even though it was mid-summer it was dark in the mill, with shadows everywhere. I thought I heard someone moaning and crying out as if in pain, but not long after that there came a shout o' laughter and then Beth called me to come inside for supper.'

Miss Priscilla's eyes glinted. 'I see, I see, mid-summer, yes, really quite a long time ago now. Oh well,' she tugged her jacket into shape, 'must be getting along and let you do the same, dear child. Don't let your father bully you. He's done enough of that in his day and now he'll have to answer for it. God bless the Sam McGuires of this world. If there is justice to be done, he's the very one to do it, and if I see him

I will tell him so and give him my blessing.'

With a triumphant toss of her head she swept away, leaving Anna to go indoors. The house was empty, grey and cold and dead-looking. Anna shivered. Going to the fire she riddled away a coating of white wood ash and placed dry kindling and coal on the hot embers.

In minutes a roaring fire was blazing up the chimney and filling the kettle from the buckets in the scullery she hooked it on to the swee and swung it over the flames.

'Anna!' The dreaded call rent the air but Anna didn't immediately answer it. Forcing herself to be calm she made a pot of tea and placing two cups on a tray together with milk, sugar and a plate of biscuits, she took it through to her father's room.

As soon as she opened the door, the heavy aroma of his pipe smoke forcibly hit her. It hung in the air in a blue haze, darkening the ceiling, insinuating itself into curtains, carpet, bedding. Despite being enveloped in a cloud of smoke, Roderick himself could only be described as immaculate. He was sitting up in bed, encased in a striped nightshirt, hale and hearty-looking, his ruddy skin shiny and fresh, whiskers neatly groomed, his well-manicured fingers clutching the tooled, brown leather casing of his own personal Bible which had his name inscribed in gold on the front and on the spine.

At Anna's entry he tapped his pipe into a heavy brass ashtray and placed it carefully on his bedside cabinet. 'Pour the tea and then sit down, Anna,' he bade politely, indicating the basket chair near the window. 'I have been doing a good bit o' thinking lying here in my bed, I realise I have never spoken to you properly before and I think it is high time you and me had a little heart to heart.'

Astonished, Anna did as she was bid, wondering as she did so what her father was up to now. Roderick always had a reason for everything; ulterior motives had been part and parcel of his lifestyle ever since Anna could remember. But for once there was nothing devious in his conversation. It was, as he had said, a heart to heart talk. His manner was confidential, friendly even. He started by apologising to Anna for his treatment of her in the past.

'Just a part o' growing up, lass,' he told her with a nod and a good-natured wink. 'Every father has to teach his children lessons in life, especially girls, one never knows what kind o' mischief they'll be getting up to next and wi' you not having your mother to teach you it was left to me to try and set you on the right road.'

He sniffed and shook his head. 'I was hard on you I know, but it paid off in the end. You're a good lassie now and you have me to thank for that, never forget it, that's all I ask.'

He went on, chatting to her about his

thoughts on everyday, rather mundane topics, after which he went on to matters concerning his health, both spiritual and physical, how he felt he had needed this period of rest to sort out his thoughts and feelings. His voice droned on, all about himself, what he wanted, what he had to have. Then the tone changed; wetting his thick lips he stared at her and told her that he felt as if everything was closing in on him, everybody was out to get him.

'They're all about me, Anna,' he said in an eerie whisper, his eyes darting this way and that, making her so uneasy she found herself following his eye movements, peering into the corners, even glancing at the space below the curtains to ascertain that no-one was hiding behind them. 'Don't let anyone into the house, girl,' he said, reiterating his previous warnings, 'especially that bastard McGuire. He's out to get me, him and that slut, Nellie Jean, after all I did for her, the filthy bitch! They'll say things about me, terrible things, Anna! Don't listen, don't believe it. None o' it's true. I'm your father, I wouldn't do anything to harm you, it's lies, all lies...'

He went ranting on, his eyes wild and staring, flecks of saliva gathering on his fleshy lips, thumping the Bible with his fists to emphasise what he was saying.

Fear invaded Anna's breast. He looked totally deranged, and she gave a little scream of relief when she heard the front door banging shut.

'Magnus!' She half rose from her seat.

'Don't let them in!' gibbered Roderick, cowering down in the bed, drawing the covers up round his shoulders till only the black slits of his eyes were showing.

'It's only Magnus,' Anna threw at him before fleeing from the room, shutting the door firmly behind her, leaving Roderick alone with the demons and hobgoblins that had sprung from the hellish imaginings of his tormented mind.

*   *   *

'Magnus!' Anna went straight to her brother and took his hands. 'Father's mad!' she stated baldly. 'He thinks everybody's after him and he's demented because o' it.'

'And aren't they?' Magnus replied bitterly. 'Serves him right if they carry him from his bed and lynch him out in the street for everybody to see. He damned well deserves everything that's coming to him.'

'It isn't just Father,' Anna bit her lip. 'The whole world seems to be going mad, Beth Jordan included. I was over there this afternoon, she's pregnant and she's blaming it on you.'

He stared. He burst out laughing. 'You're right, she *is* mad, you'll be telling me next that she wants me to marry her.'

'Don't joke about it, Magnus, she does want you to marry her, right away, to give the baby your name.'

Magnus was no longer laughing. 'The bitch,' he said harshly. 'I've never touched her in that way. You do believe me, don't you, Anna?'

She looked at his strong, sensitive face. His hazel eyes were bright with anger, a pulse was beating in his neck, and one or two curls of springy chestnut hair were falling over his brow. A rush of overwhelming love seized her. The hand that nestled in hers was rough and tough from years of physical labour carried out in all weathers; he had calluses on his fingers, and there was a tiny dent in the palm of one hand made by his shepherd's crook.

He was a young man of the soil, one who smelt of the rich loamy earth and of the misted rain blowing down from the summits of the bens. It was a hard world that he lived in. She had known better things in recent years but she knew she would always share his world. They were kindred spirits, he and she, they both found joy in the same things; they were aware of each other's thoughts and feelings.

She loved him. She had always loved him. Other girls had loved him also. Beth Jordan wanted him so badly she was prepared to lie and cheat in order to get him, but in the end all that counted was Magnus and Anna, loving and trusting one another.

'I believe you, Magnus,' she said softly, 'and

176

I'll stand by you, whatever happens.'

He gathered her close to his chest and she could hear the swift throbbing of his heart. Unable to help herself she reached up to pull his head down till their lips were touching. 'I love you, Magnus,' she told him fiercely, 'I'll always give you my support.'

His heart beat faster at her nearness. Her lips were gossamer soft against his. He gazed at her small sad face and saw the love shining from her eyes. She was so close to everything that was in his being, so near to him in every way. Something deep inside him began to burn till the heat of it spread to every nerve in his body. He gave a little cry and pulling her to him he roughly crushed her mouth with his, forcing her lips apart, kissing her deeper and deeper, passionate, intense, lost.

For a few brief wonderful moments she responded to him wildly before tearing herself away from him to rasp unbelievingly, 'I want you to love me! I've always wanted it! Your innocent little sister, in love with her big brother!' She laughed mirthlessly. 'We aren't normal, Magnus, we're heading the same way as our mother—and him through there! One big mad unhappy family!'

Her voice had risen, and she was sobbing into her hands, hysterically, uncontrollably. Magnus shook her and said harshly, 'Stop it, Anna! I'm sorry for what happened just now but . . .' He took a deep breath. 'I feel somehow

177

that it wasn't wrong, there has to be a rational explanation for our feelings about each other. I can't explain, everything in my head is so mixed up. All that talk about Beth Jordan just seemed to trigger things off.'

Anna, her own thoughts in a turmoil, had gone to sit in the ingle by the fire. 'Don't worry too much about Beth,' she quietly told her brother. 'She and Adam have been having a high old time to themselves over the last few years. This summer I caught the two o' them together in the bedroom, here in this house, so if Beth is telling the truth it's Adam's baby—or Lucas Noble's. They romped in the hay whenever they could and they weren't looking for hen's eggs! She's missed her chances there however, and since she doesn't want Adam she's picked you as the most likely choice. She's always been besotted by you, and now's her chance to get you.'

'Idiot! I'm going over there now! I'll make her eat her own words. She should know by now she can't get the better o' me so easily.'

'She'll insist it's yours, Magnus.' Anna spoke with conviction. 'I know only too well what Beth can be like when she sets her mind on something she wants. She'll say anything to get you. Beth is spoiled, in every way, and she'll be waiting, ready to fight anybody who stands in her path.'

Anna was surprised by the harshness of her own words, but she too was fighting for

178

someone she loved and she wasn't going to stand by and let Beth Jordan have everything her own way, even if she did feel sorry for her.

CHAPTER FIFTEEN

A CONFRONTATION

When Magnus was shown into the Corran House drawing room Beth was still sitting on the overstuffed sofa, looking as if she hadn't left it since Anna had fled the scene more than an hour ago. There was, however, one very obvious difference. Knowing that Magnus would come to see her as soon as Anna broke the news to him, she had changed from her rather drab afternoon frock into a pale green creation that offset her sandy red hair to perfection and even managed to quite successfully conceal her 'condition' in its generous floating folds.

Beth had not miraculously got rid of her spots, her hair was lank and as greasy as ever, and she was still wan and pale and listless. But thanks to careful applications of powder the spots were no longer quite so visible, her locks had benefited from a quick application of hair-reviving tonic, her pallor looked quite interesting, and when Magnus was ushered in by a nervous-looking Dot, Beth's lethargy was

179

rapidly replaced by an upsurge of vibrancy which manifested itself in the sparkle that appeared in her eyes at the sight of him.

'Tea and biscuits, Dot, and don't take all day about it.' Beth waved a peremptory hand at the little maid, who uttered a breathy, 'Yes'm,' and backed carefully out of the door, all folded hands and bowed head and deference oozing from every pore.

Beth fought down her excitement at seeing her visitor. After all, it wouldn't at all do for a pregnant young woman to appear as hale and hearty as a horse. That was all very well for the more robust female, a description which could never, by any stretch of the imagination, be applied to her. She had always been feminine and delicate in the extreme and that was what she kept firmly in her mind when she uttered, 'Magnus,' in a husky voice and arose very majestically to sail regally over to him and take both his hands in hers.

'Magnus,' she said again and this time there was just a tiny wobble in her voice. Taking her hanky from her sleeve she shook it out and applied the gauzy folds to the corners of her eyes. 'Oh, Magnus, dear, forgive me for seeming emotional, it's just you've no idea how glad I am to see you. I've worried and worried about this moment, going over and over in my mind the things I had to say to you, how I would say them, and now you're here it has all gone out of my head and I'm entirely at a loss for words.' Even in her darkest moments, Beth had always managed to somehow come away with statements that were so contradictory they seldom failed to bring a smile to the dourest face.

'Still in top form, Beth,' Magnus said sarcastically. 'Nothing could ever keep you down for long.'

'Oh, Magnus, how can you say that?' Her expression was one of tragedy. 'I'm at my wits' end and all you can do is make silly jokes. Didn't Anna tell you what has happened?'

'Ay, she told me,' he answered curtly.

Beth applied a corner of her hanky to the rim of each nostril. 'Isn't it all too dreadful? A thing like that happening to me? I don't want a baby. I don't like babies. I can't think why anything so horrible attached itself to me when there are so many women—real grown women— desperate to have a child. I'm still only a child myself, I'll never be able to cope, never. Oh dear, I really think I shall kill myself, it's all so hopeless, I don't know where to turn!'

'You know, Beth,' Magnus mused thoughtfully, 'you've missed your vocation in life—you would have made a fine actress. The performance gets more intriguing by the minute but I don't have the time nor the inclination to stay here and listen to all this. I have work to do, I only came over because I was so damned angry at you having the cheek to imply that the child you're carrying is mine.'

Dot came in just then, holding the door open with her back while she endeavoured to manoeuvre the tray in through the gap.

'Here, let me.' Magnus jumped up to help the little maid with her burden, earning a smile of gratitude from her and a poisonous glare from Beth.

'Can't you even bring in a tray by yourself?' fumed the daughter of the house. 'I don't know why Mrs Simpson recommended you to us, you're nothing but a little Miss Dotty Daydream and I've a good mind to tell her so when next I have occasion to speak to her.'

Dot's face blazed. She stood twisting her fingers together till Beth curtly dismissed her.

Magnus shook his head in amazement. 'By God, Beth, you're even better—or worse—than your very own mother! Your father deserves a medal living with the two o' you. I feel sorry for him, two vipers slithering about the house, a third about to put in an appearance in the guise of a baby. Surely he'll never survive three o' you because your unborn bairn is bound to be a girl. He's a man who seems to have run out o' luck a long time ago.'

'Magnus McIntyre!' Beth stamped her foot, all pretence of a helpless vulnerable young maiden dissipating like a puff of wind. 'How dare you be so flippant with me! This child growing within me is *your* child. It doesn't matter to me that you are only a farm labourer, I would be proud for it to have your name.'

'Oh, come on, Beth, you know I've never lain wi' you, even though you tried to make me often enough. You're not going to pin this one on me even supposing you talk yourself blue in the face and die in the process.'

Tears of rage danced in her eyes. 'Your word against mine, Magnus. I could make life very unpleasant for you if you refuse me this. Oh, please,' the tone of her voice changed to one of softness and seduction, 'you know how much I've always cared for you and life with me wouldn't be so bad. I could open new worlds for you. Yuffie Smythe is looking for a good right-hand man, one who is trustworthy and loyal, attributes that are inborn in you, Magnus. You would be just right for the job. Yuffie would give us a nice house in the grounds of Deerfield, probably for a nominal rent. It could be the start of a new life for us both.'

She stared at him expectantly. 'Well? What is your answer to all that? Surely you must see that it's a chance for you to better yourself?'

'No.' Magnus cocked his head at her and smiled.

'What do you mean, no?'

'Just what I say. I don't love you, Beth, and if I were to say yes to you it wouldn't be a marriage, it would be a disaster. You would end up hating me because I couldn't give you the things you wanted. You're a very pampered young lady, you've always had and you'll always want more.'

'Oh.' Beth's façade of toughness faltered. 'I'm going to cry, I shall cry, I don't know what I'm going to do, it's all too beastly for words.' With that she buried her face into the pitifully inadequate folds of her hanky and simply howled her eyes out.

Compassion welled in the big warm heart of Magnus McIntyre. Taking her in his arms he held her tight and stroked her hair, uttering soothing words in her ear and wiping her hot face with his own large, manly hanky. He crooned to her as if she was a baby, and when there was no more to be said he just stayed quiet till her sobs subsided and she lay against him, utterly spent.

'Oh, Magnus,' she said in a nasal voice. 'I really do wish you were mine. I've always admired you. You're so strong, so good to be near, Anna's very lucky having you even if you are just her brother. I wish I had someone who would love me as I am and not the way they would like me to be.'

'James Heatherington loved you in that way, Beth,' Magnus said kindly. 'He's a nice lad and he's got a good character. He would always treat you like a lady and give you everything you wanted and once he got over the shock o' your pregnancy I'm sure he wouldn't mind giving your baby his name. Haven't you ever thought of that?'

Beth's brow wrinkled. 'I'd rather end up

with no-one than marry someone like James. Oh, he's got money, but he's so boring—and he's got dandruff and spots. Poor, dear, boy, he *was* good to me and of course, I could have done worse, as Mother would say. But the spark isn't there, and I do like a man with sparkle. Besides, he's seeing someone else now, so I suppose I've missed my chances there as well.

'By the way, don't breathe a word of this to Adam. I do like Adam, he's similar to me, he doesn't mind bending the rules to suit himself, but he'd be no use at all as a husband, he's too unpredictable and wild, so what he doesn't know can't harm him.'

Without warning, and taking Magnus completely by surprise, she placed a hand on either side of his head and clamped her mouth over his. It was a kiss of soft, moist, shameless passion, and when it was over Magnus found his knees trembling and his heart thumping.

'See what you could have had?' she said tremulously, gazing at him sadly.

'In my heart I suppose I knew you wouldn't want me or the burdens I would have thrust on you, but it was worth a try, wasn't it, Magnus?'

'Ay,' he murmured, looking at her with a new liking. 'It was worth a try, Beth, and one day I truly hope you'll get what you're looking for out o' life. You're a great girl spoiled, as old Grace would say, but you could change if you tried hard enough.'

'A leopard can't change its spots, Magnus,' she replied wistfully, and soon after that she saw him personally to the door. When it had shut on him Beth gave Dot the surprise of her life by saying, 'Thank you for the tea, Dot,' in a reasonably grateful voice.

CHAPTER SIXTEEN

HUMBLE PIE

When Mrs Jordan heard her daughter's news she promptly fainted. William Jordan, always a calm man in any emergency, braced himself for all the troubles to come and summoned Dot to make tea, asking that it be served in the homely surrounds of the living room with its slightly shabby carpet and big friendly fireplace. Mrs Jordan did not remain in her supine state for long. Her husband applied smelling salts to her nose, Beth fanned her with last Sunday's newspaper, her eyes fluttered, she sat up, she looked straight at Beth's swollen stomach and she let out a long, drawn-out moan that sent the shivers down the respective spines of both Mr Jordan and his daughter.

'What are we going to do?' Mrs Jordan wailed. 'Our daughter! Expecting a child out of wedlock! And she doesn't even know who the father is! Which means ...' Her eyes bulged.

'Oh, how could you, Elizabeth? After all we've done for you! Carrying on with every Tom, Dick, and Harry. No better than a common slut! And we gave you everything that any girl of your standing could possibly want. And this is how you repay us...'

'What's done is done, Victoria!' barked William Jordan, running a distracted hand through his hair. 'It will serve no useful purpose going on and on about it.'

'How can you sit there and say that, William!' cried Mrs Jordan, wringing her hands in despair. 'We're ruined, ruined! I'll be the laughing stock of the place! I'll never be able to hold up my head again! I'll...'

'Shut up, Victoria!' William snapped. 'Just shut your mouth and listen to me for a change. It's because of you all this has happened ... I said shut up and listen and I mean it! All her life, Beth has been nagged, scolded, bullied and criticised. The poor girl has never known what it is to be loved and truly cherished for herself, only for what you could get out of her in social gain. The reason for that is simple. You cannot give love, Victoria. I myself have been deprived of it for years but for the moment it is Beth we are concerned with.'

Putting his arm round his daughter he pulled her to him and stroked her hair. 'I should have intervened more but I kept quiet for the sake of peace. Now this has happened, and I take my share of the responsibility. Your mother and me are both guilty of neglecting you, lass, and I for one have never been sorrier.'

'Neglecting her!' Mrs Jordan gasped, totally unnerved by the turn of events. 'I gave her everything, everything I could to make her happy . . .'

'Everything but your affection, Victoria. Beth is a very unhappy girl who's carrying a poor unhappy child . . .'

'How do you know it's unhappy?' Mrs Jordan had to ask that. 'It isn't even born yet.'

'With you for a grandmother, how could it be anything else?'

'A grandmother!' She hadn't thought of that. The full import of the situation struck her with renewed force, her newly returned colour deserted her once more, and slowly, quite gracefully, she swooned all over again, sinking to her knees, sprawling her length on the carpet where her husband once more administered to her with smelling salts and her daughter fanned the air with a newspaper and a notable lack of enthusiasm.

The door opened. Dot came in to announce that tea was being served in the living room. Fat Jane was hovering in the background, her double chins smoothing out a little as she stretched her neck to see what was happening in the drawing room. She and Dot had heard the family ructions from as far away as the kitchen and had been agog to try to find out what was happening. Between them they had hastily prepared tea and had taken it into the living room. They then armed themselves with mops and dusters so that they could flick them about as near as possible to the drawing room, normally the quietest room in the house but today a venue for all sorts of to-ings and fro-ings, comings and goings.

Mrs Jordan had rallied, Mr Jordan gave her his arm, and wife, husband and daughter repaired to the living room to partake of tea. Mr Jordan was shaking slightly but he felt wonderful just the same. For as long as he could remember he had wanted to tell his wife exactly what he thought of her. Today he had done just that and afterwards he had caught her watching him with a new respect in her expression.

He raised his cup to his mouth. 'By the way, Beth.' He looked at his daughter kindly. 'No-one has asked you yet what you want to do regarding your unborn child. The choice is yours, of course, and your mother and I will stand by you, whatever you decide...'

There came a strangulated snort from Mrs Jordan, but her husband carried on regardless. 'You are very young yet, my lass,' he said gently. 'A baby would be a great curtailment to you, but it might also be the making of you. You have a couple of options: as yet, very few people know of your condition—you could go away from here and have the baby adopted after it's born; or you could stay and have it here and to hell with the gossips. It's a very big decision to make and you'll have to give it some thought before making up your mind.'

Beth's eyes were misty when she looked at him. Her beloved father, so big a man in every way, so strong when strength was needed, so wasted on her mother who wasn't aware of the treasure she had under her very nose.

'I've already decided, Father,' Beth said quietly, 'I'd like to go to Gran and Grandpa's in Torquay and have the baby there. When it's born I want to have it adopted. I could never keep it ...' She moved restlessly and tugged at her hair. 'I don't in the least like babies and if I kept it I would ruin any chances that are left to me for a decent life. I know it sounds selfish, but I am selfish, and the last thing I want on this earth is a smelly, bawling infant keeping me awake at night and doing dreadful horrible things into its bloomers. Perhaps, later on, if I meet the right man, I *might* consider having a child just for the sake of perpetuation but not now, while I'm still single and much too young to know my own mind.'

Her father nodded. 'That's my girl. No-one could ever accuse you of dithering. I'll write to your grandmother at once, explain the situation, she's a sensible woman, and if I know her she won't make a fuss.' He turned to his wife. 'That's if it's alright with you, Victoria.'

She stuck her nose into the air. 'There isn't

very much left for me to say, is there? You and Elizabeth have made up your minds between you. As you say, my mother is a sensible woman who, as far as I know, has never fainted in her life, so yes, go ahead and write to her, William, I'm sure she and my father will be only too happy to have Elizabeth stay with them till all this is settled.'

Her husband left the room to fetch some writing paper. In the hall he paused in astonishment. 'Mrs Higgins!' he exclaimed. 'Whatever are you doing wielding that mop? Your place is in the kitchen—as you have said often enough yourself. In fact, I'd go as far as to say you are positively fearsome when it comes to the question of appropriate job distribution.'

'And you would be right enough there, sir.' Fat Jane was flustered at being caught out in the hall, listening. Her face crumpled. She was as honest as the day was long and seldom gave in to the more unsavoury temptations of life.

'I 'eard, sir, I listened,' she admitted, wiping one eye with the corner of her floury apron, 'and I'm right sorry about poor, dear, Miss Beth. It shouldn't 'ave 'appened to a nice lass like her but there are those 'ereabouts will always take advantage of a young girl's innocence.'

William Jordan looked at her and tweaked the folds of her pure white mutch cap. 'Keep it under your hat, eh, Mrs Higgins. It will all sort

191

itself out in the long run, as long as it's kept in the family—our family, Mrs Higgins, the one you've been a very dear part of for so long now.'

Fat Jane beamed and clutching her mop in one plump fist she waddled away to the kitchen and the belated cup of tea Dot had promised to keep hot for her. And while she was about it she gave Dot a very firm piece of her mind, warning her not to say a word about what she'd seen and heard that afternoon. 'We're a family, Dot,' she said with a proud lift of her chins. 'And families oughtn't ever to go around telling other folk things that are none of their business. Just you remember that like a good girl and don't forget to keep your 'and on your own 'alfpenny. Let what 'appened to Miss Beth be a lesson to you and one day you'll meet a good man, one who'll marry you and know that you were a decent lass who didn't go around flaunting 'erself at every Tom, Dick, and 'arry.'

CHAPTER SEVENTEEN

A LECTURE

Soon after receiving the letter about Beth from her son-in-law, Violet Jarvie travelled up to Scotland from Torquay to personally escort

192

her granddaughter back to England with her. But first she stayed for a few days in her daughter's house in Glen Tarsa, smoothing out all the ruffled feathers, lending a patient ear wherever it was needed, giving sound advice, even providing a shoulder for Fat Jane to cry on when that lady burst into sudden tears in the middle of icing a batch of empire biscuits in the portals of her very own kitchen.

Dot, taken aback and scared out of her wits at the sight of the older woman blubbering, burst into tears also and dashed out of the room to fetch Violet Jarvie, a being she hardly knew but whom she already instinctively trusted with all her young heart.

As soon as Violet Jarvie entered the cook's domain she took in the situation at once and immediately went forward to place a comforting arm round the distressed shoulders of the Corran House kitchen treasure.

'Oh, I'm sorry, m'dear,' Fat Jane wailed, frantically dabbing at her eyes with a large cake doyly from the table, the first thing that came to hand. 'It's just everything and everybody's been so upset by Miss Beth's troubles and I myself don't know if I'm coming or going. Only yesterday I got lumps in the custard and burned the gravy for the roast, me that's never burned anything in the whole of my working life.'

With that she was off again, sniffing, sobbing, howling, getting herself into such a state it took all of Violet Jarvie's persuasive powers to stem the flow of tears. But in the end she succeeded and Fat Jane was eventually installed in her own comfortable armchair by the stove, Dot perched opposite on a raffia stool, each drinking mugs of hot strong tea and eating partially-iced empire biscuits as they chatted away quite happily to the recently arrived house-guest from England.

The reason for this was simple. Violet Jarvie was a rock. People had always leaned on her and turned to her for advice and she had never yet cracked or shown any sign of weakening. It was difficult to think of her as Victoria Jordan's mother. In many respects they looked alike, but everything about Violet was softer, prettier, kinder. She refused to put on airs and graces for anyone; she was unflappable, decisive, and open-minded, and she didn't nag, fuss or do any of the things that her daughter did, and her granddaughter had always been 'most awfully fond of her'.

William Jordan was delighted to have Violet staying in his home. She had a softening effect on those around her and seemed to be surrounded by a glowing aura of light that attracted other living creatures to it like moths to a flame, even stray dogs and cats that she met in the street and tramps with holes in their boots and nothing at all in their bellies.

Violet Jarvie fed the tramps, the dogs, and the cats, but most importantly she made them feel, if only briefly, that the world wasn't such a bad place to be in after all and that it was worth going on living in if it meant meeting people like Violet Jarvie now and again. Her conversation was warm and friendly, and people from all walks of life readily responded to it because she was so easy to talk to. Fat Jane and Dot were besotted by her and loved having a cup of tea with her in the kitchen. She and Fat Jane, gourmets both, exchanged recipes and talked endlessly about food while Dot shared little confidences with her and in the process emptied her young mind of many of her small anxieties.

The atmosphere in Corran House had never been easier and mealtimes were most pleasant affairs. At breakfast Violet was quiet and withdrawn but thereafter, at lunch, dinner, supper, the talk, the laughter flowed, everyone enjoyed themselves and most of them left the table feeling spiritually lighter and mentally brighter.

But there was more to Violet Jarvie than might at first be supposed. Warm-hearted and kind though she was, she never suffered fools gladly and woe betide anyone who tried to get the better of her. She was, to put it bluntly, a tough lady when she wanted to be, and with her granddaughter on this particular occasion, she proved to be a very tough lady indeed.

On her second day at Corran House she took Beth aside after dinner and had a serious heart to heart talk with her, telling her that if she was going to be a guest in her home, granddaughter or no, she would have to toe the line and live within the limitations of her physical condition and adhere to the rules of the house.

'You were not at all a very smart or clever girl when you went and got pregnant, Beth,' she scolded that much-chastened young lady. 'That be as it may, I'm not going to judge you or lay all of the blame at your door. Your father has told me that he feels much of this is due to a lack of knowledge on your part about life's facts. If this is the case then some of the responsibility must lie with those adults who should have informed you about the workings of the human body, both male and female.

'That, however, is only a part of the problem. You yourself have been far too liberal with your favours. Men, as a rule, do not respect that kind of behaviour in young women. They can get any amount of it in the backstreets if they want it, but they seldom end up marrying those unfortunate girls; girls, I may add, who are often forced into the kind of life they lead through circumstance, not choice. You are a very well off young person, Beth, and it's high time you settled down and learned to appreciate that fact.'

At this point, Beth began to squirm in her chair and sniff into her hanky but there was to be no mercy for her as her grandmother went on relentlessly, 'I was disappointed, Beth, when you were made to leave one school after another because of foolish pranks. Your Grandpa David and I paid for you to go to those schools, as well you know, and we were bitterly let down when it became clear that you weren't going to even begin to try and further your knowledge of the outside world. Who knows, if you had, you might not be in the present fix you're in now, and I wouldn't be here talking to you like this.'

Her face softened. She put her arm round Beth's shuddering shoulders. 'I am not reproaching you, Beth, I am telling you all this because I love you and don't want to see you getting hurt any more than you are already. Basically I believe you are a fine young woman. You've got character and brains and a wonderful sense of humour, even if it is often misplaced. You and I have had some wonderful times together in Torquay and when you come to live with us we're going to be great friends and I will never again, I hope, have to lecture you as extensively as I have done tonight.'

With that Violet Jarvie kissed her granddaughter's moist, hot face and told her gently not to make herself ill through needless tears. Even so, Beth went to bed crying her eyes out but next morning, after a silent breakfast, she presented herself to her Grandma Vi to thank her for speaking her mind and to promise to be on her best behaviour while staying in Torquay.

'I'm sure you will be a model grandchild,' laughed Violet, 'but don't, for heaven's sake, be too ambitious. I want you to be really quite human, you know, and expect you to have some fun. You and I will go out shopping together while Grandpa David has a nap. He enjoys having the house to himself now and then.'

Putting her arms round her granddaughter she gave her a reassuring hug and Beth went off blithely to look out some of the things she would be needing while she was away.

CHAPTER EIGHTEEN

A CONFESSION

'You're so awfully good with her, Mother.' Victoria Jordan sighed as she watched her daughter going across the hall to her room. 'I never get her to do what I want and here you are, just arrived, and already she's eating out of your hand.'

'She just needs plain talking to, Torrie. Reproach, anger, criticism, none of these are any good to her just now. She's a child still, she needs to feel she can lean. She also needs a lot of love, and by God! I'll see she gets plenty of that from your father and me when she's living with us.'

Mrs Jordan reddened. 'Really, Mother, to hear you talk you would think I had been positively cruel to Elizabeth. I—I've given her all the fondness that I am able to give, I can't say more than that.'

Her mother nodded. 'Yes, I know, you always were a very unresponsive person, even as a child. Your father and I tried with you but you always turned away from us and you certainly never listened when I wanted to talk to you as you were growing up. If you had, you might have been able to teach your own daughter the kind of things a girl of her age ought to know.'

Gently she placed a hand over Victoria's, who quickly snatched hers away. Violet Jarvie shook her head. 'You see, that's exactly what I mean. You never liked being touched. It was as if it was abhorrent to you. No wonder Beth has been stifled and had to look for affection elsewhere.'

Her daughter's lips tightened. Without another word she turned and walked stiffly away, leaving her mother to gaze after her with a rueful shake of her head.

*   *   *

That same evening Victoria Jordan seemed loath to go to bed. First her husband, then her daughter, left the room, leaving the two older women sitting together on the sofa, sipping sherry, neither of them saying anything.

It was very cosy in the homely living room with a good fire glowing in the grate and the bracket lights on the wall giving everything a rosy ambience. The silence in the room was really quite amiable to begin with, but gradually a tension crept in.

Violet glanced frequently at her daughter, who was staring wide-eyed into the fire, winding the stem of her sherry glass round and round in her hand until it began to make small squeaky noises. Violet's stomach tautened. She stood up. She stretched. 'It's been a long day. I think I'll just...'

'No, Mother, please don't go, I want to talk to you.'

Her voice was like a steel whip slicing through the quietness. But Violet Jarvie was prepared for it. She hid a small, secret, smile. She sat down again.

'It's about me, Mother,' Victoria began, wetting her lips nervously and taking a good big gulp of her sherry. 'For years I've wanted to unburden myself to someone, but I never had the courage until now. You've only been here a very short time yet you've achieved so much since you came. You seem to get the best out of everybody without even trying. All I ever seem to do is frighten people, they shy away from me as if I had the plague. Ever since I was little I've watched you and wanted to be so much like you, but I grew up to be me instead and to be truthful I've never liked myself very much.

'Seeing you with Elizabeth, the way you handled her and got such a response from her, made me realise what an awfully sympathetic person you are and how good it would be to talk to you.'

Violet sat back in her seat and said quietly, 'Go on, Torrie, don't be afraid, starting is the difficult part, but I'm here and I'll be listening.'

It took Victoria Jordan a long while to open up and start talking, but when she did it seemed as if she would never stop. It all came pouring out, confessions, revelations, wasted yearnings, half-forgotten dreams, passions and grief that had lain buried in her heart for years.

She began with the physical side of her marriage, saying that she had always found it difficult to respond to her husband's sexual advances, admitting that certain aspects repulsed her and that she'd only had her daughter out of a sense of duty.

'I just seem to freeze up if he dares to come near me, Mother,' she said awkwardly. 'Yet, sometimes, I want to reach out and just— touch him.'

'Then why don't you admit your feelings to him and try holding his hand to begin with?' Violet suggested quietly. 'A man's hands are strong and wonderful and so reassuring. The intimate side needn't come into it, just trust and genuine liking for one another. Your

201

father and I always made a point of having physical contact, even if it was just a squeeze on the shoulder. We tried to encourage you to do the same but you didn't respond and to this day I can't understand why you are so cold and unapproachable when you had parents as loving as we were.'

Victoria's face turned fiery red. 'It all started at that boarding school you and Father sent me to.' She spoke in a muffled voice, her head downbent, as if she was ashamed to show her. 'Oh, I know you did it for the best but in the end it was the worst thing that could have happened to me. It changed my whole life ever afterwards and affected relations with my family, and other people later on.

'At the school there was a girl, one of the seniors. She looked more like a boy than a girl, but she was beautiful—an Adonis—all the younger ones put her on a pedestal and would have died for her. For some unknown reason she took a liking to me. Heaven knows why! I was gauche and naïve, anything but attractive, and I would have done anything to be near her. I used to make toast in her room on a fork near the fire and we would eat it, along with big mugs of cocoa...'

Victoria was quite carried away by this time. She sat hugging her knees as she gazed into the embers, her eyes big and brilliant in her flushed face. Her mother watched her and felt strange, as if she was seeing a vision of the schoolgirl

202

that once was, the child who had once been.

'She told me stories,' Victoria whispered in a small, little-girl voice, 'wonderful stories. I never got tired of listening to her and being near her. We touched, oh yes, I loved touching her. She was so soft, so sweet, so dear, I wanted only to be with her and couldn't get enough of her and she felt the same about me. We held hands there in front of the fire, and we kissed, petal-soft kisses; her lips were like rosebuds, she smelled of roses, everything about her was like a flower. To this day, whenever I smell roses I think of her—and I remember ...' Her voice faded away as she sat like one in a trance, gazing, just gazing into space, lost, alone, lonely.

Gently her mother stroked her hand. She jumped. 'Shush,' her mother said soothingly. 'I'm here, I'll always be here, Torrie, but tell me, you have to tell me, what happened to your rosebud? What became of your Adonis?'

'She died.' The words came out in a sigh. 'She went away one Christmas and I never saw her again. A coach ran her over in the street and my sweet dear rose of a girl was killed. She had so much to live for, so much to give ...' The tears were flowing unchecked from Victoria's eyes, coursing down her cheeks, staining the collar at her neck. Lifting up her wet face she looked at her mother and she whispered, 'We didn't do anything wrong, Mother, we just loved one another and it was beautiful. It was pure love, clean, and good and perfect. We were both so young and idealistic, unblemished by sin, unaffected by any sort of harsh reality. She will always be in my heart, wherever I go, whatever I do, I will never forget her, for as long as I live.

'For a time after her death I didn't want to go on, everything was so empty without her. I couldn't bring myself to speak about her and so I shut her away. That was the start of my remoteness, I became distant with you, with Father, with everybody. As I grew older I found it hard to relate to men but just the same I married William because it was the right thing to do. Poor William, he's such a good man, strong and reliable. He's been so patient, with me and Elizabeth, and now she's pregnant. He would have had every reason to feel sorry for himself but he's been a tower, so kind and considerate, to her, to everyone.'

'I know, I know.' Near to tears herself, Violet spoke in a husky voice, and then she gathered her daughter into her arms and held her close, thinking as she did so of a little girl of long ago who had locked her secrets away in her heart and who had borne the burden of a terrible grief alone.

'Will I ever get over it, Mother?' Victoria Jordan asked huskily. 'It's always been there, coming between me and everything I do. I want to give more of myself but how can I when my mind dwells so much in the past and I feel as if

204

chains are binding me whenever I try to reach out?'

'You've already made a start, Torrie,' Violet Jarvie said softly. 'Tonight you cleansed your mind and your heart of some of your pain. The healing process has already begun, all it needs now is patience. The days will pass, you can't expect miracles right away, but in time you will expand and open out—like a flower that has been deprived of sunlight, gradually opening its petals to the light.'

'Oh, Mother, you do say the loveliest things!' Victoria Jordan burst out, and bending down she kissed her mother on the cheek before walking straight and tall and dignified out of the room, leaving Violet to gaze after her with misty eyes and relief in her heart that, at last, she had broken through the shell that had surrounded her daughter for so long.

*   *   *

Beth had arranged to meet Anna at one of their old haunts, the big mossy boulder beside the brown trout pool, a favourite place of theirs when they had been children. Having realised, after her initial panic, that she may have upset her valued friend, she wished to make amends and had sent her a note to that effect.

It was a calm, mellow day in early October; the tiny delicate leaves on the silver birch trees were fluttering in the breeze, those on the alders were like golden pennies shining in the sun, and all around were the blood-red rowans and the yellow oaks. Down below was the umber pool, tinkling loudly as it hurried over the stones.

'Remember this place, Anna?' Beth asked. 'We used to come here at playtime to eat the slabs of Madeira cake that Fat Jane smuggled into my satchel.'

'Oh yes, I remember,' Anna replied softly. 'The Madeira cake and the big rosy apples, and in summer the great wedges of strawberry tart with huge berries dotted all round the edges half smothered in cream.'

'And the things we used to talk about,' Beth went on with a catch in her throat. 'The confidences we shared, the tears, the laughter.' She glanced all around her. 'I loved coming here with you, it was our secret, we shared so much in those days, I wish we could turn the clock back, just for a little while, just to be as we were then, children, with our whole lives before us, everything to hope and dream for.'

Anna gave a little laugh. 'You make it sound as if we're a hundred! We still have our whole lives before us, we still have everything to hope and dream for.'

Beth gave a great sigh. 'You have, I've ruined all my chances.' She looked down at her swollen belly. 'I've been so foolish—I've thrown my life away. I'm afraid of what lies before me, Anna, I don't know what the future holds for me.' The tears were glistening in her eyes but she didn't allow them to spill; instead she gave an almighty sniff, then blew her nose resoundingly into her hanky.

'Oh, Beth.' Anna's voice wobbled. 'It won't be so bad. It's a baby you're having, not a disease. You might love it when you see it, you might want to . . .'

'*No!*' Beth yelled emphatically. 'No,' she went on in a quieter tone, 'I won't, I just want to get rid of it as quickly as possible and then get on with whatever sort of life is left for me.'

She extended her hand. 'Goodbye, Anna, I—I don't know when I'll see you again but you will write, won't you? I don't think I can bear it if I don't get a letter from you now and then.'

'Och, Beth, of course I'll write.' Anna gathered her friend into her arms and kissed her affectionately on the cheek. 'I'll keep you informed of everything that's going on in the glen, even when the geese head south for the winter and the burns on Coire an Ban begin to freeze over.'

They parted company then, each going their separate ways, each footstep carrying them further from their old meeting place, where young voices seemed to whisper among the trees and the little stream seemed to chuckle as it echoed the laughter of childhood innocence.

*   *   *

On the morning before her departure Beth arose to find a note on her dressing table. It was from Dot and it read:

Dear Miss Preggy Peggy,
By the time you read this I'll be gone. I couldn't take any more of you and the dragon lady so I've helped myself to some of your jewellery to get me started somewhere else. It isn't up to much, but it should fetch a bob or two. The coral necklace didn't suit me so I've left that for you, the colour will go with your eyes. I also left you my hair clasp, the one you and the dragon lady made me stop wearing. It will always remind you of me, a small token of my generosity as a person.
I'm sorry about Mrs Simpson, she's a nice lady and I don't like letting her down, but she must know what you and your mother are like and will maybe understand.
I hope you have twins, both girls, who will grow up to be like yourself and the dragon lady.
Yours as always but hopefully never again.
Little Miss Dotty Daydream.

P.S. Tell Mrs Higgins goodbye for me. I'll miss her and her cakes.

Beth devoured the words and burst out laughing. It was just the sort of thing that appealed to her sense of humour and she began to wish that she had allowed herself to grow closer to the little maid. They might have found that they had a lot in common, despite Dot's lowly position in life! Nothing of any great value had been taken and Beth was so uplifted by Dot's connivance she showed the note to her father, persuading him not to report the thefts to the police.

'She deserves to get something after everything she's suffered at the hands of Mother and me,' Beth laughed.

'Oh, Beth.' William Jordan took his daughter's hands. 'I'm going to miss you about the place. You might be a little madam at times but you've got such a lot of life in you.'

She patted her stomach and grinned. 'Father, you've never said a truer word. More life than I bargained for, and more than any of us wanted. I'm sorry I brought this upon you, more than I can ever say.'

'It's done, Beth,' he said quietly, and there was a glint of tears in his eyes when he put her head on his shoulder and gently stroked her hair.

The following morning, Beth and her grandmother took their leave of Corran House. Victoria Jordan had held her head high all through breakfast and all through the goodbyes and the chatter of departure. But at the last moment she faltered as she looked at her daughter sitting in the coach, a tartan rug wrapped round her knees, her face pale in the morning light, her sandy fair hair falling about her young face, her poor little mound of a belly trying to hide itself under the folds of her coat.

'Elizabeth,' Mrs Jordan whispered, biting her lip. She then inserted the upper half of her anatomy inside the coach and gave her daughter a kiss on the cheek followed by a long, lingering hug.

Beth was so stunned she could think of nothing to say. Then her mother, hiding her crimson face, hurried away, leaving Beth to look enquiringly at her Grandma Vi.

'A leopard can't change its spots,' Violet said softly, 'but it's never too late for a mother to change her ways—and judging by her behaviour, yours is well on her way to doing just that.'

'What did you say to her, Grandma?'

'It was what she said to me, dear child. No, sorry, I can't reveal what it was. Enough that she said it, and rid herself of some of her sorrows in the process. She isn't nearly as thick-skinned as she makes herself out to be and is really quite soft when it comes to the bit. Now, stop chattering for a moment and let me be still for a while. It's been a trying few days. Buckets of tears have been spilled all over the place and I've had a busy time mopping them up. Everyone feels better now, however, and I feel tired. Forty winks, Beth, we've got a long journey ahead of us, and after all, at my age I need my rest—as your Grandpa David would say, when he wants a Sunday lie-in.'

The coach rumbled away. Victoria Jordan watched from her window. William Jordan came up and took her hand. It was warm and strong and she remembered her mother's advice and held on to it as if she would never let go.

CHAPTER NINETEEN

SURPRISES

Christmas and New Year, 1895/96

Anna hurried along Dunmor's high street, pulling her coat collar higher up over her ears as she went. It was bitterly cold. Flurries of icy flakes were skirling about in the wind whipping up from the sea; the hills above Gourock and Kilcreggan were already covered in white, and a slippery covering of sleety snow was starting to coat the promenade of Dunmor's east bay.

With Christmas just two weeks away the shops were looking bright and cheerful with their festive arrays of holly berries and shiny baubles. Anna had finished Lady Pandora's portrait at last, and relished this opportunity to visit the town and purchase some things for herself as well as for Lady Pandora. However she was finding it difficult to make up her mind about what to buy.

It was all so tempting, the displays of Christmas sweetmeats, gifts of every sort, the flowers, the crackers, the sweetie shop with its wonderful assortment of chocolates and crystallised fruits and plates of sugared almonds, all decorated with ribbons and bows and coloured streamers.

Great pink salmon hung suspended in the fish shop window, and in the butcher's turkeys and chickens dangled in rows, pride of place being taken by a boar's head complete with apple, looking out rather sadly at the people passing by.

Anna checked her gift list. She had managed to get something for everybody who mattered to her: Magnus, Adam, the folk of Noble House, The McLeods of Knock Farm, Beth, and Nora McCrae.

Seeing Beth's name reminded her of the beautiful card that had come from Torquay the day before. In it Beth had written:

I miss you and the people of the glen more than I ever thought possible and try to imagine the hills all covered in white and the rumble of cart wheels bumping over the snowy ruts on the road. Grandma Vi and Grandpa David have been wonderful to me. Gran keeps me on my toes but is so good at understanding how I'm feeling and Grandpa tells me stories as if I were a little girl and we all gather round the fire at night to eat toasted muffins and drink hot chocolate.

I've been to the shops with Grandma and will send you something nice for Christmas. I can't say I'm feeling on top of the world just now. In fact I feel bloated and ugly and am looking more and more like a Christmas pudding with each passing day. I'll be glad when January comes so that I can get rid of my lump and here's hoping it will arrive on time and not keep me waiting. It kicks too much.

Mother wrote me a truly affectionate letter and Father sends me little notes and cards and never ever lets me feel neglected or forgotten. I hope Magnus and Adam are well. I can't say I wish the same for your old Iron Rod of a father. Who knows, maybe someone will put some dynamite in his breakfast porridge for a truly uplifting start to Christmas! when it comes.

Yours affectionately as always,
Beth.

Anna had to smile as she remembered those last wicked lines that her friend had written. Beth had never liked Roderick nor he her, and love had certainly never been lost between them. Anna hadn't put her father's name on her Christmas gift list. He came last in her priorities. She certainly wasn't going to buy him anything. If she had the time she might make him something but at the moment she was busy knitting socks and gloves for the McDonalds, woolly bedsocks for old Grace, crocheting a lacy bedjacket for her mother under Kate McLeod's guidance.

Thinking about her mother made her pause outside the fruiterer's. Oh Mother, she thought, when will I ever see you again? Would you know me if I came to visit? Or would it be like that last time when you cried out for your baby but it wasn't me you wanted?

Mr Campbell, the fruiterer, was watching Anna from his window. Giving herself a little shake she went hurrying on her way, her steps taking her to Duncan Lauder's premises. It had been summer last time she'd had reason to visit the jeweller's. Her Luckenbooth necklace had been here all that time, owing to the fact that Duncan had been ill in hospital with stomach problems, followed by a lengthy recuperation period. So much had happened since then that it had slipped Anna's mind.

Duncan was thin and gaunt when he appeared from the back of the shop in answer to the bell. 'Miss McIntyre,' he greeted Anna. 'How nice to see you again and looking bonnier than ever, if I may say so.'

'I'm glad to see you, too, Mr Lauder,' Anna smiled. 'It seems so long since I was here and it must seem even longer for you, being ill all that time.'

He rubbed his hands briskly together, a sure sign that he was feeling better. 'I can't tell you how pleased I am to be back. I had a great deal of work to catch up on but tackled my priority items first. Your Luckenbooth was one of them, and I'm delighted to say it's all ready and waiting for you.'

Without ado he disappeared behind the bead curtain, but was soon back with her necklace in his hands. 'There you are, lass.' He placed the item of jewellery on the glass counter and spread the chain so that the whole thing was displayed to its best effect. 'Beautiful,' he said reverently. 'As fine a piece of its kind as you'll ever see anywhere. I still can't discover the secret of how to open it ...' one eyelid came down in a sly wink, 'though it wasn't for the want o' trying.'

Anna gazed at the entwined silver hearts of the Luckenbooth. For some reason that she couldn't understand she could feel herself beginning to tremble. 'I'll wear it now, Mr Lauder,' she said in a strange, breathless voice. 'I really feel I have to wear it right away.'

'Of course, lass, see here and I'll fix it on for you.'

She lifted up her hair to allow him to fasten the chain round her neck. Standing back he stared at it lying against her white skin. 'Beautiful,' he said again. 'And you say your mother gave it to you when you were just a bairn? I never knew her, I don't recall ever seeing her about the town, but she must have been a fine woman, one who loved you very much to have given you such a rare and precious gift.'

Anna's hands were shaking slightly as she brought out her purse to pay the jeweller. But he brushed the money away. 'No, take it as a Christmas present from me. I kept you waiting for it long enough and truth to tell, I enjoyed every minute o' working with it.'

'Thank you, Mr Lauder,' she whispered, 'I don't know what to say.'

'Then don't say it.' He nodded. 'Just enjoy it.'

She went to the door.

'A merry Christmas to you, lass,' called the jeweller.

'And to you too, Mr Lauder,' she called back.

Elated and excited she opened the door— and ran full tilt into Sir Malaroy striding along the high street!

'Anna!' Laughing, he held out his arms to catch her. 'I don't believe this!' he cried. 'History repeats itself! Do you spend your hours in Dunmor rushing out of shop doorways with the sole purpose of bumping into me?'

'Sir Malaroy!' she gasped. 'Oh, I'm so sorry, I didn't mean...'

'It doesn't matter.' He brushed aside her apologies. 'It's freezing out here and I was just making my way to Mrs Graham's for a cup of tea.' Crooking his arm at her in a dashing manner he went on, 'Pray do me the honour of coming with me, it's been a long time since you and I shared a little spree, and it will give us both a chance to thaw out in a convivial atmosphere.'

Without hesitation Anna took his arm. She felt uplifted. It was as if all the good things were happening to her at the one time and it wasn't even Christmas yet!

Mrs Graham's was a quiet little tearoom in a quiet little street with a discreet atmosphere and cosy tables in cosy alcoves. A waitress brought tea for two along with generous wedges of piping hot, home-baked apple pie accompanied by a jug of thick pouring cream.

'Delicious.' Sir Malaroy seized his dessert fork and dug in. Anna did the same. For a few minutes neither of them spoke, then Sir Malaroy wiped the cream from his Van Dyke beard and said, 'I couldn't have wished for a better ending to my morning; good food and excellent company, even though you've hardly spoken a word since we met.'

'I haven't had the chance,' she laughed. 'I'm just pleased to have bumped into you again. You seem always to be rushing along the high street, colliding into young women coming out of shop doorways!'

He grinned. 'I've been shopping, or trying to. I think women find it easier than men to get the things they want.' He gazed at her enquiringly. 'And what, pray, have you been up to, child? You look as if you've had a hectic morning, your hat is askew and your face is all flushed.'

Anna straightened her hat, gazing at him consideringly. 'I too have been shopping. I also took the opportunity to visit Duncan Lauder's to collect the necklace I had to leave there that last time we met.'

'Duncan Lauder's? May I ask what you were collecting? Emeralds? Diamonds? Gold?'

'No—this.' Opening the top buttons of her coat she held out the Luckenbooth for Sir Malaroy to see. His reaction was as strange as it was unexpected. His face blanched and he drew in his breath. 'Where did you get that?' he asked in a hushed voice.

'My mother gave it to me, when I was just a tiny wee thing. She told me it would protect me from evil. I've hardly ever worn it. I was afraid I would lose it and also I didn't want my father to see it.'

His mouth sagged. 'The Luckenbooth,' he whispered. 'I haven't seen that since ...' There was a pause. 'Anna.' He raised his eyes to look into hers and what she saw there made her pulses race. It was as if his very soul was exposed for all the world to see, together with pain and anxiety and a deep, deep sadness.

'It has come, Anna,' he said wearily. 'I told you that one day you would have to find out the truth about your past and that day will soon be here. I need to choose the appropriate time to speak, however, and because of that I ask that you give me your necklace, the reason being that I don't want anybody to see it until I have prepared myself for the questions that it will bring.'

'No!' Anna cried sharply. 'It's mine! I can't give it to you, not just yet. Tell me when you want it and I'll give it into your keeping. Until then I promise no-one will see it. I've always kept it hidden from my father's eyes, so that part of it will make no difference to me.'

'Very well.' Signalling to the waitress he paid the bill. At the door he collected his walking cane and in silence the tall dignified gentleman that was Sir Malaroy of Noble House, and the slender fair-haired maiden that was Anna McIntyre of The Gatehouse, accompanied one another outside, each of them very aware of the metamorphosis that had taken place in their relationship.

'Let me take you home, Anna,' he offered politely, but she shook her head, telling him that she had some things to collect for Lady Pandora.

'I'll wait,' he said huskily, taking her hand for a brief moment. 'Please, Anna, forgive me for what happened just now, I'm not myself, try to understand that. Very soon something momentous is going to happen in your life and in mine, and I find it very difficult to have to face up to that reality.'

'Alright.' Her voice was equally husky. 'And

I'm sorry too, I shouldn't have shouted at you the way I did.'

'Come along.' He began walking quickly. 'Let's collect everything and then you must come home with me. Pandora will be waiting for you and later on I want you to have dinner with us. It's the season of goodwill and nothing must stop us from enjoying ourselves. Make merry while we may, little Anna, the days of joy are brief, and, for me, they could very well soon be over.'

His cryptic remarks made her shiver and she wondered, as she had done many times before, what the future had in store for her—and for Sir Malaroy.

CHAPTER TWENTY

FINDERS KEEPERS

Lady Pandora was up early, trotting her horse, Sable, along the edge of the fields towards the bridge at the foot of the track. She often went for a ride before breakfast, more often than ever of late, for she found it difficult to sleep. The deep, satisfying slumber that had been hers when her mind was easy and her life a calm sweet harbour in which she felt safe and happy was long gone.

Over the last few years she had felt anything

but safe and rarely as happy as she had once been. Roderick McIntyre was to blame for that. Roderick, with his demands on her that left her feeling sick and uncertain. He had defiled not only her body but also her mind.

When he had been at Canon Point the situation had eased somewhat, and when he had returned he hadn't bothered anybody, having taken to his bed for some strange reasons of his own. Some had called it cowardice because Boxer Sam McGuire was back in Glen Tarsa and was out for Roderick's blood. Others said it was madness and the longer he stayed indoors in his bed the better for everyone.

Whatever it was, a blessed sense of peace had fallen over Pandora and she and her husband had found their old happiness returning little by little.

But Roderick was recovering from his attack of anti-social behaviour. Gradually he was getting back to a state of normality, if such a description could ever be applied to a violent, cruel, creature like himself. He had been to Noble House to have a long talk with Sir Malaroy. He had also arranged meetings with Pandora and afterwards she had felt all her fears and doubts returning a million-fold.

After that it hadn't been long before the gossips' tongues were wagging and the rumours flying around. She knew that her husband was aware of all the talk, though he never said anything. She could feel his coolness and his despair however, sensed his subtle withdrawal from her, his lack of participation in the things they usually enjoyed doing together.

It might have been better if he had confronted her about his suspicions, asked her outright why people were talking about herself and Roderick. But what could she have said to him? How could she have explained that her infidelity was because of her desperation to hold on to Anna, the child of her heart, the young girl who had made her life tick so sweetly for so long now.

Her thoughts turned once again to Roderick. She had noticed some alarming physical changes in him lately: a slurring of his speech; an unsteadiness in his walk; lapses in his memory; an inability to satisfy his lustful instincts for which he blamed her.

He accused her of being frigid. 'How can a man make love to an iceberg!' he had fumed, his face purple with rage. 'If your performance doesn't improve, Pandora, I'll take it to mean you're no longer interested in keeping Anna by your side. It's time she had a proper job anyway—Glasgow, Edinburgh, London, any one o' them would do. You'd never find her again. I'd make buggering sure o' that.'

But somehow her ladyship was not impressed by his threats. His words lacked conviction and didn't carry the same weight as they once had. People said he was drinking to excess and it was this that accounted for the changes in him. Personally she felt it was something more—something dreadful and frightening and nothing that she could even begin to fathom. Whatever it was, she was glad! If his health continued to deteriorate it meant he would stop pestering her so much. She didn't mind giving him the money, just as long as she could be free from his degrading attentions.

Free! She laughed mirthlessly, her breath coming out in frosty puffs in the cold still air. Would she ever be free? If Roderick were to die tomorrow he would leave her feeling tainted for the rest of her days, chained to the memories of the hateful web of deceit and lies she had spun in those last few weary years . . .

'Shine, shine, little hearts o' mine, shine like the snow and I'll be fine.'

The strangely melodious little chant, coming from the other side of the hawthorn hedge, startled her out of her reverie. It came again, soft and self-satisfied in all its enchanting simplicity. *'Shine, shine, little hearts o' mine, shine like the snow and I'll be fine.'*

Utterly mystified, her ladyship reined in her horse and dismounted. A fall of powdery snow had blanketed the countryside during the night, making the ground crunchy underfoot; the cold light of daybreak revealed a sparkling landscape of tall trees with lacy white

223

branches, and snow-covered walls marching up the hillsides, interspersed by sugar-loaf hedgerows and rickety fences capped by little mounds that looked like iced Christmas puddings. But it wasn't any of these that claimed the attention of Lady Pandora. She was intrigued by the rhyme chiming out in the frosty air, made all the more mysterious because she couldn't see the owner of the high-pitched voice that was singing it.

Very carefully she leaned over the hedge to investigate, disturbing a robin who was flitting about from branch to snowy branch looking for breakfast. There was Donal, knees drawn up to his chin as he squatted on the snowy ground, chanting out his little song, completely engrossed in something he was holding in his grimy palm.

'Donal.' Lady Pandora acknowledged him quietly so as not to frighten him away, easing herself through a gap in the hedge till she was standing in the snow beside him. 'I thought I heard the wee folk singing,' she went on in a whisper. 'A lovely little song it was too. I just had to stop and listen to it.'

' 'Twasn't the fairies—it was Donal,' he said shyly, though he wasn't too overcome at the intrusion to hastily curl his fingers round the object he had found lying at the roadside the day before.

'And what was it you were singing to, Donal?' asked Lady Pandora. 'Come now, you can show me.'

But he shook his head and scrambled several feet along the bank in an effort to get away from her. 'No,' he protested clearly. 'Mine. Donal found it. My hearts.'

Lady Pandora had followed him and now stood beside him once more, something powerful and wonderful about her as she loomed above him in her blue velvet cloak, its fur-trimmed hood framing her lovely face, little ringlets of golden hair falling down over her high, fair brow. She looked like a flower against the dawn light of the winter sky and Donal was so entranced by the sight of her he momentarily forgot himself and allowed his fingers to relax ever so slightly.

She glimpsed something shiny in his grasp and her curiosity was aroused. Everyone knew that Donal was a magpie and was forever picking up items that took his fancy; things that his brother Davie confiscated and held on to if he thought a reward might be offered for their return.

Nowadays, Donal was more devious where Davie was concerned. He had become adept at hiding his small treasures in places where only he could find them again and he didn't like being caught out enjoying his simple pleasures—by anyone, not even the lady of the big house!

Lady Pandora, seeing the expression of mistrust on his face, cleared a big stone of

225

powdery snow and sat down. 'Why, Donal, I'm not going to rob you,' she murmured soothingly. 'I just want to see what it is that makes you sing with such joy. I heard something about hearts—shiny hearts. Hearts can mean love, Donal, especially when they shine like the crystal snow. Let me see what you're hiding in your hand, I only want to look at it, just a little teeny peep is all I ask.'

She was speaking in soft, reassuring tones and Donal was so over-awed by her presence he slobbered slightly and burst out, 'Say you'll no' tell! Donal found it. Don't tell Davie. He'll hit me! He'll keep it.'

Her ladyship laid a gentle hand on his arm. 'I promise I won't tell, you can trust me, you know you can trust me. Stop worrying. I'm not going to harm you, instead I'm going to look in my pocket to see if I can find some sweeties. I often get hungry whilst out riding and that is why I always bring sweets and an apple with me. I know you like apples, Donal. Miss Priscilla told me so, and if you show me what it is you're hiding I'm going to give you mine, the very one I polished myself before I came out. It's a great big red juicy apple and it's all for you—for your breakfast.'

It was too much for Donal. Grabbing the proffered apple with one hand he opened up the other and there, reposing in the dirty folds of his palm, was Anna's Luckenbooth necklace.

When she beheld it, Lady Pandora's heart seemed to stop beating. The morning spun away in a giddy whirl; sky, earth, hills, all merged together, going round and round, faster and faster. For a while nothing made sense to her; all the country sounds that she knew and loved came from far, far away in those unreal and frightening moments and she felt so faint she had to sit with her eyes closed till her head had stopped spinning.

'My baby,' she whispered through pale lips. 'What did they do to my baby?'—She stared at the Luckenbooth necklace in Donal's hand. Tears filled her eyes. The silver hearts swam and wavered in her vision. 'Donal,' she said at last, 'may I—look at your pretty ornament? May I—hold it?'

Something in the catch of her voice so mesmerised Donal that he nodded and said, 'Ay,' in hushed tones.

Her fingers were trembling as she took hold of the Luckenbooth and held it up to stare at it. It dangled against the honey-gold sky, the light winking and sparkling on the gemstones till the whole thing seemed to grow and grow in brilliance and become like one great shining, dazzling star.

'My baby,' she said again. 'What have they done to my baby?'

She felt cold suddenly. Shakily she turned the Luckenbooth round. The inscription on the back leapt out at her: *To Anna, from*

Mother.

'Anna.' Lady Pandora's lips formed the name. 'Anna,' she said aloud, sounding so strange that Donal looked at her fearfully and began to edge away. 'Donal's hearts,' he whimpered.

She gazed at him without seeing him, but when he spoke again, this time with more urgency, she shook herself from her trance and said quickly, 'Donal, this nice necklace doesn't belong to you even though you found it. See, it has a name written on the back, not your name but someone else's. The person to whom it belongs.'

'No, it's mine, it's Donal's, finders keepers.' He began to make strange, squeaky sobbing noises that sounded uncannily like a terrified wounded animal caught in a trap. Then quite suddenly he changed tactics. 'I canny read! I canny read! I canny read!' he cried fearfully. 'Don't tell on Donal. Davie bad. He'll hit Donal.'

'Oh, come on.' Her ladyship laid a gentle hand on his shoulder. 'No-one's going to hit you, Donal, so don't cry anymore. Now, listen to me, what good is this silly old necklace to you? I'll give you something much better, a watch, you would like that, wouldn't you?'

'A watch.' He scrubbed his eyes and stared as she unpinned a gold fob watch from her jacket and held it out to him.

'Take this, Donal, yes, go on, you may have

it, it's a present, only don't let Davie see it or he'll break it, you know he broke the last watch you had.'

Donal's mouth fell open. He had forgotten the Luckenbooth. In round-eyed delight he took the proffered watch and held it to his ear. A slow smile transformed his thin, youthful-looking face. 'Donal's watch.' He gloated in happy entrancement. 'Half past five, time to rise, Don't be late, be at the gate.'

She left him there on the snowy bank, the watch glued to his ear, his voice chiming out softly in the frosty air as he recited all the little rhymes and ditties he had either made up himself or learned parrot-fashion over the years.

In a daze of wonderment, Lady Pandora caught hold of Sable's reins and led him back up the track towards the house, the Luckenbooth held tightly in her hand. The cold air seeped into her, bringing her bit by bit to her senses. Something momentous had happened in the last half-hour. The appearance of the Luckenbooth had triggered off a whole chain of questions and doubts in her mind. All the old half-forgotten memories came flooding back, the unfulfilled dreams, the heartaches, the yearnings, everything she had tried so hard to forget these last long unsettled years. And at the root of it all lay Lillian McIntyre, Anna's mother, a woman who had been incarcerated in Kilkenzie mental asylum since her daughter's early childhood.

Lillian! Roderick's wife! A mystery woman that very few people in the glen had ever had a chance to get to know properly, if at all. The message on the back of the Luckenbooth drummed in her ladyship's head. *To Anna, from Mother.* 'Mother' was Lillian McIntyre; she must have gifted the piece of jewellery to Anna. Lillian was therefore the woman who held the key to the secret of the Luckenbooth, an ornament that Lady Pandora had last seen eighteen years ago before she had parted with it—forever, she had thought at the time.

She had never expected to see it again, and now here it was, solid and real in her hand, a testament of a long-ago love, an echo of a tragic incident that she had tried so hard to forget. She had to know the answers to her questions. It was no use asking Anna what it all meant, she couldn't know anything or she would have mentioned it before now. And what about Sir Malaroy? What part had he played in all this? Had he participated in some dark and dreadful conspiracy which he had kept from her all these years? Or was he as innocent and as ignorant as she was herself? It could all have a very simple explanation of course, and there was only one way to find out what it was.

It was time for the secrets to be unwrapped, the mysteries to be unravelled and in a breathless burst of decision Lady Pandora knew that she had to go to Kilkenzie to visit Lillian McIntyre.

CHAPTER TWENTY-ONE

THE DIE IS CAST

Lady Pandora had never been one of the orthodox type of gentry. She was wont to do and say certain things that would have been frowned upon in other, more conventional large households and she didn't give a hoot about what anybody said regarding her so-called avant-garde attitudes. She was equally at home with servants and grand duchesses alike and, indeed, quite often preferred the company of the more homely type of person for down-to-earth mental sustenance.

On this particular morning, after she had installed her horse in his stable, she let herself into the house by the tradesman's entrance and thereafter made her way to the kitchen where Mary was rattling dishes in the sink and Molly the Cook was sitting with her feet up, indulging herself with tea and a hot bacon roll before preparations for breakfast really got underway.

'Just what I need, Molly,' nodded Lady Pandora. 'It's freezing cold this morning and I'm longing for a cup of tea. I could smell the

231

bacon as soon as I got in and decided I simply couldn't wait another minute to sample some for myself.'

'M'lady!' Molly wasn't unduly perturbed at receiving a visit from the lady of the house, even at this early hour. Her mistress was an entity unto herself and did what she wanted to do, and it wasn't long before she was sitting companionably beside Molly, drinking tea and eating a piping hot bacon roll, attended to by Mary who, remembering her experiences upstairs, was careful to mind her manners in front of her ladyship.

Mary had been rather subdued since that time. She didn't peep through keyholes and listen at doors nearly as much as she used to and she was altogether more respectful to her elders than in days of yore. Her allegiance to Adam had faltered after Beth's revelations of his infidelity. Even so, she was still fond of him and continued to see him, their common need for lust and companionship bonding them together, for they were both lonely, rather sad people, whom no-one else seemed to want or care for very much.

Lady Pandora was quick to notice Mary's changed attitude and seizing the teapot and another cup she said kindly, 'Come on, Mary, I don't bite, you know. Sit down, drink up, and stop looking so nervous. It's a marvellous morning, Christmas is coming, and I for one feel as if wonderful things might be going to happen at any moment.'

Mary sat, she drank tea, and even smiled a little at some of her mistress's light-hearted remarks. The sun arose and very soon the big airy kitchen was flooded with low winter sunlight streaming in through the window and the world seemed suddenly a brighter and more beautiful place to be in.

*   *   *

When Anna arrived mid-morning she found her ladyship in a strangely evasive and highly excited mood. 'I'm going away for a day or two, Anna,' she explained. 'I cannot tell you where at present but believe me, you will find out in due course. I've packed some things and had a talk with Sir Malaroy, Jim is getting the horses ready now and Neil Black is preparing himself for the journey. I know he doesn't enjoy being away from the stables for any length of time, but Jim is perfectly capable of seeing to things by himself and of course Magnus is always here to lend a hand if need be.'

'When are you going?' Anna asked with a frown.

'Now, in a few minutes.'

'So—soon?'

'Yes, yes, so soon!' her ladyship said snappishly. 'Oh ...' she put a hand over her eyes. 'I'm so sorry, I'm not myself, something urgent has occurred, something I must see to at once. Be a good child and look after things here, the Christmas dance is only a week away and there's so much still to arrange. I've made out a list—last-minute bits and pieces, do you think you could see to them?'

'Of course I will,' Anna said slowly. 'You know you can rely on me.'

'Oh well, I mustn't keep Neil waiting.' Lady Pandora pulled on her gloves, then seeing Anna's face she cried, 'Dear child! Don't look so forlorn! I'll be back before you know it. Keep busy, enjoy yourself. You and my husband can keep one another company, perhaps go out riding together. The countryside looks exquisite in the snow and the air is so wonderfully bracing.'

*   *   *

Some minutes later, Anna stood beside Sir Malaroy, waving at the coach as it rumbled away down the driveway. Anna felt desolate, somehow. Something was happening, something strange. The ground seemed suddenly rocky under her feet, and she knew instinctively that when her ladyship returned nothing was going to be the same again: everything was going to change, and she didn't know if it would be for the better or for the worse. When the coach had disappeared from view Sir Malaroy turned abruptly on his heel to go back inside the house, leaving Anna to follow slowly, her brow furrowed with anxiety.

On getting ready for bed the night before she had discovered that her precious necklace was missing. She hadn't taken it off since Duncan Lauder had fixed it round her neck, and it had been there when she had changed for dinner which she'd had at Noble House. She had walked there from The Gatehouse, along past the village, and up the track that led to the Noble House driveway. Somewhere along that route she had lost her necklace and on leaving the house that morning she had hunted high and low for it. But the snow had hampered her search, the necklace was nowhere to be seen, and there was only one other hope, that she might have dropped it within the confines of the big house itself. She hadn't expected her ladyship to be going away however, and in the flurry of the last half-hour she had forgotten to ask if anyone had seen her treasured necklace.

Now she made her way to the dining room to search for it, and she was there on her hands and knees under the table when a light step sounded and she knew Sir Malaroy had come into the room.

'Anna!' he cried when she peeped out at him. 'Once again I find you scrabbling around on all fours, like a little dog looking for a bone.'

Extending his hands he helped her to her feet and she gazed up at him, her eyes filling with an expression of tragedy. 'I've lost my necklace,' she told him quickly. 'I can't find it outside so I thought it might be in here.'

He stared at her in horror. 'You've lost it, you've lost the Luckenbooth?'

'Ay,' she answered in a whisper, feeling that she had committed some dark and dreadful deed. 'Please help me to look for it, two pairs o' eyes are better than one.'

He instantly responded to her request and the two of them crawled around on all fours, peering into the corners, disturbing the dust under the great oaken sideboard, shifting the chairs, feeling around in all the possible and impossible places until Baird the butler entered the room and simply gaped in astonishment at the sight of his master kneeling on the floor with one arm halfway up the underside of a small Axminster rug on which stood the sideboard.

'Sir,' Baird intoned stiffly, 'may I ask if you need help of any sort? If so I'll send for Daisy at once.'

'No, no, Baird.' Sir Malaroy scrambled to his feet, mustering as much dignity as he could in the circumstances. 'Please don't bother to call Daisy. Miss McIntyre and myself are perfectly capable of seeing to our own affairs and I would ask that you leave the room and shut the door behind you.'

'Very well, m'lord.' Baird positively glowered at both Anna and his master before removing his presence from the room as requested and clicking the door sharply shut at his back.

Sir Malaroy's piercing blue eyes looked into Anna's blue-grey ones. 'My dear little Anna,' he murmured softly, 'I am done for. The Luckenbooth is missing, which means that any one of the servants could find it and hand it to her ladyship. On the other hand, it might be lost forever and no-one will know its secrets. Whichever, I can't live with the uncertainty any longer. When Pandora returns you and she will have to know everything. Meanwhile ...' he held out his hand to her. 'Let me hold on to you for a little while. You always belonged to Pandora and I used to long to share in the happiness you brought her. I could never give her children and when you started coming to this house you brought her a special kind of joy. I know I never allowed myself to grow very close to you, but I always admired you and wanted to get to know you better. The reasons for my reticence will soon be revealed and when they are you will be very glad that I kept my distance from you all these years.

'Just now, I need to feel your warmth before I must let go of you for always. You will not like me very much when you hear what I have to tell you, so give me some comfort now, while you may.'

She allowed him to gather her into his arms and lay her head on his shoulder. He began to stroke her hair, his sensitive fingers caressing the long silken strands, his cheek held against the warm beating pulses of her temples. They didn't say anything, but remained like that together for a long time, just holding one another as they prepared themselves for the things that the future would reveal about the past, each of them wanting to hold on to life as it was now, both of them knowing that changes were inevitable and that nothing stood still forever.

*   *   *

Lady Pandora followed the nurse up the austere corridor to a heavy wooden door near the top. Here the nurse stopped and looked at the visitor. 'You *are* sure that Mrs McIntyre knows you, my lady?' she asked respectfully. 'She's become very distrustful over the years and won't communicate with anyone who worries her in any way.'

An odd little smile touched her ladyship's mouth. 'I can assure you, she knows me very well, nurse, very well indeed. Don't worry, I haven't come here to harm her—quite the opposite—but I would like to see her privately.'

The nurse nodded and disappeared for a few minutes. When she came back she beckoned to the visitor. 'In here, if you please, my lady, I've put her into one of the side rooms so you won't be disturbed and can be as private as you want to be.'

Lillian McIntyre was seated in the same bare little room she had occupied when she had been visited by her children two years ago. She was sitting quite peacefully on a straight-backed wooden chair, her face pink and scrubbed, her fine brown hair brushed back and held in place with slides.

'Here is your visitor, Mrs McIntyre,' the nurse conveyed in a loud voice, then turning to the visitor she said in softer tones, 'I'll be outside the door if you need me. She should be alright but sometimes she can be violent if something upsets her very badly, so please be careful with her. Kid gloves, that's the answer for Lillian McIntyre. In that way we all get peace and she stays as happy as she'll ever be.'

The door closed and there was complete silence in the room. Lady Pandora gazed at the smooth, unlined face of the woman seated before her and she felt as if she was being transported back in time.

'Lillian McIntyre,' she said softly. 'Only, when I knew you, you were Lillian Ferguson. Look at me, Lillian, after all these years I want you to look at me and remember who I am. The pretence is over with, it's time for the truth.'

Very slowly, as the pleasant cultured voice of the visitor broke the silence, the woman in the chair lifted her head, her dreamy hazel eyes coming to focus on the elegant figure standing by the door. An expression of recognition

239

flitted over the face of Lillian McIntyre, followed by one of pure and unmistakable awareness.

'No,' she whimpered, her hand going up to her trembling mouth. 'No, no, no.'

Lady Pandora came forward. 'Oh, but yes, Lillian,' she said firmly. 'It is me alright, and you know me very well indeed, you can't escape that fact any longer.'

'Yes, yes, I know you, m'lady,' whispered Lillian through lips that had gone pale. 'I—I know who you are, but I don't remember anything else.'

Lady Pandora dipped her hand into her bag. Withdrawing the Luckenbooth necklace she dangled it in front of the other woman's eyes. 'Of course you do, Lillian, you can recall everything as clearly as if it happened yesterday. You also know this piece of jewellery that I'm holding in my hand, don't you, Lillian? If truth be told you know it almost as well as I do myself.'

'No! No!' The woman crumpled. 'Go away, go away!' Fumbling in her dressing gown she pulled out a china doll that had once been a childhood plaything of Anna's, and holding it up she cried desperately, 'My baby. Don't let my lady take my baby away.'

'Rubbish!' Lady Pandora spoke briskly. Lowering herself on to one knee till her face was level with that of the other woman, she went on in a hard voice, 'Stop it, Lillian! You

240

are no more mad than I am. Stop pretending. Stop hiding. I'm not going to harm you or hurt you in any way. I'm here to help you get back to the world outside this prison you have locked yourself into. The time has come for you to unburden yourself and I'm going to sit here very quietly while you tell me exactly what happened eighteen long years ago. I think I deserve to be told. After all, it was my baby.'

A long trembling sigh came deep from within the throat of Lillian McIntyre, as if her very soul was crying out to be released from the burden of guilt she had carried around with her all this time. Tears sprung to her eyes, spilled over, and poured soundlessly down her face.

When she had finished weeping she gazed for many long minutes at the beautiful face of the woman beside her. And then she spoke. 'Yes, my lady,' she said in a voice that was meek and low but strong for all that. 'At last, indeed, it's time for the truth.'

CHAPTER TWENTY-TWO

CATACLYSM

It was very peaceful in the homely kitchen of Knock Farm. Magnus and Anna had come along to visit, accompanied by old Grace who had promised a knitting pattern to Kate

McLeod and was determined to deliver it personally, no matter how treacherous the weather.

The young McIntyres had provided her with an arm each, and guiding her footsteps over frozen cart tracks they had negotiated her around the icy puddles and stopped her from sliding into a ditch at the end of Knock Farm's road. Now all three sat by the hearth, warming their hands on large mugs of tea and eating cinnamon and nutmeg buns which Grace said gave her heartburn but which she tucked into anyway.

Magnus was soon chatting about farming to Ben McLeod, brother of Kate and Priscilla, but Anna was content to remain silent, preoccupied as she was with the loss of her necklace; Sir Malaroy's unhappiness; her ladyship's absence. Only a day and a night had passed since she had left Glen Tarsa, but to Anna it seemed like a year. She was pining to know what all the mystery was about, yet at the same time, because of Sir Malaroy's apprehension, she was dreading it as well. As for her necklace, her mind had been in a turmoil since it had gone missing. She had asked around but no-one had seen it, and no-one knew what she was talking about. Someone had suggested reporting the loss to the local policeman but in the circumstances, with Sir Malaroy behaving so strangely, she didn't want to take such a drastic step in case it might stir up a hornet's nest.

With a sigh she curled her fingers round her mug and lay back in her chair, very glad to absorb the tranquil atmosphere of Knock Farm. The warm aroma of baking filled the house; the clocks ticked; the cats purred; the dogs snored; flurries of snow outside the window made the interior seem all the cosier and everyone was inclined to congregate around the farmhouse fireplace with its quaint little bread ovens and its comforting aura of heat and sustenance.

For the last week or so, Kate McLeod had been busily engaged in making all sorts of festive fare and now, with Christmas just a few days away, she was really warming to her task and was presently involved in baking large batches of spicy mince pies.

'Enough to feed an army,' Priscilla McLeod remarked sourly, but Kate just smiled and reminded her sister that they were mostly meant to bring a bit of Christmas cheer to other people, particularly the McDonald family for whom the festive season was very much like any other time of the year.

'How very true, Kate,' Miss Priscilla said musingly. 'Things are worse than ever there just now. Sally seems to be going rapidly downhill. Anything I try to teach her she just tosses aside. She is, to put it frankly, disgustingly filthy. She won't go out of the house at all now but just wants to sit gazing up the lum, smoking her pipe, muttering and cursing darkly under her breath. Last time I was there I had to stop Davie hitting her and he started shouting that she had the devil in her and wasn't fit to be among other human beings.'

'Terrible, terrible.' Old Grace shook her head and spoke sadly. 'It's like living in the Dark Ages having that family in the glen. I feel sorry for them and I've tried to help all I can, but that Davie's a sour cratur' and spurns help as if it's a disease.'

'Ay, in many ways he's the worst o' the lot o' them, wi' his moods and thon hard buggering fists o' his,' Ben responded thoughtfully, leaning back comfortably in his chair to puff at his pipe and blow perfect smoke rings at the ceiling, earning a frown from Priscilla who had always maintained that she was 'allergic to all kinds of tobacco irritants'.

'Och well,' Kate said as she removed a tray of mince pies from the oven. 'Perhaps some o' these will cheer Davie up. I've made enough for all o' us here, plenty for the McDonalds, and a few for Todd Hunter.' Here she giggled girlishly, having been playfully wo'od by that gentleman over the last few weeks. 'And some extra for the postman, the coalman, the rag and bone man, the—'

'For heaven's sake, Kate!' her sister burst out. 'Don't you ever stop talking? You're worse than...'

244

At that moment an urgent rapping sounded on the front door, startling everyone in the room and making two snoring sheepdogs jump up as if a shot had been fired.

'Mercy on us!' cried Kate. 'Go and see who that is, Ben, my hands are all sticky from handling these pies.'

Ben put his pipe aside and rose to go through into the lobby, accompanied by his dogs who, having recovered from their fright, wagged their tails and lowered their heads to glare slinky-eyed at the door as they prepared themselves for whatever action might be needed. Ben yanked open the door—and was almost bowled off his feet by Davie McDonald who, face as black as thunder, catapulted himself into the house, hauling his screaming sister behind him.

Without a word he marched her through to the kitchen to make her stand in front of everybody, a muscle in his thin, fox-like face working frantically. So incoherent with rage was he, he could say nothing for a few moments, which was as well since Sally, wild, dishevelled and dirty, her clothes hanging from her in greasy tatters, was making more than enough noise on her own account.

Then her screams stopped, and in their place came a long, low, animal-like wailing that made everyone shiver and feel the hair prickling at the top of their spines.

'Grace, Grace!' Davie found his voice and

gazed beseechingly at the old widow-woman, his breath bubbling out of his skinny rib cage in a rapid staccato of sound. 'Grace,' he repeated. 'I'm feart.'

'What is it, laddie?' Grace came forward to lay her hands on Davie's arm. 'Why are you feart? What ails you? Whatever it is I'm here and I'll help you as much as I can.'

A fit of trembling seized Davie and everyone in the room stared at him apprehensively; it was unknown for him to lose control in this way.

'It isny me, it's *her!*' he mumbled, and with an agile flick of his powerful wrists he spun his sister round till she was facing Grace. 'Look!' he cried, an expression of disgust twisting his features as he pulled back Sally's filthy cloak to point at her stomach.

'Oh, dear God, no!' breathed Grace, and sat down suddenly in the nearest chair to look with disbelief at Sally's swollen belly. She was obviously in an advanced stage of pregnancy. Ben shook his head in bewilderment at the sight and Kate, throwing up her hands, cried, 'Davie McDonald! Why did you no' tell someone sooner? It's a bit late in the day to come crying for help now.'

'Ach, he would never know!' snapped Priscilla, so appalled by Sally's condition her first reaction was anger. 'With all the bits of rags she's got tied round herself I doubt anyone would have known—far less Davie.'

'But—what made him realise it now?' whispered Anna.

The answer came from Sally herself, who suddenly stopped wailing and emitted a piercing cry of pain instead, her hands clawing frantically at her stomach.

'God help us, she's having the bairn! The lass is in labour!' cried Kate, and she too sank into a convenient chair.

Magnus strode forward and grabbed Davie's arm. 'Who did this, Davie?' he demanded. 'Did she tell you anything at all? Give a hint o' who is responsible?'

Davie's pale eyes glittered with ice-cold hatred. 'Ay,' he spat harshly. 'All this time she wouldny tell and then the pains started and she told me it was a McIntyre—Adam McIntyre—your brother, the filthy swine that he is! Sally says he did bad things to her, but she was aye too feart to tell anybody in case he might kill her.'

Ashen-faced, Magnus recoiled as if he had been whipped, but before anyone could do or say anything else Sally tore herself free from her brother's grasp and flew into the lobby. In seconds she had wrenched the door open and was fleeing away down the road, hardly knowing what she was doing in her pain and bewilderment.

Fast on her heels went Davie and Magnus, and behind them Anna, with Grace hanging grimly on to her arm.

247

In spite of her girth, Sally was still agile and fleet of foot. The icy state of the road was no deterrent to her and she simply flew along, past the village, then the mill buildings, to arrive at The Gatehouse way ahead of the others. Wailing and screeching she pounded on the door with her fists. When it was thrown open by Roderick, she still kept on pounding, only instead of the wooden door panels it was his chest that got the full brunt of her unbridled rage.

Adam was hovering in the tiny lobby, hidden from view by his father's bulk in the doorway. Adam was in a highly excited state, his eyes snappishly alive in his glowing face and the adrenaline surging through his body at the highly charged scene he had just witnessed between his father and Boxer Sam McGuire. Sam had called in to say that old Jock the foreman was retiring at Christmas. 'I've been speaking to Mr Jordan,' he had said gloatingly. 'Tomorrow he's interviewing one or two likely candidates for Jock's job, me included. It's just a formality really, I know the boss has his eye on me and I've a feeling I'm about to step up another wee rung in the ladder. Just thought I'd let you have a whole night to fume and fret about it, Roddy, but don't worry, you'll be the first to know the results, I will personally deliver them so that I can see your reaction first hand and enjoy my wee bit glory to the full.'

Adam had hugged himself with glee at the

look of pure frustration on his father's face and he had been disappointed when Sam had said he had to be going. That had been just a few minutes ago and now, here was Silly old Sally at the door, screaming blue murder and beating the hell out of Roderick with her fists.

Adam sniggered; it looked as if he was in for some more thrills after all, and he was going to savour them to the full. Life in the glen could go on in the same vein for weeks, but as long as there were loonies like Sally on the loose one could always be assured of a bit of excitement to keep things ticking over.

After the encounter with Sam, Roderick was in a foul mood and the sight of Sally, mad-eyed and demented, her matted black hair hanging about her contorted face, made him see red altogether. 'Get the hell away from my house, you crazy bitch!' he bellowed, catching her hands and shaking her till her teeth rattled.

But in her madness she was stronger than he was. Breaking free she raised up her clenched fists and began hitting him all over again, beating a tattoo against his hard barrel of a chest, ranting at him unintelligibly.

Roderick could take no more. Raising up a meaty fist he was about to smack it into Sally's face when Magnus arrived on the scene and countered the move by lunging at his father and twisting his forearm round his back.

'You'd better leave her alone!' Magnus panted harshly. 'And if you know what's good for you, you'll get her into the house this minute and no bones about it!'

So saying he bundled everyone inside, shutting the door firmly behind him. Roderick opened his mouth to speak, but his son gave him no chance. 'Listen and listen well, Father,' he grated. 'Sally is about to have a child—*his* child.'

He pointed an accusing finger at Adam, whose face had grown white in the last few minutes. Things were turning sour on him. The sight of Sally's swollen body had brought him out in a sweat. The acts of lust he had indulged in, on that hot night of mid-summer past, came flooding back to him and his heart began to thump in a most alarming manner.

But it was his word against hers. No-one was going to believe anything the mad bitch had to say. He would wriggle out of it somehow. It wasn't the first time he'd been in hot water and it wouldn't be the last...

'You lying son of a bitch!' Roderick exploded, glaring at Magnus. 'As if *my* son would even think o' touching...' he waved his hand disdainfully in Sally's direction, 'that filthy tinker! Look at her—look at him!'

His furious black gaze swept scornfully over Davie, who was standing quietly at the door, his fists balling at his sides. 'They're mad, the lot o' them! They should have been locked away years ago and then we might all have had some peace!'

Grace, newly arrived with Anna, had collapsed on to the sofa and was fanning her face with a corner of her apron. She wasn't too breathless however to say softly, 'There's mad and there's mad, Roderick McIntyre, but we aren't here to argue about that. Magnus spoke the truth just now, Sally herself put the name to the father o' her bairn. See, how she looks at him, there's terror in the poor cratur's eyes. Ay, by God! Terror o' the de'il and no mistake, for any man that would lay a finger on that poor soul must be possessed, that's all I can say.'

Sally was staring wildly at Adam, her eyes filled with a terrible accusation that he couldn't escape. She was shaking and moaning, her mind unable to grasp what was happening inside her pain-racked body. Her baby was coming more than two months early but she wasn't to know anything about that. She was sick, she was suffering, she was in the presence of the wicked creature who had hurt her, and as well as everything else she was afraid that he might get at her and do it again.

'She had better come to my house,' Grace was saying. 'She can have her bairn there— God help it. Anna, will you come with me? I'll need your help, lassie, and Magnus, you could maybe get along to Munkirk and fetch the doctor.'

Sally had begun backing away from Adam, her fear-stricken eyes never leaving his face. When she reached the wall and could go no further she leaned against it like a trapped animal and in her dementia she began to scream, a dreadful crazed wailing sound that no-one there would ever forget.

'*NO!* Don't hurt Sally!' she yelled in agonised protest, frantically turning her head this way and that as if trying to escape the hellish phantoms of her mind. And then in one swift movement she sprang to the door, opened it, and went tearing back up the glen road, screeching as she went, dreadful sounds that echoed through the village and struck dread into the hearts of everyone who heard them.

CHAPTER TWENTY-THREE

HELL, FIRE, AND WATER

When Sally had departed The Gatehouse, Grace rose rather wearily from her chair. 'She'll be making for her own house,' she told Anna. 'You get along there and I'll be in at your back with Maggie May. She's a dab hand at seeing bairns into the world and with Sally I'm going to need all the help I can get. I'll get Nellie Jean to give me a hand along to The Coach House so you get going and don't worry about me.'

Magnus had already departed to fetch the doctor, Davie had been despatched to find

Donal and prepare him for what lay ahead, and Anna sped up the road, her heart pumping fast in her breast. She couldn't believe any of this was happening; it was a nightmare from which she would soon awaken; it was all too unreal to be true; everything had been unreal since she had lost her necklace; since Lady Pandora had left Noble House; since she and Sir Malaroy had crawled about on all fours in the dining room looking for her necklace and Baird had come in and gaped at them in astonishment.

All of that seemed to belong to another dimension now. Sally's plight had overridden all else. A vision of Adam came into Anna's head, standing there in the kitchen, staring at Sally, guilt written all over him, guilt and fear of what was to come. Roderick would get the truth out of him; make him suffer for what he had done...

A sob rose up in Anna's throat. The sound of her hurrying feet rang out on the slippery road, her hair came undone and streamed out behind her in the icy wind. She slipped and half fell, then righted herself and surged onwards. Grassy Lane, leading to the McDonalds' cottage, loomed ahead. She had no earthly idea what she was going to do when she got there. Before she reached it she heard Sally's frantic screams coming through the open door. Anna burst inside, dishevelled and panting, feeling she must be looking as wild as Sally, who was standing in the kitchen with her back to a wall, saliva dribbling from her twisted mouth.

The cottage was a dark, cold filthy hovel of a place. Daylight was almost excluded by tattered curtains hanging at the tiny, deeply recessed windows; the walls were black with dirt and smoke; cobwebs floated down from the ceiling; the only bits of furniture were three torn and rickety chairs, a huge black dresser, heaped high with papers and ragged clothing, and a tumble-down wooden table littered with greasy dishes and the remnants of a meal.

Donal was not out on one of his wanders as everyone had supposed, he was crouched in a corner of the room, sobbing into his hands like a lost child. Anna's heart went out to him and rushing forward she took him into her arms to rock him and murmur soothing words of comfort into his ears.

Sally's screams were growing in volume. Every so often she would bend double, her hands clutching at her stomach. This made the terrified Donal sob louder than ever and Anna had her hands full, trying to soothe both Sally and her brother while she prayed that someone would come soon.

Davie was the first to come rushing in, followed closely by Grace and Maggie May, the innkeeper's wife, who immediately took charge.

'Davie, take your brother down to the inn and see that he gets fed,' she ordered. 'My husband knows I'm here and will know what's happened when he sees you. Get going now, Sally will be fine wi' us, so don't worry.'

Chastened and afraid, Davie led his brother away and as soon as he was gone Maggie May, despite her huge bulk, began to move with great rapidity.

Going to Sally, she placed a beefy arm across her shoulders and said kindly, 'Into bed wi' you now, there's a dear. No' a soul is going to hurt you so just do what I tell you and you'll be alright.'

Sally followed Maggie May meekly enough, then she stiffened as another contraction gripped her. Hands clawing at the doorpost she refused to move another step, the strength of her so great that not even Maggie May, Grace and Anna between them could prise open her clamped fingers.

When the pain had receded she was spent and submissive and allowed herself to be led into a tiny dingy room that was in an even worse condition than the kitchen. A stained horsehair mattress and a dirty patchwork quilt were the only items on the bed, and Grace shook her white head in dismay.

'We'll need clean sheets and towels,' she declared. 'Anna, you come down to my house wi' me and help me carry back the things.'

'I could go and get them myself,' Anna offered, noticing how tired the old lady looked.

'Havers, I'm fine,' Grace declared

255

vehemently, adding, 'We'll be back in no time at all, Maggie May. Are you sure you'll be alright here on your own?'

'Ay, ay, away you go. I'll get these rags off Sally and wrap my own peeny round her for now. I've never seen the likes o' this place.'

Anna and Grace departed, leaving Maggie May to set about divesting Sally of her vestments. In her day, the innkeeper's wife had seen many a shocking sight, but as she removed the layers of stained clothing from Sally, her plump, good-natured face became twisted with shock and revulsion. As the stench rushed out to meet her she held her breath but kept grimly to the job in hand. Sally's pains seemed to have abated, and she lay passively, limp with exhaustion, her black eyes staring vacantly up at the ceiling. Despite the matted tangles in her nightblack hair and the grimy tears staining her face, she had a look of beauty about her in those moments of calm and Maggie May's heart was touched. Taking off her voluminous white apron she wrapped it round the young woman's swollen body and, encased in white like that, Sally looked like an innocent child whom neither sin nor sorrow had ever touched.

Her hand came out, her long fingers curling round Maggie May's arm in an oddly gentle and trusting gesture. Tears sprang to the older woman's eyes as tenderly she smoothed Sally's hair back from her brow and murmured, 'Ach, there now, poor, poor lassie, mostly you're a tormented soul but sometimes you're like a lost bairn looking for a mother. Wheesht now, it will be alright, Maggie May will stay by you, but first I'm going to heat some water and give you a wee wash. Just you lie there and don't move till I come back.'

She went through to the kitchen. Two pails sat on wooden slats under the sink but they were empty, and tutting with annoyance Maggie May seized one of them and went outside. The burn was a fair distance from the house and grumbling and panting she waddled along to the outfall that supplied several houses in the village with water.

Anna and Grace were coming along the road, laden down with clean supplies of bedding and towels. Seeing Maggie May they hailed her just as they were turning into Grassy Lane and setting down the brimming pail she went forward to meet them with the intention of helping them carry some of the provisions.

A horrifying screech stopped her in mid-track. Sally was standing at the door of the cottage, her hands pressed into her stomach. For a few brief seconds she stood framed in the doorway, then she slammed the door shut and only the muffled sounds of her demented wails could be heard as they filtered outside.

Before Maggie May could make a move Anna went running up to the cottage to try and open the door, but Sally had dropped the latch and it wouldn't move.

'Sally! Sally!' Anna beat on the door with her clenched fists. 'Let us in, please, we're going to help you to get rid o' your pain. Maggie May's here, and Grace, and Miss Priscilla should be along at any moment. You know how you love Miss Priscilla.'

Her words were met with a bloodcurdling cry of agony. Sally was in no condition to move, far less let anyone into the house. She was standing in the middle of the room, tearing at her hair, black eyes dilated with fascination as she watched billows of smoke drifting through from the bedroom.

She had retrieved her pipe and matches, from the pocket of her apron, lying on the floor where Maggie May had dropped it. But there was nothing in it to burn, no tobacco, no dead leaves, nothing to bring her a bit of comfort, nothing to help ease her torture. That was when she had started striking the matches and dropping them on to the piles of rags and newspapers that littered the bedroom floor. She liked fire, enjoyed lighting pieces of paper so that she could watch the edges curling and smouldering. The flames had spread and had soon started devouring the flimsy shreds of material that served as dividers between the makeshift beds. Sally had been fascinated at the sight, and lifting some of the burning fragments she had run with them into the kitchen to throw them on to the papers on the dresser. They were tinder dry and flared up

258

immediately.

A tongue of fire licked the cobwebbed curtains, which shrivelled up and floated to the floor; scraps of charred and burning paper were swirling around the room; smoke began to thicken and drift through the house.

Sally stood transfixed, watching it all with eyes that were mad with pain and fear. She wailed, she screamed, she cried ... And then she began to laugh, a high-pitched, cackling sound that told of a mind that had finally gone over the edge. The pains in her belly were pulling her apart. She wanted only to be rid of them, she couldn't take any more, she couldn't...

'Adam McIntyre!' The name came out in a scream of accusation, over and over, never diminishing, never stopping. Darting forward she seized the paraffin lamp and threw it against a blazing chair with all her remaining strength.

The room seemed to explode, a wall of fire roaring up towards the ceiling. Sally's screams were swallowed up as the inferno whooshed upwards and spread outwards, consuming everything in its path.

Aghast with horror, the three women outside watched as the windows shattered with the heat, sending fragments of glass flying everywhere. With a sob Anna ran forward, trying to reach the door. Smoke and flames billowed out to meet her and she felt hands

259

seizing her, pulling her away, Magnus's hands, enclosing her, his voice soothing and calm in her ear, and putting her head on his shoulder she wept unrestrainedly.

People from the village had arrived on the scene; Boxer Sam and Nellie Jean, the McLeods, Moira O'Brady the postmistress, followed by Davie, who had left his brother at the inn and had come back in time to see his house blazing like a torch.

'Davie.' Miss Priscilla put her arm round his bony shoulders. 'You must stay with us tonight, you and Donal, nothing can save Sally now, you have to see that.'

Davie's face was contorted with disbelief and he backed away, shaking his head, muttering under his breath. The men of the village were forming a chain, buckets of water from the burn were being passed from hand to hand. But it was too late. The house was beyond saving; the rest of the windows had exploded; fingers of fire were curling through the roof timbers.

Sally had stopped screaming some time ago. The only sounds to be heard now were the crackling of burning wood and the sizzling of water turning to steam on the red-hot walls.

'Oh, Magnus.' Anna clung to him. 'She was in too much pain to know what she was doing. Poor, poor Sally, what a way to die.'

'Hush, my babby, hush.' His arms were safe and strong. He stroked her hair and held her close; it didn't matter anymore that people saw them together like this. His heart was beating fast with his love for her, and still it wasn't the sort of love that a brother feels for his sister, but that which a man feels for his sweetheart.

Grace was ensnared in Maggie May's fat, comforting arms, her sweet old face drenched with tears. 'It was an act o' God, Maggie,' she whispered. 'She was a lost soul who never did find her way in this life. It was a terrible way to go—but can you imagine the bairn?'

'There, there, wheesht now,' Maggie May soothed, though her own eyes were red. 'It's over now—at this end, anyway,' she added grimly. 'I wouldny like to be Adam McIntyre when his father gets a hold o' him.'

Grace glanced at Davie, standing staring at the smouldering shell of his house, cursing under his breath, his expression one of pure murderous hatred.

Grace shivered. Maggie May was right, there was more trouble ahead, and the old lady shook her snowy-white head as she wondered if peace would ever reign again in bonny Glen Tarsa.

*   *   *

When everyone had departed from The Gatehouse, Adam and Roderick were left facing one another in the kitchen. The latter's eyes were swivelling rapidly from side to side in his red congested face, his stocky figure was as tense as a coiled spring, and his nostrils were dilated, the grey hairs in them moving up and down with the laboured working of his lungs.

Adam was well acquainted with the signs that his father's rage could generate—he had looked like that when he had beaten Anna or chastised Magnus—but never before had a deed of Adam's caused such a reaction, and he felt his knees going weak with fear, his innards turning to jelly.

He wanted only to run out of the house and never ever come back, but Roderick's looming figure was in the way, blocking the door, making escape impossible.

'So, this is how you repay all I've done for you,' Roderick began in a righteous voice. 'All these years I've coddled you, stuck by you, seeing only what I wanted to see because you were the son o' my heart. You dirty little runt! Did you rape that madwoman? Speak up, boy, I want to hear the truth from you! If you lie to me I promise, you won't live long enough to regret it!'

Adam licked his dry lips as he remembered the things he'd done to Sally. Since that night he'd experienced occasional twinges of apprehension, but time had passed, nothing had been said, so he had begun to feel truly safe—until today, and that hellish scene with Sally, her pregnant belly, her pointing finger...

Again he licked his lips and blurted, 'It was

only a bit o' fun, Father. I didn't mean...'

'*Fun!*' Roderick's incredulous roar bounced against Adam's eardrums. 'You call bringing disgrace on the good family name, fun? Lying wi' that stupid bitch! Planting your seed in her. How can I bear the shame o' it? How can I hold up my head again? I could forgive a bit o' youthful high spirits, the kind o' things I did in my own young days—but this...!'

He advanced towards his son, a menacing, frightening figure of bristling fury, apparently forgetful of all the wicked deeds he had committed.

Adam backed away, whimpering, 'Don't hit me, Father. I promise nothing like it will happen again. Please, Father, don't hurt me, don't touch me!' He fell on his knees, cowering and grovelling, begging for mercy, his arms held over his head to protect it.

Roderick grabbed him by the scruff of the neck and hauled him to his feet. The first blow knocked his head to the side and he stood there like that, waiting for the next one.

He could easily have fought back; he was taller than his father, broader, fitter, but so conditioned was he to obeying the man who had wrought panic in his breast since childhood, the idea of defending himself never entered his head. The second blow, when it came, was even more vicious than the first. It sent him flying across the room and when he hit the floor he couldn't get up again. Time and again he found himself being pulled upright by his collar to be punched unmercifully, over and over.

Blood filled his mouth, he spewed out two teeth, his head throbbed, as did his face, his limbs, his body. The fear had left him now, he was too numb to feel anything but pain, pain that throbbed and spread in a red-hot ache across his bruised and battered body.

He stood, knees sagging, in the middle of the room, waiting for the blow that he felt must surely kill him. But it never came, Roderick had collapsed into a chair, fighting for breath, trembling in every limb, the muscles in his face twitching, a tiny nerve flickering in one eyelid, almost closing it.

Adam attempted to draw air into his lungs; a knife-like pain seared through his chest and he began to pant with renewed fear because he couldn't get enough oxygen through his blood-clogged nostrils. His stomach felt weak, then quite unexpectedly his bladder emptied—he could feel it, flooding down his legs, seeping through his trousers on to the floor.

Roderick's bloodshot eyes bulged as he stared contemptuously at the puddle on the floor. 'You've pissed yourself, boy, pissed yourself like a babe in arms!' His voice became hoarse with loathing. 'No son o' mine cries like a baby and pisses his trousers. I've finished with you. Get the hell out o' my sight!'

Adam tried to stand up straight but

couldn't. His legs were wobbling beneath him, and it took every ounce of his willpower to gather up the little strength that was left to him to stagger into the bedroom where he fell on to his bed to sob unrestrainedly. Every nerve, every fibre inside him shrieked with pain; every muscle, every sinew ached and throbbed. Clenching his fists he began punching the pillows, over and over, till, exhausted, he rolled over on his back to stare at the ceiling through a watery veil.

One thought drummed in his brain, over and over, growing more insistent as the minutes ticked away.

I'll kill him! I'll kill him! I'll kill him! his mind shrieked. He nodded his head in agreement of the message that his brain was sending him and with a painful twist of the grotesque blob that was his mouth he murmured aloud, 'I'll kill him.'

CHAPTER TWENTY-FOUR

AFTERMATH

Lady Pandora stood facing her husband in their bedroom. She had returned from Kilkenzie that afternoon and had declared her intention of having an early night. Now she had bathed and was dressed in a rose-silk robe, her hair tumbling down her back in a mass of shining honey-gold curls. Although she was pale and tense looking there was a sparkle in her wondrous eyes which made her husband draw in his breath. How, he wondered, could he disclose to her the things that had been crowding his mind during the two days of her absence? She was so dazzlingly lovely standing there in the softly lit room he didn't want to do or say anything to spoil the magic that was Pandora. All he wanted was to take her in his arms and hold her close because when she heard what he had to say to her she might never come to him again.

His eyes went dull at the thought and for a moment he weakened. What good would it do to unburden himself to her now? He had kept his dark secrets locked tightly in his heart for so long. No useful purpose could possibly be served if he was to speak up now. Then he thought of Anna; of Lillian McIntyre; of Magnus; and of Roderick, the maggot in the apple, the creature who had sucked him dry for years, feeding on his faint-heartedness.

'Pandy, sit down, please, my darling, I have something I wish to tell you...'

His voice sounded hollow and shook slightly, but resolutely he went on, 'I should have spoken out a long time ago but I never had the courage, even when I knew that others were suffering because of my silence. I knew, you see, that I might lose you, and I couldn't bear the thought of that. Oh, dear God...'

Tears clouded his eyes and he looked up at the ceiling to stop them spilling over. 'I am not able to visualise my life without you and yet I can't go on with the deceit, the lies. They have already driven us apart to some extent and I feel I have lost a precious part of you.'

A silence sprung up between them that seemed to last forever. Outside, the rain was teeming down, blotting out the hills, hissing against the window panes. The wind keened round the house, moaning and wailing like some lost soul condemned to roam the wilderness for all time.

Then Lady Pandora spoke. 'Malaroy, I too have something to confess, many things in fact. We have both been foolish and weak, but I feel I am more to blame than anyone for what happened years ago, although I have suffered for my sins and paid a very dear price for them.'

She looked at him with eyes that were strange and sad and then she held out both her hands to him and when he took them she led him over to the bed and made him sit down.

'Shall I begin first?' he asked.

'You don't have to, I know it all. Lillian Ferguson—or McIntyre as she is now—told me everything she has tried to forget all these years.'

'Lillian McIntyre?'

'Yes, I've been to see her, and she isn't mad,

she's just sad, as anyone would be, living the sort of life she has. Once she started talking it was as if she would never stop. And now you and I must do the same, we must talk and talk and cleanse ourselves of guilt. Our love will never be the same as it was in the beginning, we have both suffered too much for that, and we have made each other suffer.'

Reaching out she touched his face with a tentative finger. 'I should hate you. From the start you deceived me by not telling me that you couldn't father children. Then I too turned to deceit and so it has gone on. You did terrible things to me, Malaroy, and though I may forgive you I will never forget. But what's done is done, it's in the past now, we have to go on and look to the future, and we must help one another to be happy.'

He took a deep, shuddering breath. Lifting up her hands he kissed the palm of each one and then he and she lay down side by side and talked as if they would never stop.

*   *   *

'Magnus, can I speak to you for a minute?'

Anna, hood pulled up against rain which was beating down so hard it was making froth in the puddles and rivers of mud in the yard, raised her voice against the hiss of the torrent. Curtains of drips were swishing down from the gutters and she could barely see as she peered inside the shed where Magnus was sitting on a three-legged stool, milking a large hairy cow with only one horn on her head.

'Ay, what is it?' He didn't look up from his task and she gave vent to a loud sigh, which was lost on him with all the noise outside and the drumming of milk in the pail.

'Can I come in?' she shouted. 'It's soaking wet out here.'

'Ay, you know you can come in, you don't have to ask, the cows don't bite and neither do I—yet.'

Anna wasn't amused by his words. She was cold and damp and very glad to absorb the steamy warmth inside the shed which was low-raftered and fragrant with the combined smells of hay and dung. At the far end, two farmhands were carrying pails of frothy milk into the dairy but were sufficiently out of earshot for her to say hurriedly, 'Listen, Magnus, I've just been to see Lady Pandora. I don't know how to explain this but she seems sort o' different, excited and secretive, as if she's longing to tell me something but is bottling it all up. She wants us both to be at the Christmas dance on Saturday and I said I would ask if you would take me.'

Still he didn't turn. 'Ach, Anna, do I have to? You said you didn't feel like it after what happened to Sally. It doesn't seem right somehow.'

'I know I said that,' she spoke slowly. 'But it

isn't for me, it's for *her*, for Pandora, she wants it to be a special evening. The portrait I did of her is to be shown for the first time and she wants you and me there, together, Magnus— and I want you there, for me, because I love you and need to have you by my side.'

His head came slowly round to look at her and his eyes grew tender at the sight of her golden locks escaping her hood, the raindrops glistening on the end of her nose. 'I'm just a farmhand, Anna, I don't have the clothes for these grand dances. The suit I had last summer is falling to pieces and I haven't got the sillar to buy another one.'

'You can wear one of Sir Malaroy's, you and he are about the same size...'

Angrily he brought the palm of his hand down on his knee. 'I'm not a beggar, Anna! I've got my pride and I won't dress up in someone else's clothing, not even to please you!'

A blush of shame stained her face. 'I shouldn't have said that, I'm sorry.' She shook her head. 'Oh, if only I could tell you all that's in my heart, for you, for me, for everyone. I feel that we are slipping away from one another. I can sense your restlessness and I know how much you want to break away from our life as it is now and start afresh somewhere else. I also know that you stay because o' me. You're so handsome and good, and I will never think o' you as a beggar, to me you are more noble than a prince and always will be.'

270

He stretched out his hands to her. 'Wee witch,' he said huskily, his strong face full of tenderness. 'You know how to twist me round your little finger, don't you? I'll go to the dance with you, and I'll be the proudest man there, even though you might turn up your nose at me in my threadbare suit.'

She smiled and put her hands into his, and in those trembling moments of pure awareness they could feel the love that they had for one another reaching out to embrace them in its beating, loving warmth.

*   *   *

It seemed as if it wasn't going to be a white Christmas after all, the rain had seen to that; the snow was washing off the hills and thunderstorms were renting the heavens, hurling rain to the earth with malevolent violence.

But on the day of the Christmas dance at the House of Noble the clouds rolled away, allowing the sun to shine in the ice-blue of the winter sky. It was bitterly cold but hauntingly beautiful, and lifted everyone's spirits after the grey dark of the last few miserable days.

Anna and Magnus had been asked to go early to the big house. When they arrived Sir Malaroy took charge of the latter, chatting to him, then showing him up to a dressing room where an immaculate evening suit lay over a chair.

'Tonight is a special occasion, for you and for Anna,' Sir Malaroy said with a little smile. 'Sometimes we don't feel like doing the things that we feel aren't meant for us, but ...' he spread his fine hands, 'for the sake of our lovely ladies I think we should both make an effort to please them.'

He withdrew from the room, leaving Magnus to stare at the clothes. He bit his lip. He sat down and thought everything over— and then he began slowly to get dressed.

*　　　*　　　*

Anna was swept away by Lady Pandora in a breathless whirl of laughter, up to her ladyship's own dressing room where an exquisite dress of shell-pink ninon with a cuirass bodice of satin was hanging up on the wardrobe door. And on the carpet below, a pair of pink satin dancing slippers reposed neatly, while on a nearby chair, silk stockings and fine underwear were lovingly laid out.

'I hope you like it all, Anna,' said her ladyship in a low voice. 'The seamstress at Larchwood was familiar with your measurements but we might have to make some last minute adjustments. I've asked Daisy to come up to help you get dressed.'

Anna could say nothing for many moments, then she kissed the petal-soft cheek of the older woman and whispered her thanks in a shaky voice.

'Anna,' Lady Pandora drew the girl close, her fingers playing with the white-gold strands of the hair that had so entranced her from the start. 'Anna,' she said again softly. 'I would give you the world. You have filled this house and my life with sunshine these last few years. If only I had known you sooner.' Then her tone changed to one of briskness. 'Enough of this chatter. It's time to get ready and we must both breathe in, tighten our corsets, and wear our very best smiles.'

*   *   *

An hour later, after Daisy had departed, Anna stood surveying herself in the full-length wardrobe mirror and couldn't quite believe she was Anna McIntyre of The Gatehouse. She had dressed up before, but never quite so elegantly as this. The style of her gown made her look taller, and very slender; her bare shoulders were creamy-white above the dark-green velvet bows and pink-satin flowers that decorated the bodice; the satin train, edged with ninon pleats, swirled round her feet and spread out over the floor; on her arms she wore gold-linked bracelets over long, white kid gloves; her hair was swept up into a chignon that made her look grown-up and every inch a sophisticated young lady.

When Lady Pandora appeared in the doorway she was a vision of delight arrayed as she was in a dress of pale-green satin trimmed with forest-green velvet bows; her skin was glowing; her eyes were sparkling; her upswept hair emphasised her long white neck to startling advantage.

'My lady,' Anna murmured, 'when I was a child I thought you were too beautiful to be real. Now I know that as well as being lovely you are also thoughtful and good and so kind it makes me feel like crying.'

Her ladyship said nothing. She was staring at Anna, whose delicate beauty was like a rosebud slowly unfolding its petals to the light; the colour of her attire was a perfect foil for her fair sweetness; her glowing eyes were dark in the flushed smoothness of her pale skin, her hair gleamed as richly as the satin of the dress she was wearing. That night she had left childhood behind, and even while her ladyship's heart was big with pride it was also sore with a yearning to have known more of this young girl's life.

'You mustn't cry, Anna.' She held out her hands, her face alight. 'Anna, my beautiful child, you look so grown up yet I can see you now, a little girl peeping out from Beth Jordan's ribbons, shy, wistful, and rather sad.' She shook her head. 'Oh, dear, I mustn't get morbid, here, take this.' She pressed a pink satin fan into Anna's hand. 'Now you are

274

complete, no, don't thank me anymore, all I want is for you to be happy . . .' She broke off to stare at the girl. 'You *are* happy, I hope. No, something is troubling you, I see it in your eyes.'

Anna sighed. 'Some terrible things happened while you were away, I haven't got over them yet.'

'My child, I heard. Poor Sally.'

'What's going to happen to Donal and Davie now that their house is gone?'

'Why, they'll get another, of course. Sir Malaroy is letting them have that empty cottage next to the newly-weds, Sam and Nellie Jean. She has a heart of gold underneath all her brash ways and she has said she'll keep an eye on the McDonald boys. Miss Priscilla and Kate will do their bit, I myself am going to pop in from time to time, and woe betide Davie if the house isn't clean! Donal should be happy enough, he adores Sam McGuire, so you mustn't worry any more about that.'

'I know, but I can still hear Sally's screams in my head and when I'm at home I see Adam's bruised and miserable face and hear Father nagging at him the way he used to nag me. Adam has barely spoken a word since it all happened—he just looks at Father—and there's so much hatred in his eyes it makes my flesh creep.'

'Adam is certainly reaping what he sowed,' her ladyship said thoughtfully. 'Rumours are

275

going around that Beth Jordan is going to have his child, but then both he and she had a wonderful time scattering their wild oats together.'

'Oh, you know about that?'

'My dear, I saw them once or twice when I was out riding, she and your rascally Adam, rolling about in the fields like little heathens. There was always something about Beth, she was rebelling against her mother of course, and trying desperately all the time to prove that she was an individual. She always did have spirit though, and she could be quite naughtily funny when she was in the mood.

'I know Lucas was quite taken with her, and they got on so well, but then little Yvonne came along and bewitched him. He needs someone stronger though. Beth might be a schemer but she's as stubborn as a mule and has never been afraid to say exactly what's on her mind. Outspoken to a fault, devious, spoilt, petulant, all of these describe Beth, but deep down she's lonely and sad and now she's going to give her baby away when it's born and then she'll have no-one to call her own.'

Lady Pandora sighed. Her gaze was faraway, then she gave herself a little shake and said, 'Run along now, dear girl, you mustn't worry about anything, I have many things to tell you, things that I hope will make both you and your dear Magnus happy. For now I need a few minutes to compose myself and I have to be alone for a while with my thoughts.'

Lifting the train of her dress Anna went quickly from the room. In the corridor she met Magnus and both of them stopped in their tracks to stare at one another. She had seen him dressed up before: suit carefully pressed, boots brushed so hard they shone, face shining after brisk lashings of hot and cold water, hair gleaming with the tints of autumn, everything about him shy and quiet because he had never liked crowds and only went to social functions to please her. But never had she seen him like this: handsome, tanned face glowing against the pure white of his shirt, with the elegant, dark suit making him look tall and distinguished. All at once he was a stranger to her and she blushed because she couldn't think of anything sensible to say to him.

'My princess,' he murmured, his hazel eyes drinking in her beauty. 'I—don't know what to say.'

'Me neither—except—' her dimples showed. 'For the rest o' this evening you are condemned only to happiness. If you dare to disobey this rule I shall have no choice but to turn you into a hideous toad and throw you into the garden pond.'

'Not a princess but decidedly a little witch!' He laughed, and drawing her down on to a nearby window seat he kissed her tenderly on the cheek. 'What is happening, Anna, do you know? Why am I dressed up like this? Why are you? So far all I've had are mysterious hints and cryptic remarks but no-one has really told me what all this is about.'

'Tonight, we will know,' she said, and stood up. Reaching down to him with both hands she pulled him up so that his face was level with hers. 'Will my bonny prince escort his princess to the ball?'

For answer he crooked his arm into hers and together they descended the stairs to join the colourful throng milling about in the grand hall.

The evening had begun. Neither of them knew what surprises it would bring or how it would end, although each of them was slightly nervous and apprehensive as they prepared themselves to meet whatever fate had in store for them.

CHAPTER TWENTY-FIVE

OLD SCORES

Davie had spent a good part of the evening watching a steady stream of horse-drawn vehicles making their way along the glen road to the Christmas dance at the big house. When the general bustle was over with a quietness settled over the land, except for the thundering of the swollen river deep in the woods of the powdermill.

It was a cold night, with a moon coming up in the sky to the east, and feeling in need of sustenance Davie made his way along to The Coach House Inn where Maggie May fussed over him and asked after Donal who was in Grace's care till everything pertaining to his future welfare could be sorted out. Davie had been subdued and more surly than ever since the death of his sister, but there was a subtle change in him, a grudging gratitude for the many kindnesses that had been lavished on him and his brother over the last few difficult days.

'Donal's fine,' he said in reply to Maggie May's questions, speaking through a mouthful of steak and kidney pie.

'He'll be looking forward to living next door to Boxer Sam?'

'Ay.'

'Ach, you!' Maggie May scolded in her plump, good-natured voice. 'Getting you to speak is like getting a fart out of a corpse.' She sighed. 'You'll never really change now, will you, Davie McDonald? Your sister's ashes lie in yonder ruin and you sit here and eat steak pie as if nothing had happened.'

Davie blinked but didn't comment. He had been watching the window since he had come in and now, from the corner of one foxy eye, he saw Adam McIntyre up on the road. Over the last week Davie had been watching Adam's every move and had noticed that he was spending less and less time at home, more and more at the inn.

Leaving his dinner, Davie got up abruptly and slunk outside to intercept Adam who was alone, his coterie of friends having avoided him since Sally's death.

'What do you want?' growled Adam, immediately on the defensive because he had never trusted this puny-looking man with the strength of an ox. Adam was, quite frankly, afraid of him, more afraid than ever since Sally's accident and even more so now that he didn't have his cronies around him to bolster his confidence.

But Davie, standing there with his bald head bowed, his hands hanging down peacefully at his sides, looked meek and mild in the extreme and didn't appear to be holding any grudges. Indeed he seemed anxious to be on his way and was starting to move off when he muttered hastily, 'Beth Jordan wants to see you, she said she would wait for you in number two storehouse across the river.'

Adam stared. He caught hold of Davie's arm. 'Is this some sort o' foolish joke?' he demanded harshly. 'Beth's in England! I haven't seen her for ages. How could she be back in the glen?'

Davie pretended not to hear and Adam repeated the question. 'Ay, ay,' stuttered Davie, looking vacant. 'She came home for the dance but she was sick and couldny go. She told me to say she wants to see you urgently.'

He moved off without another word, leaving Adam to shake his head in puzzlement. Beth home! Sick! Asking for him! He hadn't seen her for months. All sorts of rumours had flown about. She was going off to school again; she was trying to forget Lucas Noble; she was dying of a broken heart. It had also been said that she was pregnant and had gone to live with her grandparents till the baby was born and then she was going to have it adopted.

Adam hadn't liked the sound of that. It could easily be his child. He wasn't particularly keen to become a father at his age, but if the child was his flesh and blood he wasn't going to let go of it so easily. His head jerked up. Perhaps she had come home to tell him the truth. It might be that she wanted to marry him. It was never easy to tell with Beth. She was always playing games, making things up...

He began to walk on, then stopped. Maybe she wanted him for something else. Beth was an exciting, unpredictable girl. She enjoyed doing things in unusual places...

He remembered the woodshed and came out in a sweat. They had enjoyed themselves in that place. She had never been content with just the floor, always she was dreaming up some new position, some fresh experiment. But surely she must have heard about Sally? How he had raped and frightened her and got her pregnant.

How terror and pain had caused her to turn her own home into a blazing inferno in which she had died. Perhaps that hadn't shocked Beth but excited her! She was like him, always ready to try anything different.

He turned and re-traced his steps. Plunging through a gap in the wall of the mill he took the path that led past the buildings where the Clydesdales were stabled.

Davie watched from the trees, his being surging with satisfaction. The moon had risen higher; he could see everything quite plainly. He waited to make sure that Adam was going in the right direction, then he hurried along Stable Lane to The Gatehouse. He knew that Roderick hadn't gone to the dance. A bout of 'flu had kept him safely indoors for the last day or two, Davie knew that for certain because he had been watching the house closely and knew exactly what was going on.

At his urgent knocking the door was pulled violently back on its hinges by Roderick who had been nursing his miseries with generous tots of whisky in front of the kitchen fire, all the while cursing Anna for going to the dance at the big house and leaving him alone to fend for himself. Little madam! She was getting far too big for her boots! Neither she nor Magnus listened to him anymore. He had lost his grip on them. No matter how much he ranted or raved at them they did exactly what they pleased and to hell with how he was feeling.

Only Adam obeyed him now. Ever since the showdown over that mad McDonald woman, the lad had been too terrified to speak, never mind answer back.

Davie didn't give Roderick a chance to talk. 'Nellie Jean is waiting for you in number two storehouse, Mr McIntyre,' he imparted quickly, keeping his eyes firmly fixed on the stone flags of the porch floor.

'How the hell could she be?' snapped Roderick. 'The storehouses are all kept locked.'

'She took the keys from Boxer Sam's pocket. He was workin' late last night and Mr Jordan left him to lock up. Nellie Jean knew he still had the keys on him.'

'What the hell does she want?' Roderick growled, his bloodshot eyes raking the bald spot on Davie's downbent head, his mind racing as he wondered what new tricks Boxer Sam and his wife were up to now.

'Boxer Sam hit her, she was cryin'. She sent me here wi' a message. Number two storehouse, she wants to talk to you, she says she needs you real bad.'

Roderick's heart leapt. Nellie Jean needed him! By God! She would need him alright if her new husband had started hitting her already. A meeting with her might have its advantages, perhaps he could use the situation to ease his own. He didn't like being fleeced by McGuire one little bit and this might just be the chance he needed to get his own back on the greedy swine! Roderick suddenly felt a little better. He and Nellie Jean had been close at one time, so in her hour of need she was turning to him. She had been a bitch to him recently, but perhaps now she was regretting that and was mad at McGuire for putting him under so much pressure...

Roderick made a swift decision. Retrieving his coat, hat and walking cane from the hall stand he shut the door and roughly pushing past Davie he staggered unsteadily into the night.

Davie watched him as he walked away. The old bastard had been drinking. Davie had smelt it on his breath when he had pushed past. Well, he would need more than liquor where he was going! Nothing could help him now—nothing.

The glitter in Davie's eyes was born of ice-cold hatred and he could hardly wait for the next part of his plans to unfold. But he had to be careful; if he was to succeed in what he had set out to do he would have to be very careful indeed. Stealthy as a fox he followed Roderick through the mill, where the moon cast its shadows and the hoar frost on the dead leaves made them crackle underfoot. But Davie was fly for all that; he had been familiar with this place all his life, he was an excellent tracker, and he knew all about the ways of nature, what to avoid and what to make use of.

Roderick had no such skills. He just blundered on, the sound of snapping twigs and swishing branches making him an easy target to follow. He was cursing as he crossed the planked bridge that spanned the flooded lades. The next one over the thundering river was more sturdily built, but even so Roderick's scalp crawled as his foot slipped and he took a while to steady himself.

The noise of the water spuming into The Cauldron was deafening. Roderick could distinguish no other sound, far less the swift, stealthy footsteps of Davie flitting along through the trees.

Number two gunpowder store loomed ahead of him, the largest of several such buildings to be situated at the foot of Coir an Ban, a grim fortress of a place, protected by thick baffle walls, reached only by a padlocked, gated bridge over the river.

Tonight the bridge gates were slightly open, as was the solid wood door of number two gunpowder store. Before going inside, Roderick lit a safety lamp that was kept in a recessed area in the stonework outside the door. The hooded light was rather subdued and at first he thought the place to be empty, then he became aware of a scuffling sound coming from a corner behind the stacked barrels of gunpowder.

Adam's head popped up. He stared aghast at his father, while Roderick stared back at him.

285

'What the hell d'you think you're doing here?' he spat in most unpleasant tones.

During the walk through the mill he had carried a mental picture of Nellie Jean waiting impatiently to pour her tale of woe into his ears. He had imagined himself being rather distant with her before allowing himself to unbend. After all, the tart had been deceiving him behind his back! She deserved a bloody good hiding instead of a sympathetic ear! Still, she could be the means to an end. He was desperate to get back at McGuire, and while he was doing that he and Nellie Jean could be having a nice wee cosy time of it. He could hardly wait to meet her; if she was in the mood he might even get inside her drawers before the night was over ... And now, instead of Nellie, here was Adam, gaping at him with eyes that were black with loathing.

'I could ask the same o' you,' Adam spoke tightly. His mouth had gone dry with fear but this time the strength of his hatred for his father gave him courage. 'After all, old man, you don't own this place any more than I do.'

Roderick could hardly believe his ears. The son who had cliped, grovelled, done anything in order never to receive punishment of any kind, was talking to him as if he was a hapless two-year-old. Roderick puffed himself up. He would have to show the little bugger that he was still boss around here and with a roar of outrage he lurched forward, holding aloft the heavy Malacca walking cane that he had always believed marked him down as a gentleman of note.

In his fury he seemed to stretch and expand like a red-faced, bulging-eyed giant, totally devoid of human compassion or forgiveness, his hand raised up to strike anything that dared to defy him or stand in his way. It was this vision that had always petrified Adam into submission, but now he too was angry and filled with repugnance.

The years of bottled-up emotions spurted up, erupted out. He was bigger than his father, younger, stronger, and suddenly not afraid anymore. With a sob of fury he lunged at Roderick and wrenched the cane from his hand. In a blind, all-consuming passion of white-hot anger he raised up the stick and brought it crashing down on his father's skull.

A fleeting expression of utter disbelief flitted over Roderick's contorted features before his knees gave way and he sagged to the floor. Adam was taking no chances. Again and again he brought the stick down on his father's head, cracking it open like an eggshell.

'We've been set up, you old bastard!' Adam yelled. 'I was meant to come here and kill you! Someone wanted it more than me, more than anybody!'

Roderick rose up suddenly, his eyes wide with surprise, his bloody mouth opening and shutting like a dying fish, his blood spewing and flowing all around him.

Fear invaded Adam's face. The old fear, returning, never letting go. The old man was indestructible. He wouldn't die. He just wouldn't die! He was reaching out with one trembling hand, clawing the air, trying to reach the son who had at last dared to defy him...

'Give up, Father!' Adam screamed in horror. 'I won't go with you! I'm young! I have my life to live!'

He raised the cane once more. In a mad frenzy he kept on hitting, half-laughing, half-crying, but never stopping until the man who had been Roderick McIntyre lay inert and still on the blood-soaked floor, dead for all time to come.

CHAPTER TWENTY-SIX

PANDORA'S BOX

It seemed that everyone in Glen Tarsa was crowding in through the doors of The House of Noble for the Christmas dance, and before long the house was a swirl of colour and movement.

Halfway through the evening the portrait of Lady Pandora was unveiled at last. There was an audible gasp from the gathering, for it was even more life-like than the one which looked down provocatively from the wall above the fireplace in the hall.

Anna had captured the very essence of her ladyship's beauty: the rich blue of the satin dress enhanced the red-gold of her hair; her bewitching deep-violet eyes shone with vivacity; her full, red, sensual mouth smiled just a little; her expression was alluring yet at the same time chaste. Anna's brush had coaxed out all the vibrancy and love of life that was in her beloved mistress and everyone applauded and wouldn't stop until their hostess put her arm round Anna's shoulders and led her to the front of the crowd.

'Behold the artist!' Lady Pandora cried in a voice that shook with pride. 'Our very own Anna Ban of the fair and lovely face. You all know her. She has walked among you all her young life and painted wonderful pictures of your children. Now she has painted me. No mean achievement, considering how disgracefully I've behaved whenever she has tried to make me sit still for any length of time. Patience is certainly one of her virtues and despite many drawbacks I think she has produced a masterpiece.'

The applause intensified. Anna blushed and melted away into the crowd. But she was soon back, leading a vehemently protesting Miss Priscilla by the hand. 'This is the person you should be appreciating!' Anna cried. 'Without her I would never have done any o' it. When I was in despair she invited me into her home and in her own time, with no thought of personal award to herself, she coaxed and encouraged me to draw and paint. I spent a lot o' happy hours at Knock Farm with Miss Priscilla, Kate, and Ben, and I want them all to know how much I appreciate their hospitality.

'My paintings are what Miss Priscilla has made them and I thank her with all my heart. She has taught many of us here all that we know, yet she is too modest a lady to realise how much we owe her, and I think you should all charge your glasses and drink a toast to a very dear and talented lady in her own right.'

Turning, she kissed the hot cheek of her former teacher and for once Miss Priscilla was lost for words. Her face had turned bright red, and she was looking down her spectacles in a well-known gesture, only this time she wasn't being disapproving but was trying very hard to blink back the tears. She was surrounded by a ring of people, many of them her former pupils, all wanting to shake her hand and drink her health.

'Miss Priscilla!' the cry echoed round the hall, and then the band struck up. There was a swirl of laughter and gaiety, and the dancing resumed.

Lady Pandora smiled. She linked one arm through Anna's, the other she gave to Magnus. 'I want you both to come into the drawing room. Sir Malaroy and I have lots to tell you and I simply can't wait a moment longer to speak.'

*   *   *

A good fire was leaping up the drawing room chimney. Bottles of port and sherry had been laid out on a little table close to a very large and comfortable-looking green leather couch. The lights were soft, the furnishings quietly tasteful, and it was altogether a pleasure to be there after the bustle in the hall.

Sir Malaroy was standing by the fireplace, hands folded behind his back, rocking rather nervously on his heels, his blue eyes gazing distractedly at the ornate cornice bordering the ceiling.

'Please sit down, Malaroy,' Lady Pandora requested softly. 'We must all sit down and be as comfortable as we can, we know one another too well to behave formally.'

She saw the look of bewilderment that passed between Anna and Magnus and she smiled, albeit a little uncertainly. 'Forgive me, I'm talking too much, it's just there is so much to say and I really don't know where to begin.' Getting up she went over to the bureau. With her back turned she unlocked a small drawer, and taking something out she held it in her hand for several long moments. Turning round she uncurled her fingers and there, dangling at the end of them, was Anna's necklace.

291

'Where did you get that?' Anna could hardly believe the evidence of her own eyes. 'It's mine, the necklace Mother gave me! I thought I had lost it forever. I'm so relieved you found it.'

Lady Pandora shook her head. 'I think in a way it found me. Yes, after all these years, I really do believe it found me.'

Her husband too was staring at the shining ornament. 'Pandora's box,' he whispered, his lips white. 'Anna showed it to me a few days ago. Until then I thought you had hidden it away because you couldn't bear to remember.'

'No, I didn't hide it away,' Lady Pandora spoke very quietly. 'I did what I said I would do with it when you gave it to me in the beginning. I hung it round the neck of my firstborn child— and I thought it had gone with her to the grave until last week when I came upon Donal with it in his hand. He had found it in the lane where Anna had dropped it. When I saw the inscription on the back it was the first indication I had that my child was alive—and Lillian McIntyre gave me the rest of the answers.'

Anna and Magnus were completely baffled by all this and her ladyship went to sit beside them. Taking her engagement ring from her finger she held it up. 'This is the key, the only key in the world that will open the back of this piece of jewellery which was always known to both Sir Malaroy and myself as Pandora's box.'

While she was speaking she had inserted her diamond ring into a star-shaped niche in the heavy metal backing of the Luckenbooth. There was a tiny click, and magically the back flew open on minute springs to reveal a gold disc nestling in a bed of red velvet. With shaking fingers she lifted out the disc and handed it to Anna. 'Read it,' she directed gently.

Anna gazed at the lettering on the disc. Then her lips moved, as she whispered, 'Love protect thee from evil. Love keep you forever. Divine Love be with you and bring you peace. Malaroy to Pandora. 1863.' She looked up, her eyes full of the awareness that something incredible was about to be revealed. 'What does it mean, my lady?' she asked in a wobbly voice.

'It means, my dearest, dearest Anna, that you are my daughter.'

Anna, her face devoid of colour, took Magnus's arm and held it tight, and Lady Pandora cried out, 'I'm so sorry, I didn't mean to spring it on you quite like that, please forgive me and let me explain. On our engagement, Sir Malaroy gave me a Luckenbooth brooch that had been in his family for years. He decided to have it made into something special so he took it to a craftsman in Cumnock and asked him to make a hollow backing for it with a carving on the metal to match the stone in my ring—

effectively the only key in the world that would ever open it.

'Oh, it was just a foolish notion of sweethearts, we were young and very much in love and when the little box was ready Malaroy took it to a jeweller and asked him to fix it to the back of the Luckenbooth. It was, by now, rather heavy, so a chain was fitted, turning it into a pendant which my husband gave me on the day of our wedding.'

'Mr Lauder said he thought it had started off as a brooch,' Anna said dazedly. 'But, I still don't understand ...'

'Hush, let me finish, Anna. When Sir Malaroy gave me the pendant I vowed to place it round the neck of my firstborn child. The Luckenbooth was believed to be a protection to babies against evil ...'

Her voice broke and she stared down at her hands, unable to go on. Her husband took up the story. 'Everyone knew that I couldn't father children. I didn't tell Pandora this till after we were married, it was a dreadful thing to do, but I was afraid I might lose her and I also thought that we would always be enough for one another. Pandora, however, adored children and wanted a family. My news devastated her, relations became strained between us and it was round about then that a young artist of Irish origin came to the district. He painted my wife's portrait, the one you see hanging in the hall. She became infatuated

294

with him and she and I grew more and more apart...'

'I was unfaithful to Malaroy,' Lady Pandora broke in, not looking at anyone. 'The young man was here for a few months. When I found out that I was expecting his child I didn't tell him, and he went away never to return. Unable to bear my burden of guilt alone I confessed all to my husband. He didn't want anyone here finding out, and neither for that matter, did I. We planned that I should have the baby in England where it would be brought up. Even though we seemed to discuss every detail it was all quite unreal—I was being fanciful to think I could spend half my time here, and half with my baby in England. Sir Malaroy went ahead of me to arrange for a private nurse to deliver and look after the baby. That nurse was Lillian McIntyre, only then her surname was Ferguson.'

'She was a woman I had known earlier in my life,' his lordship took up the story once more. 'A person of great discretion whom I trusted implicitly. She had knowledge of both nursing and midwifery to her credit and I brought her to our house, Wheatley Manor in Devon, to deliver the baby. My wife didn't have an easy childbirth, it went on and on, and she was practically unconscious when at last the child, a girl, was born, healthy in wind and limb.

'It was only then that Lillian realised a second baby was yet to be born, that Pandora had been expecting twins without any of us guessing. The next little girl was stillborn—and it was then that I saw a hideous way out of my dilemma. I was foolish and proud, afraid of my reputation. Pandora's idea of raising the child in England was quixotic, I knew she would eventually want to bring it back to Scotland, and so I set the scene for my devilish plan of deceit—God forgive me.'

A deathly hush had fallen over the room. Anna was leaning weakly against an ashen-faced Magnus, and Lady Pandora too was pale, as if she had stepped back in time and was re-living the nightmare hours of childbirth.

'I put my proposals to Lillian,' Sir Malaroy continued. 'At first she was shocked and refused to do as I asked, but she was in dire straits at the time, her husband had just died, leaving her with an infant son to rear ...' Magnus gave a cry and the older man nodded. 'Yes, Magnus, you were that infant, Roderick McIntyre is not your father, your father was a fine man, a Scot who went by the name of James Ferguson. You were barely three years old when he died and that is why you have no memories of him. Your mother, Lillian, was torn apart by grief, also she was very poor. I offered to pay her and pay her well if she would take my wife's daughter and bring her up as her own and eventually she agreed to my suggestions.

'When Pandora awoke from her oblivion

Lillian took the dead baby to her. Oh, how cruel it was of me to do that to my dearest wife, but it was a very bad time in my life, I was full of weaknesses, and when I saw her grief I almost told her the truth. But of course I didn't, and so it has gone on. I will never forgive myself for what I did and my heart is sore within me for all the suffering I've caused since then.'

His wife seemed not to hear him; the tears were pouring down her face as she stared unseeingly into space and whispered, 'I put the Luckenbooth pendant round my dead daughter's tiny neck and when Lillian took the little mite away I wanted to die myself. Part of me did perish with that waxen scrap of innocent flesh. I thought I was being punished for my sins. I never saw the pendant again, never expected to see it. I had thought it to be mouldering in the ground with the bones of my little baby—then, suddenly, it was there, in Donal's hands, after all these years, it was just … there. I almost fainted when I saw the inscription on the back and went immediately to Kilkenzie to see Lillian. She admitted everything, how she had taken the pendant from the dead baby and kept it to give to you, Anna, my living daughter.'

'How did she come to meet *him*?' asked Magnus tightly. 'The man I took to be my father?'

'She met him soon after Anna was born,'

explained Sir Malaroy in a low voice. 'I was sending her a regular allowance for the child's upkeep, and when Roderick came on the scene he scented money and wooed Lillian. He can be very charming when he likes and they were speedily married. Bit by bit he got the story of Anna out of his wife and the notion to blackmail me took root in his mind. Lillian must have regretted marrying him quite early on, for she discovered, when it was too late, that his older sister was in an asylum and that his family was cursed with a hereditary mental illness for which there was no cure.'

'He told us it was Mother's sister who was mad!' Magnus burst out furiously.

'Ah, yes, he would, he wanted to close his mind to the black future that awaited him. Your mother was quite sane and normal until he drove her to the edge of darkness. In all innocence she conceived a son, and then before he was born she found out about the lineal madness. She almost went crazy herself, knowing what she did about Roderick's family and what she would be helping to pass on.

'After the boy was born, Roderick came here to Glen Tarsa and applied for the post of under-manager of the mill. That was when he told me what he knew, when the demands started. He brought his family here to this place and Lillian was terrified to go anywhere in case my wife saw her. She became a recluse, bullied and beaten by McIntyre. Her life became a hell. In pain and misery, unable to face reality, she retreated into a lonely shell—you know the rest.'

'But I think now that she is going to get well,' said Lady Pandora. 'It will take a long time and much patience. Years of self-imposed solitude cannot be wiped out in a few days.'

Anna, her mind in a whirl, said wonderingly, 'This means that I am in no way related to Adam—or Magnus?'

As she spoke she glanced at the young man whom she had always imagined to be her brother—and yet, hadn't they both known that this wasn't so? They had always loved one another, not as brother and sister, but as two people whose instincts had told them that they were not of the same flesh but individuals without blood ties.

The full realisation of this news was beginning to hit home. Love, joy, relief, all struggled for expression in their eyes. Anna got slowly to her feet. 'You aren't my brother,' she murmured, shaking her head as she looked at Magnus. Then turning to Lady Pandora she went on, 'But you are my mother, my real mother, I can hardly believe it. I will need time to get used to the idea. To me, just now, you are my dear, dear, friend and companion—give me time, my lady.'

Tears sprang to Pandora's lovely eyes. 'You have all the time in the world, my beautiful, beautiful, daughter, to me you have been special from the first moment I saw you. When you told me that you had been born on the Hallowe'en of 1867 my heart almost stopped. It brought it all back, and I thought of my own little girl who had come into the world on that date never to draw breath, never to say my name. From then on, every Hallowe'en night, I filled my house with children, little knowing that someday, one of them would be you—child of my heart.'

Anna put her hand to her mouth. 'Oh, my lady,' she breathed, and going forward she gently kissed her newfound mother on one soft cheek.

'Go back to the dance,' her ladyship said quietly. 'We all need some breathing space. So much has happened so quickly.'

Magnus took Anna's hand and led her out of the room. The sound of music and laughter came to them. Through the archway Anna could see the portrait of Lady Pandora looking down at the dancers in the hall. Anna's heart beat fast. Her father had painted that picture, her real father, not the cruel and grasping sham she had lived with all her life, but an artist of Irish descent who had loved Pandora and who had painted her picture, capturing everything about her, his brushstrokes even allowing the onlooker a glimpse of the enigmatic qualities lurking in the depths of her eyes. He hadn't stayed long enough to discover what those secrets were, he had never known about his

300

little twin girls, one of whom had never drawn breath, the other...

Anna turned to gaze at Magnus and her heart beat faster at the look of tenderness shining out of his hazel eyes. 'We are not brother and sister,' she whispered.

His strong hands came out to take hers. 'I know,' he said, and his voice was filled with gentle joy. 'It wasn't wrong—what we did—it was right, Anna, for you and me it has always been right.'

Her eyes became misty. 'Everything is turning out for good for you and me, but what about Adam? I feel so sorry for him. I can't deny he worries me a lot, but he doesn't deserve...'

Magnus gripped her hand tighter and the strength of him flowed into her, enclosing her in a love that had known its beginnings in the fragile seedlings of childhood affection, growing ever greater till now, when it was ripe and ready to burst into flower.

'I love you, Magnus,' she said, savouring the sound of those simple words, able to be said now without making her feel tarnished and guilty.

'And I love you, Anna, with pride, with delight. We're free now, we don't have to hide our feelings any more, from each other, from the world.'

Leaning forward he kissed the soft, ripe sweetness of her lips and when he drew away from her she saw in his eyes the look of a man who was drunk with the excitement and enchantment of that wonderful night of unlocked secrets and shared discoveries.

*   *   *

Left with his wife in the drawing room Sir Malaroy was unable to look her in the eye. 'Oh, if it could be as easy for us as it is for these two young people,' he murmured. 'Tonight brought everything flooding back, I can hardly bear to think of the heartaches you suffered because of all this. When I saw Anna with the Luckenbooth I knew it was nearly over for me. And then you went to see Lillian and I felt it was the end. I think I ought to go away for a while, give us both time to recover.'

'Malaroy.' She took his head between her hands and gazed deep into his eyes. 'We've been through this before. When I came home from Kilkenzie we agreed to help one another. We've both behaved foolishly, but if we don't try and rescue what's left for us we'll just end up destroying ourselves completely.'

He cleared his throat. 'I know, my love, we must go on being honest with each other. There is, however, one thing we didn't discuss. I told you how McIntyre threatened and extorted me, but you haven't told me your side of it yet.'

She evaded his eyes. 'He was blackmailing me for Anna's companionship. He knew I would do anything to keep her and—the price for that was very high indeed. Money is his god, he worships it, but now, as far as we are concerned, he can't touch us anymore. Of course, he may say things to get back at us, we must be prepared for that, and the truth about Anna will have to come out, it can't be kept hidden any longer.'

He took her hand. 'I can't deny it, I'm not looking forward to that part of it. You'll have to help me, Pandy, we'll both need to be strong to carry us through, but as long as we're together everything will be alright.'

A deep contentment swept over her. Putting her head on his shoulder she sighed and felt happier than she'd been for years ... and then she became aware of something happening within herself, a fluttering deep in her womb. She held her breath. It was nerves. It wasn't the first time, it had been there before, it would pass. It came again, stronger, a quickening, a pulsing thread of life, stirring, awakening. A wave of nausea washed over her. It couldn't be! Oh dear God, it couldn't be! It was cruel, too cruel!

She tried to think back. For the last three months there had been an alteration in her womanly rhythms. She had imagined it to be a natural thing even though she had rebelled against the idea. She was forty-three, an age at which any woman might begin to expect changes. That those had included a slight thickening of her slender waist had seemed to her a sign that her girlish body could not escape maturity forever. But it was more than that. Something much much, more. She wasn't to be allowed to escape Roderick McIntyre after all. His seed was growing inside her at this very moment, and each day it would get stronger, bigger...

The bitter twists of fate shook her to the core. The world seemed to open beneath her feet and suck her into an abyss from which there was no return.

CHAPTER TWENTY-SEVEN

KINGDOM COME

The explosion, started by a flashing trail of gunpowder laid and lit by Davie, was only a small one compared to that which was to come. Not even Davie himself had expected quite such spectacular results and it was as well for him that he had stayed his distance from the vicinity of the store sheds. Minutes earlier, he had thrown a flaming wad of paraffin-soaked cloth into a snaking grey ribbon of gunpowder that led over the bridge into the number two storehouse.

Adam had just dropped the Malacca walking cane that he had used to kill his father and was backing away in horror from the blood-spattered huddle on the floor. 'Oh, my God!' he whispered unsteadily. 'You made me do it, you made me do it, Father. You never gave me a chance, you should have given me a chance, I was your son, your son...'

He began to run to the door—just as the trail of fire reached the first barrel of powder. It split apart like matchwood and the full blast of it caught Adam in the doorway, lifting him off his feet, never giving him time to know what was happening, hurling him to the lip of the riverbank which rocked and cracked into fissures as the storebuilding blew up in a series of earth-shattering bangs that spat tons of rubble and flames into the air. The lower slopes of Coir an Ban heaved and shuddered, causing an avalanche of mud and boulders to slide down, thudding into Adam as he lay helplessly on the ground, carrying him over the edge of the riverbank and into the boom and churn of the deep dark pool known as The Cauldron, twenty feet below. The seething water grabbed and held him, his head span crazily, then disappeared, only to bob up a few seconds later. But there was no mercy for him. The pool was deeper than usual, swollen by acres of melting snow coming off the hill; the currents were pulling him, the water pounding his bruised body, forcing him to submit to its power.

Round and round he whirled like a spinning

top, gasping and choking. His hands came up to claw at the air before the whirlpool sucked him under once more. Ice-cold water filled his nose, his ears, and finally flooded his lungs.

Mother! His heart cried out the name. When he came up for the third time he was not aware that he was floating lifelessly on the surface, like one of Sally's matchsticks.

*   *   *

Boxer Sam and Nellie Jean had wandered outside Noble House to get a breath of air and were strolling arm in arm along the moonlit riverbank when the explosions shook the ground beneath them. Through the trees they saw plumes of smoke and belching flames and without ado they took to their heels and were the first to arrive on the scene.

They both stood, utterly horrified, surveying the wreckage before them. Nellie Jean peered down into The Cauldron and her stomach lurched when she saw the blur of Adam's dead face staring up at her out of the torrent.

Beside her, Boxer Sam gave a cry and made to scramble down but she drew him back. 'He's dead, Sam, and you'll die too if you land up in that whirlpool.'

Her husband shook his head. 'Poor, demented, young bugger, he didn't stand a chance, did he? Not in this lot.'

He gazed at the crackling remains of the

storehouse. The roof had been blown sky high, a portion of one wall was missing but, miraculously, the greater part of the stout structure had remained intact.

'You know,' Sam said thoughtfully, 'I once swore I'd blow McIntyre to kingdom come but I'm thinking young Adam's beaten me to it. For days now he's been swearing vengeance on his old man, but I didn't think he had the guts.'

He looked again at the pale mask of death bobbing down below. 'Seems I was wrong after all. I think it would be a safe bet to say our Roddy is lying yonder in smithereens—only thing is, he took the boy with him, he couldn't get out o' the shed fast enough. Och, I know he was a swaggering young lout, but I had a soft spot for him, Nellie, there was good in him, it just needed bringing out.'

She put her hand in his. 'It's maybe better this way, Sam, if he'd lived he would have gone cuckoo like Roderick. It might have been later, it might have been sooner, but there was no escape, it was in the family.'

'Ay, you're right there, Nellie lass.' He grinned suddenly. 'Only thing is, because o' what's happened, the lad's inadvertently cheated us out o' a few bob. I was going to soak the old man a bit more before I let go, make him pay for what he did to everybody.'

Voices echoed through the trees; people were flooding the scene to stare in shock, horror and wonder at the devastation that a few barrels of gunpowder could cause when ignited by fire.

*   *   *

Davie slid silently out from his hiding place further up in the woods. A satisfied smirk touched his mouth. It was finished. He had avenged his sister's death; the violation of Donal's innocence; all the cruel injustices dealt out to his family by these two mad McIntyres. Their accursed reign of terror was over with, peace would come back to Glen Tarsa, fear would never stalk the powdermill again. He gave a last long look at the smouldering ruins at the foot of the hill before making a stealthy detour out of the trees to the comforts that awaited him at The Coach House Inn.

*   *   *

It was the strangest Christmas Anna had ever known. Everything had happened so quickly: joy, sorrow, delight, and death. She was sorry about Adam, he had spent his life being afraid of the terrifying bully that was his father. He had never been truly at ease, always he had looked over his shoulder, afraid of the dark, unsure, unhappy.

Even so, there were quite a few mourners at his funeral. Anna, Magnus, Nellie Jean, Boxer Sam, Mary weeping quietly into her hanky,

308

forlorn and lost looking. Adam and she had been alike, unloved, unwanted, except for the comfort they had given one another. Now there was no-one for Mary and she was overcome with quiet gratitude when Anna came over to her to put a sympathetic arm round her shoulder and give her a little smile of understanding.

Neither Anna nor Magnus could grieve for Roderick. He had terrorised and cheated them too much for them to feel anything but relief that it was all over. Anna remembered too keenly how she had suffered at his hands all through the years. She recalled her darling Peter, and how he had died in the flower of his life because he had innocently become involved in the aftermath of Roderick's vengeful murder of Andrew Mallard.

Roderick had caused too much pain, both mental and physical, for anybody to care very much that he was gone. Most of the villagers tried to be discreet in their opinions, but not so Moira O'Brady, the postmistress. She had always hated and feared Roderick and when she heard about his demise she threw her moth-eaten felt hat in the air and yelled, 'Good riddance to bad rubbish!' completely forgetting herself in the euphoria of the moment, echoing the sentiments of the neighbourhood in general though some said it was bad luck to speak about the dead in such a flippant manner.

Very few of them attended Roderick's funeral. Those that did only went out of a morbid sense of curiosity and a desire to make sure he was well and truly six feet under.

Justice had been done; the sort of justice that Roderick himself might have understood if he had been a spectator at his own funeral.

CHAPTER TWENTY-EIGHT

LETTERS

As soon as Beth heard about the latest explosive happenings in Glen Tarsa she wrote Anna a letter.

May Iron Rod rot in hell. He had it coming but I do weep for Adam. We had some good times together, he and I, and there was a funny, generous side to him that was often very touching. So much is happening there in Glen Tarsa. Fancy you being a lady of truly Noble blood after all, with Lady Pandora as your real live mother. I'm longing to come home to hear everything properly, meanwhile I languish in this bloated ugly body of mine and look forward to THE day in fear and trembling. Your friend, always and ever.
Beth.

310

Another letter quickly followed:

It's here and it's a boy! It was hell having it! I hated every minute, but when I saw it I couldn't believe that I, Elizabeth, Victoria Ellen Jordan, could actually produce something that looks so human, even though it is exceptionally ugly. But it has a rather nice mop of jet black hair and a mouth like Lucas Noble's??? Also, it definitely looks blue-blooded in the right sort of light. It doesn't matter anyway, it won't be with me very long. Mother will see to that. Next episode soon.
    Beth.

The 'next episode' arrived a few days later, and this time the baby was referred to by his rightful gender.

When Mother saw the baby she burst into tears and Father had a dreadful job getting her to calm down. It was pretty earth-shattering. Mother actually crying! As if she were a real human being! Grandma Vi and Grandpa David led her away sobbing and Father just sat looking stunned by all the changes that were happening in his life. As for me I keep thinking, I made this child, he is mine, I simply can't give him away. When he nuzzles my breast and wants to suck I feel as if I'm drowning in pain and want to die.

That was last night. Mother is behaving most strangely. She keeps telling me the baby is my flesh and blood and is therefore also hers and Father's. She's weakening, there's no doubt about it.

Two hours after lunch. Mother wants me to bring the baby home to Corran House! Father just smiled and nodded. We all cried a bit and looked silly but it was good to get it all off our chests and to be a real family for the first time ever. I'm not saying very much but secretly, Anna, I'm thrilled. For once I feel as if there's some meaning in my life, someone to care for and love. I've decided to call him Leopold, the little lion, my son.

   I never thought this could happen to me but it has, and I'm glad. He's so little he'll just do little messes to begin with. When he gets older they'll get bigger but by then I should be used to it and ought to be able to cope.

PS: You'll never guess, the strangest thing! Dot came to see me! Remember! Little Dotty Daydream, who nearly had a nervous breakdown when she was with us at Corran House and paid us back by taking some of my jewellery. She's working as a maid in a hotel near here but says she misses Glen Tarsa and Fat Jane and her nice little room in our house. Her conscience must have been bothering her because she offered to give me back my jewellery as she got a job quite quickly and

312

hadn't sold it yet.

I asked her if she would like to come back to Corran House and help me to look after the baby and she accepted—on the condition that both myself and 'the dragon lady' as she calls Mother, learn to treat her with some respect and stop bossing her about so much.

I ask you! Next thing she'll be wearing my clothes if I let her! I said yes because I really like her and feel I ought to give her a chance after all that I put her through. I feel good, Anna. I feel alive and well. Hoping to see you all sooner than soon. My love to Magnus. Wish he were mine. You were born with a lucky spoon in your mouth after all.

Always your friend.
Beth.

Lady Pandora sat at her writing desk, her pen poised uncertainly over a blank piece of paper. What could she say? How could she tell Malaroy about the thing that had caused her such mental torture since its discovery three weeks ago. Three weeks or three years? It seemed as if she had been putting on an act of normality forever.

And Roderick was dead! She no longer had to bear the sight of his lecherous eyes raking over her body or the sickening feel of his hands pawing her. Oh, bitter irony! She was free of his physical presence but was still fettered to him even as he rotted in hell!

313

She would never be free of him. It was her final punishment. To have, at last, everything that meant happiness to her only to know that soon she must lose it . . .

Inside her body the child twisted and turned, pulsing with life. Roderick's life! He was living on in the innocent flesh he had planted in her womb. She gave a little cry and put one slender hand over her eyes.

'Dear God, help me,' she whispered. 'Show me what I must do. I am not brave, my Lord, I need your help. I need you to make me strong. If I give birth to this helpless babe growing within me I will be unleashing another poor, unhappy mortal into the world, I will bring more disgrace and shame on all those I love. If I were to die, I will bring unhappiness to my dear ones but at least they will be able to hold up their heads after I am gone. Please guide me, my Lord, oh please . . .'

The tears poured down her face. She fumbled for her hanky and cried into it for a long time, then she wiped her red eyes, straightened her shoulders and began to write:

6th January 1896

My dearest Malaroy,
I feel very alone as I write this letter. Despite everything, we had some good years as husband and wife, and I really believed that we could look forward to a happy and contented future together.

I see now that this wasn't meant to be. Influences are reaching out to me from beyond the grave. Inside me grows the seed of Roderick McIntyre. I feel the child moving as I write. I paid a high price for Anna's companionship and this is the result. Never tell her that though, it would break her heart and she would blame herself forever.

There is only one door open to me now. I cannot bring more disgrace upon the family nor can I bring a baby into the world with a destiny too terrible to contemplate.

Tell my darling daughter I love her. She mustn't grieve for me, I want only her happiness and she will find that with Magnus.

Be brave, my love, I have had a wonderful life and feel very privileged to have lived in this beautiful house in the heart of God's country.

I don't want to leave it all behind, I don't want to leave you. We knew such enchanted love in the beginning and some of it is touching me now as I pen these words.

May God be with you always.
Pandora.

She read the letter over then with an angry sob she crumpled it into a ball and threw it into the fire. She couldn't, she wouldn't, leave her husband with such bitter memories. It would do no good to burden him with the dreadful secret she carried. Far better to leave quickly, without a word, without a goodbye.

Clasping her cold fingers together she put them up to her mouth. Could she do this? Go without saying a farewell to any of the people she loved? She went to the window and stood gazing out. A fresh fall of snow covered the countryside. The fields were virgin white, the wooded hillsides like fairyland. Down below, Anna was building a snowman, her hair gleaming in the cold rays of the winter sun. She was staying at Noble House now, filling it with everything that made life worthwhile. Sam McGuire was now under-manager of the mill and had moved into The Gatehouse with Nellie Jean. So much had changed, most of it for the better...

The figure of Magnus was coming along the track from the home farm. Soon he was beside Anna, gazing down at her, his strong young face alight as he greeted her. Their laughter drifted, the laughter of youth, bubbling with happiness. They were very much in love. It showed in every glance, every gesture. He was presently living in one of the shepherd's bothies but one day—soon—he would be sharing his life with Anna and moving with her into a wing of the house. He would help Sir Malaroy to run the estate but he had also expressed a desire to keep in close touch with the home farm. It had been his life for a long time, he didn't want to let go—and besides, he had said with a laugh, the animals would miss him too much if he didn't go back from time to time.

Lady Pandora went into a muse as she watched Magnus bending to kiss Anna on the cheek. How sweet they were in their youth and innocence. One day they would have children. The house would ring with little voices; the swift careless clatter of rushing feet...

Pandora's eyes grew misty. Anna glanced up and saw the lovely face of her mother at the window. Pandora raised her hand, all the while drinking in every aspect of the girl she had recently discovered was her daughter. They were both still getting used to the strangeness and wonder of that fact—and now it was all going to be taken away from them once more. She hesitated. Could she do this to Anna? It was so cruel after all that she had already suffered. Then the child within her moved violently, her heart accelerated, and she held her breath...

Sir Malaroy had joined the young people in the garden. Their voices mingled, laughter crackled in the frosty air. He had been so buoyant of late. With Roderick's death a gloomy shroud had been lifted from everyone—all except her.

'Goodbye my dearest loved ones,' she breathed, and went to change into her riding habit. No-one saw her leaving the house to make her way to the stables. Jim, the stableboy, got her horse ready and led it outside.

'You goin' far, m'lady?' the boy enquired, his rosy cheeks glowing in the cold fresh air.

'Wherever Sable's nose takes him,' she answered evasively. 'It's a marvellous day for a gallop. I always liked riding in the snow.'

Sable's hooves rang out as he cantered away from the yard. She guided him along the edge of the fields and on down to the bridle path which the trees had protected from the worst of the snow.

It wasn't long before the lady and her horse were moving over the foothills of Stor Mhor, whose white-capped peaks reared majestically into the cold blue sky. The crags of Ben Corsa rose up, cradling the dour dark Pass of the Coffin into its rugged shoulders.

Up, up, the noble horse and his mistress climbed, right into the heart of the hills. It was a breathtaking place to be, awesomely wild, stunningly beautiful. The sun was shining into the corries, warming the rocks, throwing the gorges into deepest shadow.

Sable whinnied and pawed the ground, as if sensing some impending disaster. He tossed his head and seemed unwilling to go on but his rider urged him forward, guiding him to the lip of a ravine where she sat gazing down at the boulder-strewn river far below.

The sun was warm on her back, and the dream-like stillness enclosed her; the bracken rustled, the streams gurgled down through the stones. Everything that was life was all around her, the endless sky stretching to the infinity of the horizon; a buzzard gliding majestically in the blue; gulls soaring in the air thermals high above the peaks.

Solitude touched her like a living thing; her heart went quiet within her as she could almost hear the echoes of voices from ages past. Argyll was a land steeped in history, a country of great grandeur, remote, aloof, endlessly enchanting, and if she raised herself up in her stirrups she could see the tall chimneys of The House of Noble, the roofs, the sweeping curve of the lawn, the lands of Leanachorran all covered over in a snowy white quilt...

'My lovely land, you are tempting me to stay,' she murmured huskily. Closing her eyes she rested her hands on Sable's silky black mane. He was solid and strong beneath her, patiently waiting on the lip of the gorge for a flick of the reins that would tell him it was time to move—but instead, the hold on his mane grew tighter.

Then the grip slackened. Sable threw up his head, and his hoof slipped on an icy rock which gave way beneath him. He reared up in panic, flaying the air, snickering and whinnying as he tried to re-gain a foothold.

*   *   *

Lady Pandora lay where she had fallen, on a rocky shelf of the ravine far below, her eyes staring up at the blue sky far above. A vision of Anna darted into her mind, Anna, her daughter, fair of face, a child whose existence had been a struggle but who was now happy and secure of mind and body...

The vision blurred and faded. Lady Pandora gave a little cry as blackness engulfed her; her limbs relaxed and she lay still, her honey-gold hair soaked in the blood that spilled from a wound in her head.

On the ridge of rock high above, Sable whinnied and pawed the ground, then, with trailing reins, he turned and re-traced his steps down the slopes of Ben Corsa to make his way back to the stables.

CHAPTER TWENTY-NINE

COMING HOME

Strange things happened in the afterlife. Things that seemed of the heavens yet were still of the earth. Floating sensations; hills and skies; people with great elongated heads and big noses circling round, staring down, talking in hushed voices.

Movement; flying, like a bird; up, upwards, then down, downwards, into the pit ... it was warm in heaven, great fires were burning, she could see the flames, growing bigger and bigger. Perhaps she hadn't gone to that higher place after all but was burning in hell...

Roderick would be there! Roderick *was* there, reaching out to get her, clawing at her, pulling her further down into the pit of blackness.

She let out a small scream of terror ... and opened her eyes to see Doctor Alistair Minto peering down at her, shushing her in a soothing voice and telling her that everything was going to be alright.

Her vision began to focus. Moving her head slightly she saw that she was in her own bright airy room in Noble House, where a big fire was burning in the grate, the flames flickering and leaping up the chimney.

'You've come back,' the doctor said with a little smile.

'I thought I was dead. I—I thought I was in—hell.'

'Perhaps you were,' he said gently. 'You've been very ill. You lost a lot of blood, and ...' Discreetly he turned away. 'You also lost the baby you were carrying.'

'Oh!' Her hand flew to her mouth. Grabbing hold of the doctor's sleeve she said urgently, 'My husband, please don't tell him about it. He mustn't know, he mustn't...'

The door opened and Sir Malaroy himself walked in. Going immediately to the bed he said quietly, 'I do know, Pandora, I couldn't help knowing, you were in such pain.' A mist of tears veiled his blue eyes. 'But you're back now and that is all that matters.'

'Oh God,' she turned away, 'I'm sorry, I'm so sorry, I tried to spare you, I tried to.'

'I know what you tried to do, Pandora, but thank God you didn't succeed. When Sable came back we all went out looking for you. Jimmy Johnson the gamekeeper was the first to spot you and climbed down. We tried to get you up but it was too difficult and so we lowered you down instead.'

'Heaven and hell,' she murmured.

'What did you say?'

'Oh, nothing, just raving.'

Gently he took her hand in his and held it as if he would never let go. Doctor Minto gave a little cough and quietly left the room. The heart of The House of Noble seemed to have started beating again now that her ladyship had returned to fill it with her life and her love.

*   *   *

Anna and Magnus walked hand in hand along the road to Corran House. It was March; the fields were hazy in the spring sunshine, daffodils lined the verges, and the golden slopes of Coir an Ban rose up into a misty sky. Anna looked with affection at the mountain that had given her strength and hope when she had been a vulnerable and frightened child.

Her gaze travelled downwards to The

322

Gatehouse, where woody-blue smoke was billowing from the chimney. There was a barrow load of freshly cut logs by the door and a dainty little black cat was sitting on a windowledge washing its paws. It all presented a serene picture against its majestic backdrop of moor and mountains. The walls that had once harboured sorrow and pain seemed now to breathe of contentment and peace. Evil had departed along with Roderick McIntyre. His influence no longer stalked the rooms or lay in wait for innocence to appear.

'Strange,' said Magnus quietly, 'there was a time when I thought we would never escape from that house. We had a lot o' unhappiness there yet I don't really hate it as I thought I would.'

'It will always be a part of us,' Anna replied slowly. 'Despite everything we found love there. It was fear of Roderick McIntyre that made everything so hateful.'

She shivered. It was over, all over. Boxer Sam and Nellie Jean were making sure of that. All traces of Roderick McIntyre had long disappeared; even the smell of his pipe smoke had vanished under Nellie Jean's determined attacks of polish and paint in all the rooms, corners, and cupboards. For a moment Anna remembered what it had been like with her father and Nellie Jean, the resentment, the dislike of a woman who didn't belong in the house, but the moment passed quickly, she and

Nellie Jean got along well now, there was no reason to hate her anymore.

They were at the garden gate of Corran House. Beth and the baby were home, their arrival causing a great stir of interest and gossip in the glen. The Jordan family reacted in different ways to this. William Jordan still wore a flower in his buttonhole and held his head up with pride. Victoria Jordan kept her head down but was learning to cope with her life as it was and not as it had been, and Beth kept her chin up, far too busy to care about anything as trivial as idle chatter when she had a real, live, bouncing baby to look after.

'Are you coming in?' Anna asked Magnus.

'No, it will be all girl talk and baby chatter. I'll go in and see Sam and have a blether with him.'

*   *   *

Beth was in her room, brushing out her long sandy hair in front of the mirror.

'It's great to see you back again, Beth,' Anna said warmly. 'So much happened while you were away, not just to us, but to you as well. I think you've found the one thing in your life that you really wanted but didn't know it.'

For a long time Beth said nothing but just kept on brushing her hair, her back turned to Anna. Then suddenly she spun round and her eyes were big and brilliant with joy when she grabbed hold of her friend and hugged her so hard she gave a yell of protesting laughter. Beth paid no heed. Taking hold of Anna's hands she whirled her about and danced with her all round the room till they both collapsed dizzily on the bed, panting and giggling.

'Oh, Anna,' gasped Beth, 'I can't tell you how good it is to see you. And you're right, I have found what I wanted, my little Leo, my son. I'd do anything for him and he loves me back, it's all there in his eyes when he looks at me and gives me one of his big gumsy smiles.' She gave Anna a long, considering look. 'It took me a while to discover what I wanted out of life. You were the one who always had everything.'

'Me?'

'Yes, even when you were a poor wee thing with nothing to call your own. Oh, yes, you can gape at me with those fascinating eyes of yours but it's true! When you thought I had it all I had none of the things that really mattered. Everyone loved you and hated me. I've always been jealous of you, Anna, and did some ghastly things to get back at you. Strange how it's all worked out. All along, you were the daughter of a fine lady and now that you've found out that Magnus isn't your brother, you even managed to get him too.'

'No more bitterness, Beth, promise.'

Beth shrugged. 'I can't, I'm me and I can't help myself. I was always a little schemer and it got me nowhere. I used to look at you, in your ragged dull frocks, and I could never understand how you managed to look better than me for all my finery. I disliked you very much for that, yet—' her voice broke, 'I loved you too, like everyone else. Oh, I know I've said this before but I'm going to say it again. Those were the best days of my life, Anna, those long-ago days when we were the bestest friends on earth...'

'Oh, Beth, we'll always be bestest friends!' Anna cried. Both girls looked at one another and then they melted into each other's arms and cried together for far off days of whispered secrets by the brown trout pool when the most important things in life were slabs of Fat Jane's cakes at playtime and their dreams of all the wonderful things they would do when they grew up.

They drew apart, and Beth fingered the Luckenbooth necklace at Anna's throat. 'The twists of fate. I remember you showing it to me on one of your birthdays. I thought then it was something special and I suppose everything that's happened to you owes itself to this. You thought your mother gave it to you and all along your real mother was Lady Pandora. How is Lillian McIntyre by the way? It seems she's not mad after all.'

Anna's chin tilted. 'Oh no, she's getting better all the time. One day she'll come home, Magnus and I still love her very much.'

Her attention was caught by the initials on Beth's case, which was only half unpacked. 'Your initials, I never realised, the initials of your name, Elizabeth Victoria Ellen, make "Eve"'

Beth gave a funny short laugh. 'Perhaps I've still to find my Adam . . .' A flush crept over her face. 'But I did find him, didn't I? We tasted the forbidden fruits together, he and I. Poor Adam, in a strange way I miss him. Perhaps if he had lived he would have become my Adam after all, but no, it couldn't have been, the poor creature was destined to go mad like Iron Rod. Never mind, I have my handsome little Leo. I think you should see him, I'll get Dot to bring him in.'

The baby arrived, carried through from his room by Dot who was looking as pleased as if she had produced the child herself. The little boy was perfect in every way, dark-haired, chubby-cheeked, and there was something about him that was familiar and recognisable.

'He's got Lucas Noble's mouth,' Beth spoke quickly. 'Anybody can see that. One day Lucas will see the child for himself and know that it's his. I've been hearing things about him and Little Miss Chastity Belt. Their marriage isn't idyllic by any means, he'll come back to me, in the end I know he'll come back to me.'

She was trying to convince herself, but Anna wasn't really listening as a quite unbidden memory came to her: her first Hallowe'en party at Noble House, games, customs, all the little girls throwing apple peel over their shoulders to make initials of future sweethearts and husbands. Beth's had taken an 'A' shape, while Anna's had looked like a 'W', but it wasn't...

With sparkling eyes she kissed Beth on the cheek. 'It will be your turn to visit me next. Bring the baby, her ladyship—my mother—will love having him in the house.'

With that she walked away, out of Corran House and down the path to the garden gate where Magnus was waiting for her.

'It wasn't "W" it was "M"' she greeted him breathlessly. 'All along it was "M".'

His hazel eyes crinkled with laughter. 'You talk in riddles, my darling little princess.'

She linked her arm through his, the heat of his body beating into hers. 'Let's walk,' she said joyously. 'I'll explain on the way.'

Together they made their way through golden Glen Tarsa, their laughter ringing as they walked and talked, their footsteps taking them past the Clachan of Corran and on towards the tall beckoning chimneys of The House of Noble.